# *Everyone Loves Ronald McDonald*

## *A Novel*

Andrew Grof

CITI OF BOOKS

**CITIOFBOOKS, INC.**
3736 Eubank NE Suite A1
Albuquerque, NM 87111-3579
*www.citiofbooks.com*
Hotline: 1 (877) 389-2759
Fax:            1 (505) 930-7244

Ordering Information:

Quantity sales. Special discounts are available on quantity purchases by corporations, associations, and others. For details, contact the publisher at the address above.

Printed in the United States of America.

ISBN-13:        Softcover        979-8-89391-130-5
                Ebook            979-8-89391-132-9
                Hardback         979-8-89391-131-2

Library of Congress Control Number: 2024909853

Oh, man.

Everyone loves Ronald McDonald. That's a fact.

And the last thing you want is to argue with facts, facts the very stuff of life, argue with facts and you just bash your head against the wall to get it bloodied, the blood just dripping then oozing down your forehead, temples, which reminds me of my old man of course, now there was a bird, a rare specimen, but not now, not just yet, but my first or most vivid memories of this clown, this Ronald McDonald, by then they must have had a whole bunch of them all over the state, the nation, perhaps even the world, a whole bunch of different guys dressed up as Ronald McDonald and showing up at the different restaurants all over the place, a crummy job if you think of it, no more than minimum wage I bet, I mean you might think you're a star or something, at least for the half hour or hour you show up at a particular restaurant, and the kids, you know, the kids swarming all around, but just put yourself in their shoes, the clowns' I mean, I mean all you are is this man, this bum in this crummy clown's outfit, and working for a fast food chain at that, I mean not even a clown working for some circus which might be considered something like a profession, it just might, and for the rest of the time, your life you're just this bum who can't land another job, I mean it's sad, really pathetic, but as a kid this sort of thing never occurred to me, how could it have, Ronald McDonald like my personal buddy and savior rolled into one, and as far as I was concerned there was only the one, this particular Ronald McDonald in the entire world, and I didn't even give a damn about the other kids, I really didn't, it was just Ronald and me, and I really felt safe and happy, now there's a notion for you, happy, but I really felt safe and happy in his presence.

Gotta stop smoking. That's a fact.

Been smoking since I was twelve or thirteen, like father like son I guess, but damn if I'll ever resemble my old man in any shape or form whatsoever, but chain smoking, smoking like a chimney just like my old man, God bless him wherever he might be, alive or dead, it really doesn't matter, but in some jail no doubt and sleeping it off, talk about your menace to society, to himself and his so-called family, drunk or sober I can't even picture him without a cigarette dangling from his lips, my mother the same of course, poor white trash from the Panhandle, I'll give you just one example, they named me Bingo, my mother or father, I don't know which, but they named me Bingo, their one and only child, Bingo Sherman, now there's a name for you, all because of my mother's addiction to the game I guess, no imagination, but Bingo Sherman, now there's a hell of a way to go through life, now and again my father going on and on about the Sherman part, mostly when drunk and not sober, it worked better when he was drunk and not sober, but this whole link, this connection to the Civil War general, all in his imagination, I was pretty sure even then, I mean we were southerners to the core so what the hell was a northern general doing in our midst, part of the family tree and all, but my father a great one for making up stories to suit his moods, my father about the biggest story teller or liar I've ever met in my life, I guess he couldn't quite see making it in life other than through his stories and lies, but I don't begrudge him, I never have, my father just this out-and-out loser from the get-go, and that's the only comment I have for the moment. I smoke like a chimney.

Stunt your growth. That's a fact.

But at twenty what sort of growth left to be stunted, I'm six-one at any rate, taller than mother, father and all the cousins all over the place, so what's the diff, and thin, as a rail, unlike the rest of them I could eat from morning till night without putting on any weight, and I'm not talking all the healthy stuff, no, lots of grease, sugar and starches, my protein-free diet, it's like I'm burning up calories as soon as I ingest them, and I don't even have to be doing anything in particular, you know, run, work, work out, nothing like that, I could be just sitting perfectly still and smoking the way I am now and still I'm burning up calories like mad, a kind of nervous disposition I guess, great for keeping the weight off, and how's that, you know, how's that for a blessing in disguise, life just full of blessings in disguise if one knows how to recognize them. Watching the ships, the cruise liners in Miami Harbor.

Man, oh, man.

Lately I've been coming here Saturday afternoons, one of my days off from my so-called surveying job, but all the ships, the liners lined up then, it's like time standing still before it starts to move again, you know, at a snail's pace when all of them start to move out towards the ocean, like giant hotels I guess, which is exactly what they are, which is exactly what everyone wants out of life I guess, those that can afford it, to be on some giant hotel floating out to sea, out to nowhere, I mean personally I don't know if I could stand being cooped up with all those strangers, hundreds, maybe even thousands of them, I mean muggers, rapists, murderers, who knows, although by the looks of them they're really just these ordinary people from the midwest or New York or wherever, but even ordinary people in large enough numbers will give you the heebie jeebies, shout for time out or help, I mean what is it that makes them want to crowd together like that, be fed and entertained like cattle, and as for the open air and so- called exotic ports of call, there's open air wherever you are, provided you're out of doors somewhere, and as for the exotic ports of call, I bet they're not so exotic if you happen to be living on them, all in the eyes of the beholders I guess, I'm not knocking, just saying, and watching from a distance, from across the bay is really not a bad way to spend a Saturday afternoon, I could and have done worse, you know, some Saturday afternoons and nights when I couldn't even tell you what I was doing or even where, the whole thing a blank, you know, certain periods, certain times of my life that are nothing but blanks.

A sound mind in a sound body.

I really am a firm believer in this, not always, not in the past, but now I mean, right now, this is the new Bingo Sherman you're looking at, new and improved, the cigarettes aside of course and the boozing, the occasional boozing as well, but a man must start somewhere, you know, and Rome wasn't built in a day, no, not Rome or any other place I can think of except for certain sections of Miami which look like they were built not only in a day but an hour or even under perhaps.

So.

I start talking to this bum, this homeless guy, I'm always ready to talk to just about anyone at all provided they don't look too threatening, you know, have that crazy look in their eyes, "I hope the birds shit on all of them," he says apropos nothing, he means the gulls of course, all these gulls forever circling the ships especially when they start moving, "Shit on all of their fucking heads," he adds for good measure, but means no harm, he really doesn't, just letting off a bit of steam, I mean he's even smiling for Chrissake, and the thing about bums in general or some bums at any rate, they can be quite philosophical about life, you know, that's been my experience, I mean the way they live and all, hand to mouth and from one day to the next, what else but be philosophical about everything around them, I mean you don't find a responsible man or a woman with a job and all and a family to support being philosophical about anything at all, they have neither the time nor the patience, I mean their one concern in life is getting on with things whatever those things might be, and bums, exactly, what on earth do they have to get on with, you know, but that's just my opinion, you can take it or leave it.

He's got this cat in his lap, this nondescript furry cat or kitten in his lap, holding on for dear life it seems, the bum I mean, I mean that cat or kitten couldn't get away even if it wanted to, not that it wants to by the looks of it, but it really couldn't if it ever did. And bums, quite a number of bums I've met are just like that, they seem to need to have something in their lives, something to hold on to beside themselves, some mangy cat or dog, you name it, but something they can call their own and care for in a manner of speaking.

"What's its name?" I ask, and, "Cat," he replies. "Just Cat." And that shows a certain lack of imagination, it really does, and I doubt he even knows or cares whether it's a male or female, it's all the same to him, but that's really none of my affair, in general bums with a certain imagination in some areas but none, absolutely none in others.

"So, what do you say we blow them up?" he asks. "Blow those fucking ships right out of the fucking water," and, "I'm game if you are," I tell him and leave it at that.

I'm wearing this black T-shirt and jeans, a black cap as well. I've always had this thing for black, you know, shirts, T-shirts, caps whatever, I mean I really don't care what they are or even if they fit so long as they're black, it says 'Chicago Bears' on the cap and 'Ask Me What I Want' on the T-shirt, white on black, and for some reason this guy, this bum becomes suddenly fascinated by my attire, I mean he's staring at me now just the way he stared at those ships before, and, "'Ask Me What I Want,'" he reads in this really slow, this meaningful way, like he is trying to penetrate this important question or puzzle, and, "So, what is it you want?" he finally asks, and, "To get laid the same as everyone else," I tell him just to be saying something, really, nothing more than that, and, "All women are cunts," he says, but in this matter-of-fact and not at all vicious fashion, and I can just see the wheels turning in his head, I mean he is ready to delve, to dig into this topic, explore it from all sorts of angles perhaps, and all he needs is a comment, some bit of encouragement from me to get started, but right now I'm not in the mood, and at any rate I'm noncommittal about whether women are cunts or not. I mean it's still too soon to tell as far as I'm concerned, once I've lived another twenty, thirty or even fifty years, yes, maybe then, maybe then I'll say, 'All women are cunts,' or, 'Some women are cunts,' or even, 'No women are cunts,' who knows, but right now I don't feel up to the task, truth is I don't even feel like thinking about it.

So, "Look at those clouds," I just tell him instead, really magnificent, dark, heavy and low to the water and the land, about the best clouds in the country, in the world perhaps, and, "I think it's gonna rain," I tell him, "we're in for it," and I can tell right away he doesn't like my switching topics on him like that, I mean no doubt he's still got this women being cunts on his mind, so, "You're full of shit," he says, and, "What the fuck do you know about the fucking weather?" he asks and we just leave it at that.

And, 'High time, Bingo,' I tell myself, 'high time to be off somewhere else.' Which I do now and again, from time to time, things about some situations, I don't care what, but just things about some situations getting to me, like I can no longer breathe, swallow or think straight.

"You take care now," I tell the guy, and I leave him the bay, the threatening skies and all those ships, he can do with them what he likes, sit here until doom's day for all I care.

And off, off I go.

The weather really does look like it's threatening although in Miami you can never tell, it might be threatening or even a downpour one minute and bright sunshine the next, so in a sense it really doesn't matter, but off I go to hop some bus across the causeway and then up, up on Biscayne, I just have this yen and all to see and talk to Grace, Grace this prostitute, this hooker on Biscayne, wheelchair-bound, you know, which is pretty amazing for anyone but especially for a hooker, for someone in her line of work, I often wonder about people who go on, carry on with their lives stuck in a wheelchair, there was this kid I used to know, doesn't matter where or when, but this kid who took a dive into some pool in the middle of the night, and no water you know, just some three or four feet of water which he didn't know, the pool drained for some cleaning or repairs, and this kid goes straight down, you know, not a flat dive but straight down, and as soon as he hits bottom with his head and all he knows there's something terribly wrong, he doesn't knock himself out but he knows instantly something's terribly wrong, breaking his spine or something, I mean he can only move his arms a bit but not the rest of him, imagine, you know, just imagine what that must feel like, and right then and there he must decide, you know, he's still under this three or four feet of water and he must decide whether to come up or not, I mean does he go on living like this paraplegic and all or just let himself drown in this three or four feet of water, I mean just put yourself in his shoes or whatever, I know I couldn't, but then he just comes up, you know, makes this all-important decision about the rest of his life, and I often wonder what that must be like, to be in this position to make this all-important decision about the rest of your life.

Ah, well.

Public transportation really a mess in this city. That's a fact. You can wait forever for some bus to show or two or three show up at the same time, but then you learn to take things like that in stride, I mean all you do is just sit or stand around and now and again look into the distance to see if some bus is or isn't coming, I mean it's no use complaining, it doesn't make a bit of difference.

But back to Grace.

She's like this Avis or something, you know, if you're number two you have to try harder, but she's out there hustling practically every day and night, like she deserted time or time deserted her, either way, but sooner or later I nearly always find her whenever I mean to, and she's got this really terrific face and all, practically angelic, and this great, really great head of hair, and her hands, her fingers, I mean it's like they're sculpted or something, sometimes I just can't help staring at them, the rest of her a mess of course, like she's just poured into this wheelchair, liquid you know, and she often tells me about her Johns, it takes all types I guess but there's usually a certain type that gets attracted to a woman in a wheelchair, sometimes she knows right off the bat she tells me, she can tell just by the way they're looking at her, and it's really no hard sell, no, nothing like that, I mean if a guy wants a woman in a wheelchair then that's just what he wants and all she has to do is be around for him to see her, and she's got this really great attitude about herself and her work, I don't know how but she does, not always of course, no, but most of the time, in general I mean, and talking to her nearly always makes me feel good about myself and just things in general, "And how's my lovely Bingo Man today?" she says, you know, things like that, and I don't even have to do too much talking if I'm not up to it, I do sometimes but not always, it depends, and she's got all these stories about her Johns, you know, most of them humorous but, no, not all, and the really great thing is that I'm not, you know, never was nor ever could be one of her Johns, not that she disgusts me, no, nothing like that, but I'm just not, and she knows it as well as I, our relationship of an entirely different nature I guess.

Now, here's the thing.

Grace not around. Nowhere to be seen.

This happened before of course, not often but every once in a while, and then I just hang or walk around for a spell and sooner or later I see her wheeling down the street or assisted out of some car, you know, but this time different, I mean the whole feel of it different, now and again I get this certain feeling about some things, like this sixth sense or something, and most of the time it's about things gone or about to go wrong, even terribly wrong, and half, yes, I'd say roughly half of the time I'd be right, and this feeling about Grace right up there with just about the worst feelings I've ever had, and I'm not saying it's right or wrong, just that it's there, that I have it, but what am I to do, I mean really, usually with feelings like that there's nothing but absolutely nothing to be done, I mean I guess I could start looking for her, but really, just where would I start, I mean I know nothing about where she lives, what she does with herself when she's not out on the street, out on her spot, and it's really like that with most people I guess, I mean you know some things, just some specific things about their lives but not others, I mean they could be just about anywhere and doing anything at all, still, I do start walking around a bit, up and down Biscayne and even along some intersecting streets, going by the different store fronts, mini-malls and some so-called professional buildings, and I pass by this one place that advertises services for illegal immigrants, you know, all you have to do is walk up some stairs and this law office or whatever will start the proceedings to make you legitimate and all, good luck, you know, I mean all these lawyers, whatever care about is pocketing the little money you've got and as for the rest you're pretty much on your own the way most people usually are, I mean I don't care who you are, really, it doesn't much matter, but whoever you are and no matter what people say or do for you, sooner or later you realize that you're pretty much or basically on your own, I mean people, some people might help you a bit here and there but really, basically you're on your own, and I just start thinking about these miserable illegal immigrants and all, I see some of them standing, lined up in front of some office upstairs, and in my mind they merge with Grace and all, you know, the way one set of miserable people will sometimes merge with another, and here again what's to be done, you know, that's the thing, what's to be done.

And about the most, the best I can do right now is head back to the beach, head back home, call it an afternoon, whatever, I mean I could walk up and down Biscayne here for the rest of the afternoon and even the night with my chances of running into Grace just about the same as they are now, which is practically nil the way I feel, so I just look out for number one, which is really a crude, an awful way of putting it but nevertheless true, yes, I'm pretty sure, true in spite of what I might think or tell myself.

Right now, for the moment I'm living two blocks off Ocean Drive, somewhere to the back of Ocean Drive, living with my cousin Frank, it's really his place, his apartment, he's been living there practically forever and I'm just shacking up with him for the time being, "Yeah, man, whatever," he said to me when I first called and suggested it to him, Frank this really laid back, easy going guy which is really strange considering the rest of the family we both come from, but the truth is he is out of it, really, kind of out of it most of the time, I mean when he's not drunk or high on some dope or other he is this smiley and well meaning zombie or something, not that I mind, not really, I mean a zombie is okay for a roommate, about the only kind of roommate who could put up with me I guess or I with him.

But the thing, you know, the thing is that Frank is both there and not there for practical purposes, I mean it's practically impossible to have a decent or even any sort of sensible conversation with him, not that I'm this great talker, nothing like that, but once in a while I really do feel like having some sort of intelligent conversation, not with Frank of course, I mean he's got these set phrases, comments to just about anything you might say to him, like now, you know, just now when I walk in, "Home so soon?" he says without really looking at me, I mean I bet he doesn't even know I was gone or gone for as long as I was, and by his eyes I can tell right away that he's been drinking and all, mixing his beer with this god awful whiskey he buys at this discount liquor store, the empty cans of beer all over the kitchen which is usually where he does his drinking, and, "Happy days are here again," I just say to him, I mean I really don't mind too much about the empties, I'm not this neat freak, nothing like that, and it's his place, you know, it really is, but now and again I just wish, you know, I really don't know what I wish, but, "You feel like going down to the pool?" I ask him, this rinky-dink pool in the courtyard which is about the only place we've ever had anything even vaguely resembling a conversation, I guess I'm in the mood just now to talk a bit about Grace or whatever, but this pool this really overblown bathtub where people from the building come just to sit and bullshit for a spell, I mean in all the time I've lived here I've never seen anyone actually swim, take the occasional dip but never an actual swim, and sitting by the poolside which Frank and I do now and again, I always get the feeling that life, you know, life is really somewhere else, up and down Ocean Drive but really somewhere else, that this place, by the poolside I mean, is like this limbo where people do nothing but sit around and wait for something to say or do, I mean nothing very much ever gets said or done, nothing of any importance that is, about the only curious or even vaguely memorable thing that ever happened was this old Russian guy, not quite right in the head, but this old Russian guy walking up and down and saying, "Mama dead, mama dead," as if to himself, you know not waiting for any response or whatever but just walking up and down and saying, "Mama dead, mama dead," and you really had no idea whether his mama died a day, a week or even years ago, I mean there was really no way to know, and I told Frank at the time that maybe we should just stop the guy on his rounds and ask him the details, you know, for his benefit if not exactly ours, but Frank just shook his head and said, "No, leave him, just leave him be," and that's what we did, we just let him continue his rounds and saying, "Mama dead, mama dead." The thing about Frank though, you know, whenever we go down to the pool and all, which isn't that often but now again, but whenever we go down to the pool he thinks he's this beach boy or something, in his red shorts and his flowery, cheap looking shirt, I mean I think he imagines he's out there on Ocean Drive or something and looking for action, but about the only action he's going to get around here is some old lady tripping over his outstretched legs or something or some old man coming around to ask him the time of day or month or even year, I mean this place practically infested with the aged and forgotten, I'm not complaining mind you, just observing, I mean some of my best conversations with these old geezers who now and again are pretty good at pretending to listen even though they probably can't hear a thing you're saying, and Frank just glistening with this Hawaiian Lotion number fifty or something, but the thing is I wouldn't mind going down to the pool with him just now, I really wouldn't.

So, "Frank," I tell him, "Frank," without really knowing what I'm going to say to him or how I'm going to say it.

But it's really no use, I can tell right away, you can usually tell even as you're about to say something, anything at all that it's going to be no use, I mean the feeling I get is that I'm in this one world and Frank in another, I mean all he does is sit there and stare at me with blank eyes and this totally expressionless face, I mean I could be Mother Teresa or Shaq O'Neal and the stare, the look would still be the same, he is basically just sitting, drinking and mulling to himself, his past and future so-called business deals I guess, Frank this small, but really smalltime pusher of drugs, a bit of hash and some pharmaceuticals I guess, but he exists on the periphery of the real thing that's going on all around us, this kind of nowhere middleman, a kind of metaphor for a loser, I mean he basically sells to tourists or kids from the burbs who come down here without a clue as to what they or this whole scene is all about, I watched him make a sale once to this pimply faced kid who looked like he would have bought anything from anybody just so he could think himself being with it or something, but in his eyes, I mean in Frank's eyes he fancies himself this big time dealer or something, you know, a regular Al Pacino in 'Scarface' or something, and the thing about that is that he must have watched that movie about sixty times to say the least, in any case Frank with a way of doing things, certain things over and over and over again, like he's trying to get it right or something, and now and again he'll even do this imitation, this really bad imitation of Pacino in the movie, I mean his, that is Frank's so-called Cuban accent is even worse than Pacino's in the movie, and he'll say something really stupid before he starts, "Okay," he'll say, "okay, guess who I am," and he's always this really bad, this miserable imitation of Pacino in that movie, but I don't mind, I really wouldn't if just once in a while we could have something resembling a serious conversation.

"Frank, Frank." So, I just leave him alone after a while. You know. What else? But this feeling, you know, brought on by Grace or her disappearance or the sight of all those illegal immigrants lining up in front of that office, who knows, I just can't shake this feeling that the world should or is about to explode, I mean it just comes over me every now and again like now I guess, I mean with everything I've seen, heard, done, thought and felt I don't see why it doesn't, and I'm not saying that I've already lived this really crazy, topsy-turvy life, although in some ways I have, enough to make a guy puke, to fart, to piss and shit in his pants, but I guess I've still a ways to go, a bit of time still before I can honestly say or ask why the world just doesn't explode, I mean according to some scientific types the world, this whole thing began with a bang and all and I see no reason why it just doesn't end that way, right now I mean, but enough, I guess, really, enough of that for the time being.

And here, yeah, here's another thing.

Once in a while I toy with the idea of changing my name and all, and not just the Bingo part which is about as ridiculous a way to go through life as one can possibly imagine, but the whole thing, the Sherman part as well, I mean once in a while my crazy old man, drunk or not, it really made no difference, but once in a while he'd say something like, "Oh, how we burnt Atlanta," or, "how we marched to the sea," like he really knew what he was talking about or was even there at the time, I mean all this crap and pseudo- crap that had nothing but absolutely nothing to do with him or us, and by changing my name I guess I occasionally get the feeling that I'd be stepping out of all of that crap, all of the past I mean, but I never take it any further than that, I mean I don't even know how one goes about legally changing his name and all, a lot of bureaucracy, a lot of paperwork I bet which is about the last thing I want in my life, I mean I can just see myself walking into some government office and going from one clerk to another and just repeating, "I want to change my name and all," I mean what would be the difference between me and that crazy old Russian going around the pool and repeating, "Mama dead, mama dead," no difference at all as far as I'm concerned, and at any rate at the sight of the first clerk I bet I'd just high- tail it out of there the way I have in the past, once when applying for unemployment money and another time for the GED, the so-called high school equivalency diploma, different cases, different offices I guess 'but the clerks, you know, the clerks all the same, but all I'm saying is that it's one thing to think, to dream about changing one's name and something else actually doing, going through with it, and I'm usually pretty good on the thinking, the dreaming part but absolutely hopeless on the going through with it one, the obstacles practically insurmountable, but at any rate it's doubtful whether changing my name would make all that much difference, make me feel better about myself perhaps, although who knows, really, who knows about something like that.

As to the GED, the so-called high school equivalency diploma. There is this guy at work, this Bruce Steadman, the foreman and my immediate boss I guess, he is forever after me to get my GED, I mean it's like it's uppermost in his mind or his primary goal in life perhaps, he'll say things like, "What's wrong with you, Bingo?" or, "You're a smart kid, Bingo, so, why not just do it?" I mean he hired me without it, you know, just after talking, spending a bit of time with me, and he'll often say I'm about the best guy on his crew, the most dependable, and this includes a bunch of old geezers who've been at this surveying thing since before I was born, but this Bruce, you know, he thinks I'm the one with the best eyes and hands, and ditto for showing up on time or doing overtime without batting an eye, and even though the business, you know, the surveying business is kind of precarious right now, that's a great word by the way, precarious, but it really is, another instance of everything depending on everything else, you know, if there's no construction, roads, buildings, whatever, then there's no surveying, so more and more we've been going out of town or out in the middle of nowhere, out into the Everglades, but in any case Bruce makes sure I'm on the job, that I'll be one of the ones he'll use for whatever job there is, most mornings he'll even come and pick me up because he doesn't live all that far from here, like he really cares or something, this kind of father son relationship or something, who knows, and I don't think he's gay or queer, I'm pretty sure, I mean I've had dealings with gays or queers before but I don't think Bruce is one, all or most of the signs missing I guess, and I don't, I wouldn't care one way or the other, I mean everyone's sexual preference is his or her own business as far as I'm concerned, but still it's better if one knows, I mean knows in advance about something like that, knows what to expect, but the thing is sometimes it's hard, nearly impossible to tell, I used to know this guy once, this body-builder type and in the end he turned out to be gay, and then this other, this really swishy type who wanted nothing but pussy out of life, I mean the whole thing was just an act, you know, his modus operandi I guess, so you never really can tell, but this Bruce this married guy and all, two kids, I've seen the photographs, but the thing is one never knows, never really knows for sure.

But back to the GED.

"It's nothing, really, nothing at all," Bruce tells me, " all it is is a bit of studying, a bit of preparation," scared I guess, I think he really is, that without this GED and all sooner or later he'll have to let me go, union rules about things like that, "And let me tell you, Bungo," he says, sometimes he calls me Bungo instead of Bingo, but, "let me tell you, Bungo, with this GED you'll be on your way, a knack," he says, "I think you've got this real knack for surveying, and who knows, take a couple of college courses, get a degree and you'll be set for life, start surveying for some bigger firms and maybe even the government," but I don't know, I really don't, surveying is all right I guess, I mean you're out of doors and no one's really on your back, you're just doing your own thing and for the most part just taking your sweet time about it, but survey for the rest of your life, or do anything for the rest of your life, I mean I really don't know, I just don't.

Get your head clear. That's it.

Now and again I tell myself, 'You need to get your head clear, Bingo,' regardless of the circumstances, the situation, but, 'You need to get your head clear,' I just tell myself, easier said than done in most situations, like my father and mother, just to take two examples, I don't think their heads were ever clear for a single day or even a single hour of their lives, I mean they go through life or whatever it is they do through this fog or something, living on the outskirts of this nowhere town in the Panhandle, population a hundred twenty or something the last time I looked, you know, hunting coons, rabbits, turtles, whatever, like it's really important or something, and my father forever tinkering with other people's cars, pickups like he's this really savvy mechanic or something which he never was nor will be, and my mother, yeah, well, that's another story, just clipping coupons and growing her own so-called vegetables, they're really these small, these shriveled looking things, and that's whether they're drinking or not, which at any rate they are most of the time, it's like they're these professional drinkers or something if drinking can be called a profession and all, but never mind about them, 'You need to get your head clear, Bingo,' I tell myself, like now when I'm just standing here and looking at Frank gazing into the void or something, like he's locked, really, locked in his own world or universe or something with no way out, his own world of dreams I guess, and, "Come on, Frank, come on," I tell him, "let's just go out, we'll walk to the beach or something," and it's like I'm talking to myself, that much is pretty clear, I mean I could just shake him or turn him upside down and his reaction would be about the same, which is nothing at all, although now, right now he does look up, he just about manages, and says, "Hey there, Bingo boy, what do you say, what do you do?" and he's got this really idiotic smile on his face, the Sherman smile I call it, like I can just imagine that Civil War general have the same kind of smile when he burnt Atlanta and then marched to the sea, I'm merely guessing of course, and at any rate that Sherman with nothing to do with us I'm pretty sure, and no sooner does Frank look up and say, "Hey, there, Bingo boy, what do you say, what do you do?" than he's looking down once more and gone, really out of it for practical purposes, don't laugh but I'll tell you whom he reminds me of at times, Ronald McDonald, that's a fact, and I don't mean the clown, you know, the clown himself but that miserable bastard playing the clown, that poor slob who other than playing this clown and all hasn't a clue about life or anything at all, I mean all he knows, all he does is to dress up like this clown and all and for the rest of the time he's like this lost soul or something, not that he isn't this lost soul when he's playing this clown but for the sake of the job he can put it on hold, forget about it for a spell, and that's Frank all over, with his booze and pills he can put his miseries on hold for a spell like this Ronald McDonald with this idiotic smile painted on his face.

But here's the funny thing.

Once in a while, not often, but once in a while I'll still go into a McDonald's, there's one not that far from here, and it isn't because I expect to run into Ronald McDonald, not a chance, I mean I go at these odd hours, the middle of the night or just before dawn I guess, and the reason I go is to catch a glimpse of these odd, these really curious types, I mean you'd be surprised at what washes up there in the middle of the night or just before dawn, this one time this really tall, this really gorgeous black hooker and all, I mean she was obviously dressed like a hooker and all, no way she could have been anything else, but that didn't matter, I'm just telling you, I mean everybody has to be something, make a living the best one knows how, but what did matter was that suddenly here was this really tall, this really stunning woman right out of the Arabian Nights or something, I mean right there in McDonald's and right smack in the middle of the night, in between Johns I guess, just taking a break, it didn't matter, but the way she looked and moved and even talked, you know, for a minute or two I was standing right next to her by the counter, but the way she just stood there it was like she was from another world or something, and I just froze, practically, I mean I just couldn't take my eyes off, and right then and there I was ready to follow her just about anywhere I think, I mean after she got her order and all and walked to this booth it was about all I could do not to trail behind and slide into that booth right opposite, and then tell her, yeah, that I would give her all the money I had on me, which wasn't much of course, not by a long shot, but give her all the money in the world just to be permitted to sit there and stare at her for a spell, really, nothing else, just to sit and stare at her, and no doubt she would have found that ridiculous and me as well, so in the end I didn't, of course I didn't do it, but that's what I'm talking about, that sometimes in the midst of this miserable world you get a glimpse of this other, this totally different one, and I don't want to make too much of this, I mean no doubt this gorgeous hooker had her problems the same as everyone else and perhaps even more, but occasionally there are these glimpses, you know, these sudden glimpses of I don't know what, and then you don't know what to do with them, how to fit them into anything at all, and that's just what makes them so special I think, that you don't know how to fit them into anything at all.

Once, just once I'd like to meet someone with his head clear, you know, his head perfectly clear about something, about anything at all.

The fact is I never have, not in all my life, a bunch of people I guess who were pretty good at pretending, but after a while you could tell, no question, you could always tell, but once, just once I'd really like to meet someone whose head was perfectly clear about something, anything at all, or to even have my own head clear about something, that'll be the day, but just once I'd like to see that happen.

Ah, well.

But, "Later, Frank," I just tell him, I mean there are times in our living together when his very presence depresses the hell out of me, mine him I suppose although I don't know, with Frank there's really no way to tell, but, "Later, Frank," I just tell him and off, off I go. 'The evening, the night is young, Bingo,' I tell myself just to raise my spirits a bit, but I head for the beach, Ocean Drive, the works, and for the moment I don't even care that the place, the whole scene is about as fake as you can get, all I want is to get out of the apartment, out of Frank's depressing presence and all.

And then.

I head for the beach but I do zig-zag a bit, pass a bunch of tacky stores, head shops, sex shops, what have you, strictly for the gullible, the tourists who have nothing better to do with their time than to gape and be amazed and all, I mean they come here expecting I don't know what, and then whatever they find has to do, you know, it has to be good enough for them, and then I'm even asked to snap a picture of these homey-looking girls in front of a sex shop and "Smile," I even tell them, "smile now," like an idiot, and one of them even asks me to pose with her friend and all, like it's this big joke or something, like I'm this native or something, part of the local atmosphere and all, but I don't mind, I really don't, I even get a kick out of imagining myself in some fancy album, and all this without their knowing who I am, knowing a single thing about me, but that's all right with me, it really is, as a matter of fact I sort of prefer it that way.

And on I go.

And passing this sunglass store or shack or something I'm even tempted to go in and browse a bit, you know, maybe even buy a pair, I've always had this thing for sunglasses, the same as everyone else I guess, you know, that with the right, just the right pair I'd be this new person or something, this new me, never happen of course, I mean I look pretty good in some of them but never quite good or new enough, like in just the right pair of sunglasses I'd be Tom Cruise or Richard Gere or someone, I mean it's just this stupid game I play with myself, I mean there are really no pairs of sunglasses to ever make me look like Tom Cruise or Richard Gere or someone, and I'm not even sure that's what I really want, and anyway those things are priced way out of my range, the ones that I want or think I want, so I just walk on by, you know, like later, later for that.

And it's great, really great to smell the ocean and all.

And you do, you really do, at first without even being aware of it, but suddenly there, there it is, and you know it's the ocean, it just couldn't be anything else, and this in spite of all the other smells in the air, you know, fried food, suntan lotion and who knows what combinations of perfumes and cologne, but the thing about the smell of the ocean is that in spite of all the other mixtures in the air you can't, you really can't mistake it for anything else.

This one time, you know, I dragged, I practically dragged Frank to the ocean in the middle of the night, I mean the beach itself never sleeps but I dragged Frank past Ocean Drive and right across the sand to the water's edge, you know, dragged him out of whatever dream world he was inhabiting at the moment, and I don't know what I expected to happen but something I guess, although who knows, all he did was moan and groan about the sand in his shoes, like it was such a big deal to take them off which he refused, absolutely refused to do, and then the darkness, yeah, even the darkness getting to him, "I feel like I'm going blind, Bingo, like I'm going fucking blind," he kept complaining, and it really wasn't all that dark, nothing like pitch black, in fact a kind of sparkle about the ocean and even the skies, I mean all you needed was just a bit of patience for your eyes to adjust and all, and Frank really not this patient type, I mean he's out of it most of the time but that's not the same as being patient, and right at the water's edge I felt like we were at some kind of boundary between worlds, I mean I don't know what Frank felt if anything at all, but right at this boundary I felt like I didn't even exist at all, you know, like everything else existed, the stars, the ocean, whatever but I didn't, or that there was just this looking, this observing and all but no looker, no observer to speak of, but then, "Fucking cold, Bingo," Frank said, "don't you think? The fucking wind picking up," and it really couldn't have been colder than sixty degrees, I mean this was fucking Miami after all, but Frank with this really poor constitution, I mean he feels chilled when the sun ducks behind the clouds or something, so we just turned around after a while and headed back, I mean the whole thing seemed like this huge mistake, dragging Frank to the ocean in the middle of the night and all.

I get comfortable on the veranda of this renovated Art Deco hotel and bar, I mean that's all you've got around here, all these renovated Art Deco hotels and bars, and I'm not that crazy about them, not really, they may have been something in the past, the twenties and thirties I guess, but now it's like they're trying to recapture or reinvent the past or something, I mean who the hell knows, and the people, all the so-called beautiful people are the same, living neither in the past nor in the present as far as I'm concerned, but whenever I come here it's always to this one veranda this one hotel and all, and, here's the funny thing, sometimes I think it's because they've got this really terrific, this really amazing blow dryer, hand dryer in the bathroom, I mean I've never seen anything like it anywhere else, this really jet age blow dryer that just about takes your hands, your arms off, I mean the sheer power is just amazing, you can just see the skin on the backs of your hands just flap around like it was a sheet of paper or something, but anyway I order one of these tall mojitos, like I'm this really with-it guy drinking mojitos and all, and I can drink three or four at a time without feeling a thing, it doesn't matter, except I do get a buzz, you know, just a little buzz going, but I still keep my 'Chicago Bears' cap on, and I don't care whether it's cool or not, it probably isn't, but I just do, and what I do, I mean all I do is just look, stare at things all around me, people mostly, I mean the more I drink, the more I look the weirder they become, and I don't mean weird in a bad way, just weird, curious I guess, I mean I'd bet I'd have nothing but absolutely nothing to say to anyone of these so-called beautiful people, nor they to me, but that's all right, it really is, I mean the people around here just want to be seen and all and not necessarily talked to, although there is this young German couple, you know, at the table next to me and they seem to be in something of a deep conversation, I don't understand a single word of course, but at least someone, you know, some people are having some kind of conversation after all.

And it's like two or three in the morning when I finally stagger, no, not stagger, just kind of float out of the place, I mean where does time go, I often get the feeling that it just dribbles through your fingers, and I'm feeling neither good nor bad but more good than bad I suppose, and I head back to Frank's place, to our place I suppose, and it's like I'm on automatic pilot or something, you know, just walking without really feeling I'm walking, and I just bet I could keep this up for hours, the entire night even, and I could head just about anywhere at all, north, south, east, west, you name it, without ever arriving, I mean spend the entire night just moving without ever arriving anywhere at all, but then what would be the point, I guess no point at all, so I just head home, and I don't know if it takes me a second or an hour to get there, I really don't.

And Frank's really at it tonight.

He's got all these types, these certified weirdos in the apartment, I mean I don't know where they come from but now and again they just appear, show up out of nowhere at the apartment, friends of Frank's I suppose or 'business associates' he once called them, but all they do is just hang around and talk in these monotone tones and all, I mean I doubt anyone of them listens to what anyone else is saying, it doesn't matter, but they just keep it up like they can't stop, can't help themselves, "Here's my Bingo man," Frank says but the others barely look up to acknowledge my presence, I mean they're just boozing, dropping pills and continuing with their endless monologues, and, "Don't let me interrupt or anything," I just say and head for my room, and the thing about Frank is that at least he keeps my room off limits to anyone else, I mean he keeps my door shut whenever I'm not around and makes sure no one gets in there, I mean his so-called friends, his business associates can spill over the entire apartment but at least my room is off limits to them, and the thing is if I didn't have this private space in Frank's apartment I don't think I could hang out here for very long, I'd have to go somewhere else, I don't care where, just somewhere else, I mean about the last thing I could deal with is Frank's so- called friends or business associates spilling into my room, which I'm sure they would do if Frank didn't keep my door shut and all, or even Frank himself, but Frank knows enough not to come in here unless I expressly ask him to which is once in a blue moon I guess, and it's not that there's anything important or special or whatever that I'm guarding in this room, unless it's me of course, my privacy, my private space, but that's it I guess, that's about all.

And then here's what happens.

No sooner do I go into my room, my private space and all than I start feeling dizzy, just out of nowhere like that, I mean I don't even bother turning the light on, nothing like that, just head for my bed I guess, and then, again, no sooner do I lie down, flat, just flat on my back than I start getting the shivers, the shakes, and I'm reminded of my mother, you know, who got the shivers, the shakes more than anyone else I've ever known, still does I suppose, but her shivers and shakes a lot more understandable than mine with her constant boozing and all, I mean if such a thing can be said to be understandable at all, I mean who, really, who knows what goes on in your body, at any one time all the things that go on in your body, it doesn't matter, but my mother just comes to mind, she's the last thing I think of before I go crashing into these bizarre dreams and all.

And Frank and his cronies are still at it outside, this humming or buzzing noise that's their pointless conversation, but it's like they're in this one world and I'm in another, this bizarre or bizarro world of dreams where I'm still shivering and shaking I suppose without really being aware of it.

'Come here, come here, Bingo!' I hear someone call.

But it's really no one at all, like I'm calling myself or something, and I'm in this really flat, this nowhere landscape, which could be Miami I suppose or maybe even all of Florida, but it really isn't, it's more like a desert or something, nothing but sand all around, and for some reason I've got all my surveying equipment with me, all the tools of the trade I guess, and, 'What the fuck,' I say to myself, 'what the fuck?' and I know, I just know I'm supposed to start surveying and all, I mean no rhyme or reason, I just am, I mean it's this really flat, this nowhere landscape so just why and what the hell am I supposed to survey, I mean I can't even tell where the land stops and the sky starts, there seems to be no separation or anything, but no sooner do I start setting up my stuff than I'm suddenly back home, back in the Panhandle, it's like I've got nothing to say about it, and surveying here with this really odd but also intense feel about it, like the sooner I start, the sooner I finish the better for everyone concerned, like I really have to get this right, survey it exactly right or else, but the thing is I'm just fumbling about, I'm even having a hard time just setting up that stupid tripod and all, and my old man and my mother are watching, you know, like, 'Let's see how he'll fuck this up and all,' and I can't even get properly started, no way, and even though I know this is about the most important thing in the world, to do this surveying right, to get it over and done with, I can't even get started and all.

And so on and on for the rest of the night, just one stupid and impossible surveying job after another, but there's no escape, not really, not until the early morning when I just sort of survey myself out of these idiotic dreams or something.

And I finally find myself on the floor when I wake. You know. Not on the bed at all but on the floor when I wake.

Frank talking to me about the Amazon.

This one day, this one evening Frank just talking to me about the Amazon, I mean I have no idea where this is coming from unless he'd been watching one of those silly National Geographic shows that take you all over the globe like you're this armchair explorer or something, but now and again Frank takes it in his head to, "Educate my fucking self," as he puts it, and what that usually means is that after he's high and all he'll watch some idiotic National Geographic program or something, it must have been on the Amazon this time, but this other time, about a month ago, it was some special on genealogy, you know, and then all he could do was talk about genealogy for days afterwards, like how we should explore the branches, unearth the roots of our family tree, like all the way back to this supposed connection to General Sherman and perhaps even further, which of course as far as I'm concerned doesn't exist, and Frank without a clue in the world of how we should go about such a thing, I mean he watched this stupid show on genealogy and all but still he hadn't a single clue, and anyway all you have to do is to look at the surviving, the living members of our family to realize that these aren't the sort of people with a genealogy worth a damn, I mean even if we knew what we were doing, even if there were records and all, which I doubt, about all we'd discover in the past would be more odd characters, more losers. like them, and perhaps even odder and bigger losers, the chances pretty good, "And what's the past got to do with us," I asked him, "got to do with the present?" to which he couldn't reply of course, just give me one of his idiotic smiles, but now it's the Amazon, you know, if it's not genealogy it'll be the Amazon or something like that, "There are something like four hundred fucking different tribes in the jungle," he tells me, "maybe more, undiscovered and shit," "So," I ask him, "so?" "And then all these medicines and shit, you know, herbal medicines," and then he's got this idea that one day, not now, but one day he and I should take this trip down the Amazon and visit all these known and unknown tribes, gather up all the herbal medicines we can find, you know, known and unknown, "Cure all the fucking ills of the world," he smiles, "Yeah, right," I tell him, but I know just what he's thinking, I mean saving the world not one of Frank's major priorities, what he really wants is to discover some kind of potent drug never before on the market, you know, corner the market, make a killing with this new kind of hallucinatory crap, and, "I'm sorry, Frank," I tell him, "but I just can't see you in this safari outfit and shit," and I'm breaking his heart, his dreams, I know I am, but, "We don't need a fucking safari outfit," he comes back at me, "all we need is this fucking loin cloth and all," and it gets better and better as we go along, it really does, "And I guess the natives will be overjoyed to see us," I tell him, "Damn right," he smiles, I mean sometimes Frank's like this child of ten or twelve of something, especially when he's high and some inane TV program got him all worked up, I mean there's really no sane, no rational way of dealing with him, "And what makes you think some medicine man of one of those tribes won't just kill your ass and serve you up as a ceremonial meal," I tell him, I mean such things have been known to happen, one of the Rockefeller boys I think some seventy years ago, and if they can kill and eat a Rockefeller they sure as hell can kill and eat Sherman," and then I get this vision, you know, I don't know why, I just do, but this picture of Ronald McDonald showing up in the jungle, in the midst of one of these tribes of the Amazon, and I wonder, I really do, what on earth they would make of him, I mean this symbol, you know, practically this symbol of western civilization showing up in their midst, I mean you can take your doctors, your political leaders and even your scientific types and as far as I'm concerned they don't hold a candle to Ronald McDonald as far as a symbol of western civilization, but then here's the thing, judging strictly by his dress, his appearance and not at all the poor drunken slob he really is, that tribe may well think this Ronald

McDonald the chief medicine man of some other, more developed tribe or something, perhaps even this great clown god of the jungle, I mean who knows, and that could be Frank I suppose, Frank as Ronald McDonald and this great clown god of the jungle, and who knows but that he would find his place and all right there in the jungle, it's just a thought, but then Frank just whistles through his teeth the way he sometimes does, his way of both emphasizing as well as nixing whatever we'd been talking about before, and you just have to love when he does that, I know I do, and that's as far as his dreams of an Amazon exploration go, really, about as far as he can carry it for the time being.

"There's been an accident," Frank tells me one evening when I return from this surveying job in the Everglades, "your mother, she's in the hospital," later it turns out he didn't get the story quite right, he rarely does, after a bunch of calls and all I finally find out what happened, it's my mother all right but it wasn't an accident but a heart attack, which makes a lot of sense, I mean what else but a heart attack after all the boozing, eating and just sitting around, and it's massive I'm told, too late to operate and all, but she's still hanging on, you know, just about, hanging on at this hospital, and I just tell Frank, "I gotta go," just like that, I mean I don't even bother thinking about it, and he, "All right, all right, let me go the fuck with you," but that's the last thing I need and want, you know, keeping an eye on Frank while thinking, worrying about my mother, so, "No," I tell him, "no, you just stay put and I'll be back, back as soon as I can," even though I have no idea what the hell I'm talking about, I mean I have no idea what I'm getting myself into, and anyway the last time Frank saw my mother he was just this little kid and all and I bet he doesn't even remember what she looks like, so I just pack a few things in this airline bag and all and take this stupid cab to the bus station, I mean they've got buses running day and night, I'm pretty sure, and while I'm getting ready Frank is just moving up and down the apartment like he doesn't know what to do with himself, like he's really out of it, which I guess he is, I mean if there's one thing Frank can't handle it's death or even the idea of death, he really has no grasp on things when it comes to death and that may be jumping the gun a bit, although, no, I don't think so, but, "So long," I tell him, "so long," and I'm out the door.

And it's like I'm heading right smack into the middle of the night, smack into the middle of the unknown. Just this feeling I have.

The bus ride's to take about eight hours or so, dawn by the time I'll arrive, you know, journeying right through the very heart of the night, and a lot, I tell myself, a lot can happen on a journey like that, although I really have no idea what I'm talking about, but I get comfortable in my seat by the window, 'Just get comfortable, Bingo,' I even tell myself, 'that's the main thing,' and I'm just staring into nothingness out the window, like I can't even see or feel or think, just staring into nothingness like that.

And the thing, yeah, I guess the only thing that saves me after a while is that this cute, this really cute young woman climbs aboard and sits down right next to me, "Is this seat taken?" she even asks, I mean the bus is half empty and all so it's really this pointless question, but, "Only by you," I reply like I'm this really suave, this sophisticated guy-about-town, which is like the biggest joke going as you must know by now, but then we don't talk for a while, later, later I guess, but we just sit there in silence as we pull out of Miami, both of us lost in our own thoughts or something.

And I'm doing my best to picture my mother and all. No rhyme or reason, I just am.

And sometimes, you know, sometimes when you try to picture something or someone, that's when it becomes the hardest, practically impossible, I mean all I get is this blurry image of a large woman who just sort of moves about, or sits, you know, just sits in this ratty chair like it's impossible for her to get out of it, and no face, no, nothing at all, the face comes a bit later, shows up on its own, and the thing is do I love her or have I ever, or she me, I mean has either one of us ever made it easy for the other and then at about the same time I start thinking about my father, I mean what I have in common with my old man, which is practically nothing at all, but the thing is maybe you can love someone even when you have nothing in common with her, you know, I mean maybe love has nothing to do with whether you have anything in common with the person or not, I'm just thinking, but maybe love is something entirely apart from that, I just don't know, but then a bunch of images do start, some good I suppose and some bad, but mostly bad I guess, like I just see her lying practically senseless on the floor when she's dead drunk and all, I mean what sort of a relationship with a person who's dead drunk and all, but then some other images start to come as well, and not all of them bad, no, not all.

And I'm just heading into the night. And it's like at times I don't even know where or why.

And luckily, yeah, I guess luckily that's when this young woman and I start talking, conversing a bit.

And it's funny how every once in a while, not always and not even that often, but how every once in awhile depending on the circumstances and all you start talking to this total stranger and the words just keep corning, I mean you don't stop, the words just keep flowing, just one topic after another, and it just seems, you know, it really does, that all the topics in the world are somehow related, I mean you think of this one topic and then another and it just seems that there's a link, I mean you may be jumping all over the place, you probably are, but it doesn't seem like that, no, not at all, and I'm just discovering all these things about this young woman and she about me, and not just our names and all, hers, by the way, is Yolanda, which I think is this pretty cool, this pretty unusual name, and I almost hate to tell her mine, Bingo, you know, but she just nods and smiles, like she doesn't think it's funny but just a bit odd perhaps, but anyway she's this model type, you know, studying nursing or something on the side, but really this model type, and that's something I can certainly believe and even tell her so, and she's just going to the west coast of Florida, Tampa or someplace for this modeling job, and I don't even ask her why Tampa and why in the middle of the night, it really doesn't matter, and here is where it gets just a little bit odd, curious I guess, but she also happens to be this courier for drugs and all, but strictly part time and not on any great scale, I mean she's got this doctor friend, two, really, one in Miami and the other in Bogota, and what they do or have done is to make this incision across her belly, "Horizontal, you know," she says, and she's ready to show it to me, in the end she doesn't, but she's certainly ready to, 'Like a pouch," she says, and that's where the packets of drugs go, one or two I guess, and heroin I'm guessing, and then she gets sewn up in Bogota and sliced open again in Miami, I mean that's how it's done, "But it's really a small cut," she assures me, "practically invisible," and I'm thinking, Christ, Frank should be here to hear this, I mean I bet neither he nor any of his so-called business associates ever thought of this particular mode of transportation, "But I'm going to stop," Yolanda assures me, "just one or two more trips and that'll be it," and I believe her of course, no reason I shouldn't, but for a while I just can't get her belly out of my mind, her pouch with the drugs and all, I mean it's this pretty unusual and even exciting picture, and then I tell her about my own so-called trip to the Panhandle, the mother probably dying if not already dead in the hospital, and, "Oh, no," she says, "oh, no!" like she's really this sensitive, this caring person, which I'm sure she is, and on and on I go, I mean Yolanda is not just this great talker but a great, or at least a better than average listener and I'm painting this really awful picture of my family for her which I don't think I've ever bothered painting for anyone else before, you know, not even for myself, and she's listening, I mean she really appears to be, and then she says, "Come, come here," and she lets me put my head on her shoulder, but it's really her breast, her left breast because I slide down a bit, she doesn't mind, no, not one bit, and this is how we ride through the night, that's pretty much it.

And then just before she leaves, gets off in Tampa, she writes down her name and phone number on this slip of paper she hands me, and, "Don't be a stranger," she says with this really cute smile, and I just wish she said something else or even nothing at all, I mean people are forever saying, "Don't be a stranger," to one another and they mean nothing, but absolutely nothing by it, but in her case I don't really mind, I guess I don't, but, still, I wish she said something else or even nothing at all.

Let me just say this one thing, this one positive thing about my visit back home, my so-called visit to the Panhandle.

I'm in time, still in time to see my mother alive. And the first thing I do, really the first, is to hitch a ride to the hospital, the people here are pretty friendly, they'll pick you up no matter what, I mean you can look like a serial killer or something and still they'll pull over and pick you up, "Where you headed?" they'll ask and off, off you'll go, and it's this really terrific dawn and all, morning I guess, the sky all red, orange-then yellow, something like that, and this guy, really no one special, but this guy even goes out of his way to drop me off by the entrance to the Mercy of Christ hospital, and the thing about that name is that it really gives me the creeps, I don't know why, it just does, I mean who knows whether Christ was truly merciful or not, there's no way to tell, and I bet, yeah, I just bet that even the people around him at the time he was living, the apostles, I bet even they didn't know whether Christ was merciful or not, I mean as far as they were concerned he was just this really charismatic and energetic prophet, and other than that, no, I bet they didn't know a damn thing about him, and let's, you know, let's just say he was merciful, for the sake of argument, but let's just say he was, I don't see how that makes a damn bit of difference to my dying mother right now, I really don't.

Still.

The place is pretty much deserted, it being early in the morning, but this woman, this nurse I guess gives me a hard time at the reception desk, I mean I guess her role in life is to give a hard time to just about anyone who comes here to visit, I mean she just looks me up and down and then points to this clock on the wall and says, "Do you know the time?" like I'm this creature from another planet who hasn't a clue about earth time or earth rules and regulations, so,"My mother is dying," I just tell her, or shout, yeah, maybe I shout it, nothing terribly clear at the time, although somethings, yeah, somethings painfully clear, and the thing is my shouting does achieve something, it has an effect, I mean what it does is jolt this nurse awake, like now my mother's dying is no longer just my problem but hers as well, hers in the sense that she can't just disregard it, not with this crazy guy shouting at the top of his lungs, I mean she could call security I suppose but in a place like this what sort of security can they have, some old geezer I suppose who's sleeping it off in some utility closet or somewhere, can barely hear or see and with his gun embedded in his holster because he's never had to use it, so the nurse must figure it's just her and me, and who knows, she certainly doesn't, but who knows what sort of unbalanced person she's got to deal with, I mean around here every other person is unbalanced in some way with the rest just out to lunch, and the thing, about the only thing I regret is that I haven't got this tattoo on my forearm with a skull and dagger and 'MOTHER' in flowery letters across, I think that would just about clinch it, but the thing is I was never a great fan of tattoos, and not just the tattoos but the whole process with the needles just about giving me the creeps, Frank now and again raises the possibility, the idea, like he's got this idea of flames or some heart in a flame right across his chest, but, no, not even Frank would go through with something like that, I'm pretty sure, no matter, but the the nurse, yeah, the nurse finally does take me my mother's room, I mean it's really no skin off her back, and it's three sixty-nine, this really great number, practically impossible to forget, and then I even smile, why not, but I even smile at the nurse and say, "Many thanks," or something like that.

My mother all alone.

Which is about what I expected.

I mean even though it's early in the day, the sun, I guess, yeah, the sun just about peeking through her window, but even if it weren't I wouldn't expect anyone to be by her side, standing death watch or whatever, I mean everyone in my so-called family with this deathly fear of hospitals, I mean once you're in there you just don't come out they all figure, and in my mother's case that's probably right, no matter, but my mother just all alone and hooked up to these tubes and all and breathing through a mask, but other than that she really doesn't look all that bad, I mean I've seen her look a lot worse at various times of her life, I mean not that she looks great, I don't think I've ever seen my mother look great in her life, this one time maybe when out of the clear blue she decided to attend Sunday church, but it was only that one time, but the thing is she really doesn't look terrible, not like someone who's about to pass from this world into the next.

Asleep. Yeah, I guess. All the signs. Although who knows, really who knows? And I just sit down by her side, pull a chair over by her head to be more precise, and then just stroke the top of her head, her face, whatever, and, "It's Bingo, Mom," I tell her, "it's Bingo," and after a while, you know, but after a while she does open her eyes, and there may or may not be a sign of recognition, maybe there is, but then she shuts her eyes again, like having seen me it's now okay to shut her eyes again and get back to the business of dying, and then there's nothing, really nothing for me to do but just sit there for a spell, and my preference would be that she expire right then and there while I'm still around but you can't rush a thing like that and maybe you shouldn't, but it would be best I think, it really would, if she would expire while I was still here.

Not that she's in any pain. I don't think so. Her face though, yeah, her face does twitch a bit every now and then, but that could be from anything, really, anything at all.

"It's Bingo, Mom, it's Bingo," I tell her again but this time she doesn't even bother opening her eyes.

And then here, here's what I'm thinking.

What sort of a life and death for a woman like this, I mean it doesn't make a hell of a lot of sense to me and maybe not even to her, although I wouldn't presume to say, to judge, but still, what sort of a life and death, I mean I guess you're supposed to get things out of life, just certain things, and don't ask me what exactly, I'd be hard put to say, but just certain things let's just say, and what did this woman ever get out of life other than being born and then living, existing from one day, from one hour to the next, and her dying pretty much the same, I mean it's like she's not even around to witness, to experience it, out of it is what I'm saying the way she was for much of her life, but I really don't want to think about that too much, it doesn't help, but sometimes you can't help what you're thinking, you just can't.

And I just stay like that for the rest of the morning, pretty much so, a couple of hours at the very least.

And then this nurse, this really cute nurse comes in, Rose, and that's this really terrific, this appropriate name for her, and she doesn't even ask who I am or what I'm doing here, I mean it's like she can tell at a glance what's what, and then, "Would you like a cup of coffee?" she asks and I just shake my head, I mean I'm neither hungry nor thirsty, no, nothing like that, and the thing is I haven't even taken a piss in I don't know how long, and most of the time I piss fairly regularly, every hour on the hour I'd say, I mean even Frank noticed it, "You do anything but piss, Bingo?" he asked this one time, but nothing now, it's like I've shut down or something, and I'm not even tired or sleepy, it makes you wonder I guess, I mean no drink, no food, no sleep for I don't know how many hours and still I'm okay in a manner of speaking, I guess I am.

But then, you know, then.

I see this cockroach out in the middle of nowhere, out on the floor I guess, on its back, you know, with just its legs and antennae twitching a bit, I mean it's dying, that's pretty obvious, and then just the sight of that cockroach dying and all, that's what really gets to me, and I get nauseous like from one moment to the next, and before you know it I'm in the bathroom and throwing up into the toilet, I mean I don't know what I'm throwing up, there isn't much but I'm really going through the motions, and it's that dying cockroach, not my mother, but that dying cockroach that's making me puke my guts out.

And, "You all right?" the nurse asks when I come out, and, "Fine," I tell her, "perfectly fine," which in a way I am now that I've puked or tried to for all I'm worth.

And, "It won't be long now," she says, "I don't think it will." But the thing is I just can't stay around any longer, and even though my whole reason for coming her was to be with my dying mother, I just can't, so I just hightail it out of there, I really do, but not before I embrace this Rose and all, no rhyme or reason, I just do, and then I'm out of there, head for the hills, which is a laugh of course, given the hills around here, but I'm out of there, that's the main thing, I really am.

So.

I just check into this motel, not a motel really, just some guest house or something with a couple of rooms off the highway, I mean the last thing I want is to go back home, my mother's so-called house where for the last couple of years she's been living by herself, my father off on his own somewhere else, who knows, but the last thing I want is to be there with all her so-called things about me, her smells and all, and it's not that I'm disgusted, no, nothing like that, but right now I just don't want to have anything to do with that, so this guest house, whatever is just about perfect, I mean a time in my life when I did nothing but live in these motels and all, some for shorter, some for longer periods of time, so this is fine, really, perfectly all right.

And sometimes, you know, sometimes I just think that this is or will be the story of my life, just spending my time living in all these motels, just one after the next after the next, I mean right now I'm living with Frank but that's not a solution, in no way is that anything like a permanent solution, and say whatever you want about Frank, at least he's got this place and all, it hardly matters what and where it is, but at least it's his own is what I'm saying, and when I think about me, yours truly, I can't even begin to imagine myself with a place of my own, and it's not just a place I guess but everything, yeah, all the things that go with having a place of one's own, I mean this feeling of being settled or grounded or whatever, and then who knows, and I know I'm reaching here, I really am but for the moment I just don't care, but maybe some woman, some female companion, and even, don't laugh, but later even a kid or two or maybe a bunch of them, I mean all these little Bingos or Bingettes just running around, and the thing is I've always been crazy about kids, no rhyme or reason, I just have, like the other day on the beach I saw this kid, this little girl of ten or eleven on roller skates, I mean she was gawky as hell and wearing this stupid looking striped T-shirt to boot, and it was about all she could do to keep from falling, to skate a couple of feet, rest and then skate some more, I mean maybe it was her first time on these skates, it's entirely possible, but I just kept looking, staring at her like she was this really terrific or beautiful sight, I mean all around her there were these stunning, these drop dead gorgeous guys and women, like models or would-be models just zooming by, but for some reason I didn't give a damn about those, no, not one damn, I mean all I did was look, stare at this gawky little kid, but all I'm saying is that I just have this thing for little kids, and the gawkier the better I even think, but can you just imagine me with one, even just one of these, I sure as hell can't, I mean I'd be worried to death all the time about raising, bringing them up the right way, and I don't even know what that might mean but so long as it wasn't the way I was brought up, I mean my old man and my mother just had me was all, the result of some accident no doubt, and for practical purposes, as far as they were concerned that was about it, I mean the idea that raising a kid involved some care, some planning never even entered their minds I bet, and I'm not knocking them, I'm really not, too late I guess, really, too late for that, but all I'm saying is that I'd do it differently, I really would.

No. I have no idea what I'm saying thinking.

'Ah, the story of your life, Bingo,' I just say to myself and leave it at that.

And then.

What I do is go into the bathroom, no window, and when I shut the door, it's dark, but absolutely dark in there, and I don't bother with the light but just sit on top of the toilet in this absolute darkness, and that's all I do, just sit in the dark like that.

And I don't know how much time passes or even if time passes at all, sometimes I feel it doesn't, like now I guess, but then I just come out after a while and lie down on the bed, flat on my back on the bed, shut my eyes, and then I just fall fast asleep like I haven't slept in days or even years perhaps, I mean all there is is this darkness but deeper, a lot deeper than the darkness in the bathroom before, and I have no idea of anything at all, no dreams, no images, just this deep sleep like I'm dead or something.

And then.

It's early evening when I return to the hospital, and I find my mother's room empty, and I'm told she passed away that afternoon, the orderly or whoever quite precise about the time, he even looks at his watch like he's reading it off or something, "Four twenty-two this afternoon," he says, and I don't know what to do with that bit of information, I really don't.

And then, who do I see there but my old man, my so-called father, and all we do is just kind of look at each other, like 'It's you, is it?' and then he just says something like, "We've lost her, Bingo, we really have," and for some reason I just hate him then, for what he says and the way he says it, and I don't even know whether he's drunk or not, he probably is but at times with him it's impossible to tell, but I just hate him for what he says and the way he says it, I mean he doesn't even bother to ask how I am or where I've come from or where I'm staying, not that I expect him to at a time like this, but, yeah, maybe I am, but I just hate him for what he says and the way he says it as much as for what he doesn't say, doesn't ask.

And we just sit there for a spell on this bench or something right outside her empty room, and, "I guess we'll have to make some arrangements," he says, which means that I will, it's fairly obvious, but I don't mind, not one bit, but again it's just what he says and the way he says it.

And I don't much care to go into details about all the rest. I really don't.

Funerals really give me the creeps, not dying or death so much as funerals, there's something really fake and unreal about all the ones I've ever attended, not that many I guess, but all the ones I've ever attended, like people don't know what to do with themselves, they really don't, like everything they do or say with this feel of fakery, of unreality about it, about the only real, the only genuine thing is the dead person in the coffin, and no one can touch that, no, no one even comes close.

And I don't stick around for long afterwards. No.

No reunions, strolls down memory lane, nothing like that, I just check the schedule for the bus and wait in the depot, I mean if I had to wait for days and nights I'd still do it in this depot and nowhere else, I've just about run out of energy for anywhere else, just sitting and waiting in this depot about all I can manage.

And the thing is there's this mangy dog right inside the depot, just lying on the floor I guess, and I call him over, like, "Here, boy, here," and after a while he does, just ambles over and flops down by the foot of my bench, and I'm grateful I guess, yeah, truly grateful for his so-called company, like in this entire place his is about the only company I care for while waiting for my bus, like his seeing me off is the only thing that makes any sense at the time.

Nothing special.

The ride back to Miami.

Really, nothing special at all. And then.

As soon or almost as soon as I get off the bus I run into this guy who looks like he's got nothing to do in this world except to stand around and look dumbfounded or just plain dumb, and then I hear him saying to me or, really, to no one in particular, "This is like a fucking foreign country," meaning Miami of course, what else, but, "This is like a fucking foreign country," he repeats while looking at me this time, and I figure I better reply, just say something, with this type of person you're usually better off replying, just saying something although, no, not always, so I just say, "You bet," and let it go at that, it seems to do the trick, but the thing is as I leave him I start thinking, that fucking or no fucking foreign country this is still a hell of a lot better than up there in the Panhandle, I mean I'll take the Cubans, Colombians, Haitians, whatever over those rednecks any time of the day or night, and until I'm actually thinking this I didn't even realize that this was the way I felt, and it's not that I'm crazy about Cubans, Colombians, Haitians or whomever but they're a hell of a lot better than the rednecks up north, and this is something like a discovery, a revelation to me, I mean anytime you find out how you really feel about something and it's not at all the way you thought you felt it's really something like a discovery or revelation, and then I feel okay, almost okay I guess about being back in Miami.

So then I just head for the nearest McDonald's.

I mean it's like I haven't eaten for days, which in a way I really haven't, and hunger, this tremendous hunger has just caught up with me, sort of like after holding your breath underwater you suddenly take this big, this really deep breath on surfacing, although that's not a good analogy, it really isn't, never mind, but what I do is order two Big Breakfasts like I know that just one won't do, but two Big Breakfasts with the eggs, the sausage patties, hotcakes, biscuits and hash browns, and I don't even care that it takes them like under a second to give them to me, like the things have just been sitting around for god knows how long just waiting to be microwaved, I mean how good can they be, but it doesn't matter, and anyway I was reading the other day, I forget where, but I read that McDonald's is like the biggest fast food chain in the entire world, and that's something I suppose, it really is, I mean right now as I'm eating this shit there are people in London, Paris and maybe even Outer Mongolia eating this same shit, who knows, maybe even in certain places along the Amazon, who knows, you can never tell, which for some reason makes me think of Frank, but, no, not just then, but all these people more or less like me, some more and some less I suppose, and in different time zones of course, it doesn't matter, but all these people eating the same shit I am, like Latin I guess, you know, all these people speaking Latin one time, in the Middle Ages I guess, pretty close to it, and I don't exactly know how that makes me feel, good I suppose, more good than bad at any rate.

And then of course, I just start thinking about Ronald McDonald, how he's this universal symbol or something, I mean he really isn't but he could or might as well be, I mean if you have to have a universal symbol why not Ronald McDonald, I'm not saying either way, but, you know, why not.

And then I can't, I really just can't wait to get home.

I mean everything is relative, I guess it really is, but I don't even want to think about all that stuff right now, all I want is to get back to Frank and all.

Like here we go, you know, here we go and the rest of all that shit. "How time flies," Frank says to me.

Nothing, really, meaning nothing by that at all, but once in a while he'll just come out with something like that, just out of the clear blue like it's something deep, philosophical, which it really isn't, just something to say I suppose, I mean Frank without a philosophical bone in his body, that much for certain.

Still.

Nothing lasts, that much clear enough, and we know as little about beginnings as we do about endings, I mean both beginnings and endings sudden at times and more or less confusing, like Frank has this friend and all, had I suppose, but this friend or acquaintance who was a garbage man one time, not a bad job, really, given the pay and the little background required, but it's all who you know, the union pretty exclusive, but this acquaintance of Frank's who, judging by the one time I met him, had his shit together about as much as Frank, which is to say not at all, but, still, he was this garbage man and all, or sanitation worker which sounds like you're this goddamn professional, but, you know, on the job, what, two, three months at the most, and then he gets killed, from one day, one hour, one moment to the next he just gets killed, and he's on the job when it happens, that's what I'm getting at, that he's on the job when it happens, I mean I don't care who you are and what you may or may not be doing but when your time is up your time is up I guess, and this kid, Dick I think his name was although I'm not sure, but let's just say, but anyway this Dick may have thought he had it made in a manner of speaking, with the steady pay, relatively short hours and only the occasional periods of exertion, I mean the whole business so damned mechanized it's like the eighth or the ninth wonder of the world, just as an aside, some mornings when I have the time I just go out there to watch these mechanized monsters do their thing, I mean garbage collection, I really do, I mean you can have your Mars or whatever robots, you know, these mechanized little gadgets directed from the earth but for my money I'll take these really amazing, these stupendous garbage trucks, not to mention the garbage men, sanitation workers I guess with practically nothing to do, the barest minimum I guess, a little pulling, lifting, then some tossing is about all, I mean about all they need to do is make sure that everything goes according to this preordained plan or something, which is how I think of it whenever I see them, but apparently there's something else that's required, I mean you still need to have your wits about you which apparently neither Dickie nor the driver did this one time, the driver just backing up without looking around and Dick, you know, Dick putting himself between the truck and this building the way Frank told it, and then squashed I guess, yeah, like a bug, which is really an awful way to go when you think of it but maybe, maybe not, because it's probably over in a second or two, I mean that's my guess, but the thing is, on my way home from McDonald's I just start thinking about death and all, life and death both I guess, I mean if the one then the other I suppose or if the other then the one, and the thing is no one but no one knows what to make of either, not really, although we have a better shot with life, that's my guess, because we're smack in the midst of it, whereas with death, well, death this great unknown, even though in a manner of speaking we're smack in the midst of death as well, but, still, death this great unknown, and it's pretty amazing that a lot, quite a few people will opt for death while still in the midst of life, and I'm not saying Dick was one of those or even me, no, but once in a while I'll start thinking, just fed up with all the shit around me, but then here, now here's the interesting thing, the next thing I think is that what if you had death, you know, something like death right in front of you, would you choose it then, I mean while you were still alive would you be capable of choosing death, death being this absence, this nothingness although I'm not entirely sure, but still, it's a legitimate question, and in the end who knows, really, no one is my guess and I'm pretty sure I'm right.

And then for some reason I want to share this with Frank, this line of thinking I mean, and good luck is about all I can tell myself, really, because what I don't want is to start talking about my mother's dying and death but what I do want is to share just some kind of thought about death with Frankie boy, anything at all except my mother's dying and death, and I'm just hoping against hope that some of it will still be clear in my head and Frank will be in some kind of condition to listen, so, good luck as I said, but the thing is as soon as I get home I can see right away that Frank is truly out of it, I mean I can tell by just the look in his eyes that he's on this ten or even fifteen hour high or something, tell also by the way he says, "Damn, how time flies," in lieu of a greeting, and then so much, I guess, so much about sharing some of my ideas about life and death, mean I may as well share them with the walls or the refrigerator door for all the good it'll do me, and that's about it, yeah, pretty much it for the time being.

But back to McDonald's for a moment.

And it's nothing, no, really nothing to do with Ronald McDonald now, let's just forget about him for now, but the thing is there's this really, this truly amazing camaraderie among all the workers there, and I don't know if it's just down here because of all the Latinos and blacks and all, I really don't, but the thing is all these workers just kidding, joking around while flipping the burgers and frying the fries, and when one of them comes on his or her shift or leaves, you know, he or she will embrace and kiss all the others, practically all the others, I mean it's like this one big happy family which is weird, really strange considering the circumstances, and occasionally I'll just stare at them and think, 'Ah, so this is what a big and happy family is like,' I mean this is how they act and all, and it's not that I'm envious, no, although yeah, maybe just a bit, but for all that I still wouldn't want to be one of these workers, I mean they have a kind of job security but on the whole I'd rather be a garbage man than go on frying fries and flipping burgers all day. But the thing about job security.

My surveying job may be down the tube soon, the handwriting's on the wall, you know, we go out into the Everglades only two or three days a week now, Bruce just trying to stretch the job as far as he can, and, "Keep your eyes open, Bungo," he'll say to me, "just keep them open," and he'll start talking to me about these other fairly remote jobs, that is if I mean to stick to surveying which I expect he expects, but this job in Kuwait for example, I mean Kuwait of all places, which is a part of the world I haven't given much if any thought to, and this in spite of the fact that that region, you know, that part of the world is constantly in or on the news, which I don't much care for, the news I mean, written, oral, visual, it doesn't much matter, what I'll do is just read the advertisements or watch the crappy commercials, I mean I get at least something out of those even if it's just mindless entertainment, like the other day this advertisement in the paper about meaningful cremations, you know, 'Have you ever thought about a meaningful cremation?' it asked and that just killed me, it really did, but, anyway, back to Kuwait, I think Bruce is sorely tempted to go, his so-called company can get this contract, I don't know how but I think it can, and he's ready and wants to take me along, "Let's leave this shit behind," he said to me, "and take off into the great unknown," and I'm not sure just what he meant by all this shit, but I guess everything, this country, this city and maybe even his family but I don't think I'm ready for that, no, not like Bruce is, I guess I might consider a move to Canada or somewhere in the Caribbean, but even that's just a maybe, I mean I think there are still possibilities to explore around here, I'm just guessing, and even if that's just a vague, a blurry idea in my head it's still an idea, what I mean is I'm not ready to give up on Miami just yet like for now it's still Miami, as far as I'm concerned.

So I have this conversation with this fish. I'll explain.

This really blue, this shimmering fish, I mean all it is is this guy dressed up in some fish suit and standing not far from this liquor store and holding up a sign that says, 'GET YOUR DISCOUNT LIQUOR HERE,' I mean how's that for a job, really, dressed up as this fish for I don't know how many hours a day, rain or shine I guess, it doesn't matter, but the thing is no one bothers to talk to it, him, he's all alone out there right off the highway, at any rate not that many people doing any walking around here, some but not that many, most of them in cars and just driving by, you know, a few of them will wave I guess, like some automatic reflex at seeing this fish, and I guess the connection, you know, between this fish and the liquor store is that here you can drink like a fish at rock bottom prices, but no one will stop to talk to him, a few blocks down the road I've seen this Statue of Liberty, this woman dressed up as the Statue of Liberty and advertising this income tax place, like having your taxes done is about the most American thing you can do, but I have seen people talking to her, like it's easier to talk to the Statue of Liberty than to some fish, but I do stop to talk to this fish, this guy, and he's not at all what you'd expect from a guy dressed up as a fish, although when I stopped I didn't know what to expect, I am usually without expectations I guess, but I soon enough find out that he's got this master's degree in social work from Columbia, you know, everyone down here is from somewhere else, that's a fact, the original Spanish, French, British, whatever, they were from somewhere else as well, and that includes the so-called Native Americans, the Miccosukees who were brought or chased down into the Everglades by the U.S. government at the time, but the thing is I do stop to talk to this fish, and he's really grateful, I can tell he is, he even puts his sign down while we have this really interesting, perhaps even meaningful discussion about Miami and life in general.

Which reminds me.

I've always had this thing for animals, and that includes guys in fish suits I guess, and the thing is Frank is pretty much the same, he really is, I once dragged him to the zoo in South Dade, and don't ask how we got there but we finally managed, and you should have just seen him with all these animals, I mean neither of us really crazy about their being confined, although some in these really large enclosures made to resemble their natural habitats, but for practical purposes they were still these enclosures, no matter, but you should have just seen Frank with these tigers, gorillas and even some of the more exotic antelopes, I mean animals, even caged ones can communicate pretty directly sometimes, about all you have to do is just stand there a bit and look and you'll find none of the fakery that's common or fairly common among human beings, and Frank was just standing there and taking it all in, and I couldn't even tell if he was or wasn't high at the time, it didn't matter I guess, but Frank just standing there and getting this other kind of high which was a hell of a lot better than the other kinds he's usually on. But back to the guy in the fish suit.

As I said we really have this deep, this meaningful conversation, fish or no fish he's remarkably well informed, I really can't tell you all the things we discuss but they include greed, nuclear energy and sexual politics to name just a few, "The problem with the world is our egos," he says at one point, "our egos forever getting in the way," and I can't agree more, I mean he's really this thoughtful, this serious type, "Look," he says, "just look around, it's everyone for himself as far as I can tell," and so on and so forth, I mean it's just shit like that one after another, and at some point, yeah, at some point I'm even tempted to bring up my idea about life and death, you know, of death within life with him, it never happens though, I haven't the chance, because the thing, the only bad thing with this guy, this fish is that once he gets going he doesn't know where or how to stop, I mean if it's not the problems of the Palestinians it's poverty, hunger and eradicable childhood diseases, I mean there's really no end to it, and after a while I just stand there nodding and except for some brief comments here and there he doesn't leave much for me to say, and it's not that I disagree with anything he says, pretty much the opposite, but I'm like in the midst of this avalanche of words where I can barely move or even breathe, and in the end it's all, really, about all I can do to get away from him, I mean guy or no guy, fish or no fish my head's just swimming, and it's a shame, it really is, because there are all these ideas in my head I never get the chance to run past him, but what, really, what can I do, so, "Well, I've got to get going," I just say to him, and then what he does is wave his fin at me, he really does, and says, "Take care, you take care now," and while I don't for a minute regret my having stopped and talked to this fish guy, I regret leaving him even less, I mean enough is enough, it really is.

And later, not too long after I leave this fish, but later, this is what happens.

I find this shoe, this single red sandal with a broken strap in the middle of the street, you know, plastic but, no, not entirely cheap looking, and I don't pick it up, why should I, but I do stop and stare at it for a while, and then this, this is what I start thinking, and it's funny how something, some small thing will start you thinking about another thing or person which may not be small at all, but out of the clear blue I just start thinking of Yolanda, the girl, the young woman on the bus, and once I start thinking I can't just dismiss her the way I can this red sandal with the broken strap, I mean she's there or here to stay for a while, in my mind I mean, and I've got her phone number in my wallet somewhere, and then I start thinking about that, this slip of paper with her phone number in my wallet somewhere, and then it's just one thing leading to another, you know the way it usually does, and the next thing I know I'm calling her, the number I mean from this really awful half phone booth that smells of rotten eggs, and there aren't that many left in this city or anywhere else I suppose, but there is this one by this gas station, just my luck I suppose, or not, and at first it doesn't even look like the damn thing's going to work, I mean the receiver is just hanging like a hanged man in mid-air but after a while, after some banging I do manage to get a dial tone, and then I just punch in her number, and careful, really careful about getting all of it right.

And once again I don't, I absolutely don't know what to expect.

I mean I seem to go through life without expectations, from just one thing to another without any major or even minor expectations, what will be will be I guess, but basically, for the most part I find myself without any dreams, hopes or any sort of plans, and, I hate to say this, but who do I remind myself of in this, who else but Frank, and even though we're at different levels and all, I mean Frank as if innately incapable of dreams, hopes or any sort of expectations and I don't think that's the case with me, but basically we're the same in this, no dreams, hopes or any sort of expectations.

And then the phone starts ringing, it does, and it keeps on ringing for quite a while.

And I'm thinking, 'Thank god, Bingo, thank god, you're off the hook I guess,' apparently Yolanda without an answering machine, just this phone that keeps ringing for something like an eternity, but I don't mind waiting, listening, I mean the more I wait and listen the clearer it becomes that I'm off the hook and all, but then I hear this click and all and then a voice, and it's hers I guess, although it bears little or no resemblance to the one from the bus, and, "Hulloh?" she says, real sleepy like it's the middle of the night, which it isn't, high noon or something, like one of us really confused about time or the two of us as if in different time zones, and, "It's Bingo," I tell her, "Bingo from the bus," and it occurs to me that she probably doesn't know Bingo from Jingo or Dingo or Zingo, and anyway she sounds really out of it and probably thinks she's dreaming this call or something, and, "What? Who?" she says, and there's nothing worse than repeating your identity to someone, like if they don't get it the first time what's the point and all, but, "Bingo," I repeat, "Bingo, Bingo, Bingo, Bingo," like I'm pounding it into hear head or something, and then, "On the bus," I add again, and then silence, this really long silence on the line, like I'm ready to hang up and all, but, no, not really, not yet, and then, "Ah, the Chicago Bears," she says like a revelation, like she's suddenly awake or something, and, "That's right," I tell her, "that's right, the Chicago Bears.,"· and then we have this bit of a conversation, you know, like trying to pick up where we left off which neither of us quite remembers, I mean all that I truly and clearly recall is resting my head on her breast for a while, and her pouch I guess, her horizontal cut across her belly which played on my mind for a long time afterwards, "So, what're you up to?" she finally asks, and, "Nothing, nothing special," I tell her, "So, why don't you, why don't you just come over?" she asks, "Now, right now?" I ask, and, "Now, why not now?" she asks, so I just take down her address and all, write it on the palm of my hand with this pen I happen to find in my pocket.

And the thing is this isn't like a date, not at all, as a matter of fact I don't believe in dates, never have, I mean I've been with girls, with women but never on anything like a date, I mean I never once asked a female, 'Will you go to the movies, the dance or the whatever with me?' no, not once, not even, 'Will you take a walk with me?' which is about as simple a date as I can think of, no, I simply hung out, spent time, whatever, and then either one thing led to another or it didn't, it all depended, I mean the last thing I ever did was force the issue as far as, you know, sex was concerned, I mean the one thing I didn't, never wanted was to initiate sex and then create, leave this wrong impression, like, rest of that, or, 'I am yours and you are mine,' you know, all the 'I will love you forever,' things like that, like I don't even have a conception of what forever might be, you know, I really don't, and as for love, you know, I'm as much in the dark about it as the next guy, even more would be my guess, which doesn't mean that, you know, I guess you know what I mean, but the thing is the last thing I want are complications, my life complicated enough the way I look at it without my adding to the list.

I mean the example, the perfect example of a so-called loving couple is or was my father and my mother, may she rest in peace, I don't have to look very far, and I'm sure, just about sure that in their so-called loving days, their initial couplings and all my father must have whispered god knows what to her, you know, 'Donna, this and Donna, that,' all the usual things, my father perfectly capable of whispering these things when under the influence and at times even when not, and as for my mother, your guess as good as mine, but in the end what else did she do but spread her legs, and I don't mean to be crude or anything but my mother not at all this romantic type, you know, but romantic enough to have spread her legs when called upon I suppose, and in the end, in the very end what did it get them, I mean my father off on his own and my mother as well, I mean they could hardly stand the sight of each other, and so much, I guess, so much for a so-called loving couple, but all I'm saying is don't say anything you don't mean, you know, say nothing you don't mean, just screw and all which I guess everyone sooner or later has to, but just screw and say nothing at all.

You know.

But all the time I'm thinking this, you know, but all the time I'm resurrecting this image of this young woman, this Yolanda and all, it isn't at all difficult, it just sort of happens, and all the time I'm making my way to her apartment it's like she's there, right there in front of me, and it's not even anything specific, her hair I guess, rich like chestnuts, and her eyes, I've always had this thing for warm, for dark eyes, I mean most guys will go for blonds with sky blue eyes, not me, not that I recall, although when you come right down to it I don't see what difference it makes, I really don't, no matter, and her boobs of course, the left in particular which is the one I felt, the one I rested on, relatively large I guess, although it wasn't the size so much as the firmness, I mean really firm, and I don't even want to think about whether it was natural or with something done to it, you know, I just don't, but it's really nothing specific like I said, just the presence, the feel of this Yolanda as I'm walking along, I mean I couldn't dismiss her, the image, the feel I guess as I'm walking along, and I get to this really old, this amazing neighborhood and all, Red Road I guess, there are these really ancient, these magnificent trees with tremendous branches and leaves, and I don't even know their names, you know, my mother might have, I mean in spite of being this hopeless drunk and all she certainly knew her trees, shrubs, plants, what have you, no matter, but then, 'You get around, Bingo,' I say to myself, 'you certainly get around,' and that's a fact, whenever I'm not working and all I just take off in one direction or another, mostly without a purpose but sometimes with like now, but, 'You get around,' I say to myself, and for some reason that makes me feel good I guess, you know, pretty good about myself and just things in general.

And the house is not that hard to find, and it's really like a mansion or a mini-mansion let's just say, and, 'Jesus Christ, Bingo,' I say to myself and, 'holy shit,' things like that, and by the outside gate I have to ring this bell, pull this chain and all to ring this bell, and then the gate, you know, the gate just opens as if by magic, and then there's this walk, this really long walk along this stone path with all the stones, the slabs of stone, all smooth and carefully laid out, and that's something as well, and the door to the house itself is wide open so I just walk in, like what am I supposed to do, and inside there are all these tremendous rooms, all Spanishy looking with these paintings of bulls and crossed swords on the walls and shit, and once again, 'Holy shit, Bingo,' I say to myself, but then after a while I actually say, "Hello? Hello?" out loud, I mean what else can I do, the place is really like a maze and the last thing I want is to get lost while looking for Yolanda and all.

And then out, out she comes.

From somewhere I guess, I really have no idea. But out she comes.

And she's wearing this housecoat, but I mean attractive, more like a kimono with these flowers and dragons or whatever, and, "Ah, the Chicago Bears," she smiles, and it just makes you melt the way she smiles and says it, it does me, and then, "This is quite a palace you've got here," I tell her, which is this really stupid, thing to say but at the moment I can think of nothing else, and she says, "Come, come with me," and she takes me by the hand, she actually does, and it's then I realize that she's quite short, I mean barefoot and all, no shoes, five two or three if that, but with some people, women it doesn't matter, so long as they've got all this other stuff I suppose.

And then she just takes me into this bedroom or sitting room or whatever, I mean the furnishings are pretty much that of a sitting room, also Spanishy but with something of an eastern flavor as well, I don't know, and in the middle of the room this tremendous bed covered with this silken spread and all, although I'm not sure it's silk but it might be, and these pillows, these really soft pillows all over.

And she can tell I'm impressed.

I mean I've got this 'Gee, shucks' expression on my face, I've been told by several people that it's this habit of mine, you know, depending on the circumstances, and I'm trying to be conscious of it, you know, not have it at all, but sometimes I can't help myself, I just can't.

And, "It's not my place," she says as she flops down, you know, just to break the ice, "it belongs to this doctor friend of mine," and I just say, "Oh, oh," and leave it at that.

"Drink," she asks, "nuts?" and, "Sure," I say, "why not," and up, up she goes again, and as she rises her kimono partially parted to reveal her knees and calves, and there's this scent, this tremendous scent of jasmine or whatever, I'm not sure, and she mixes these drinks by this bar against the wall, I mean she doesn't even ask what I'd like but just mixes these drinks and all and brings them over, and then the nuts, she goes for this bowl of nuts, most of them Brazilian.

And, "I hope you're not allergic," she says, meaning the Brazilian nuts I guess, and, "What, are you, kidding?" I reply, which again is this really stupid, this inane remark.

And the thing is we get comfortable, we really do, I mean what else are we supposed to do, just lying on these pillows and all, lying next to each other, touching you know, touching just a bit, and then we just watch this stupid reality show or whatever on this large screen TV built into this wall unit past the foot of the bed, I mean she must have been watching this all along, even when I called, and personally I don't much care for these idiotic shows, you know, faking reality and all, but whatever anyone watches is their business I guess, not mine, like Frank will stay up into the wee hours of the morning just watching stupid CNN, you know, the guy trying to look mesmerizing, and it's not that he knows anything of what's going on, he really doesn't, he just reads these cards, like for him CNN is just another fake reality show personally, me, you know, about the only thing I'll ever watch are westerns, the older the better, these old black and whites with people like John Wayne and Gary Cooper, you really can't beat those, Christ, the Duke, now and again I'll go through binges just watching these old flicks with the Duke and others, but to each his or her own I suppose, so we just go on watching this stupid reality show, but the thing about these old westerns and especially the ones with the Duke I guess, is that fake or not, and let's face it, everything you see on TV or in the movies is fake, only there are degrees of fakery I suppose, but the thing about these John Wayne westerns is that there are the good guys and the bad, with a few exceptions I suppose, I mean there are exceptions to just about everything under the sun, but right and wrong, and the good guys and the bad, and you don't get this on the reality shows or even CNN, I mean the thing about these reality shows and even the so-called news is that right forever turns into wrong and the good guys into the bad or vice versa, and then the fakery on top of all that, but that's neither here nor there I guess, only I sort of wish we'd be watching some old western with the Duke and not this stupid reality show, whatever it is.

And, "Is everything all right?" she asks.

Because I'm just lying there, I mean I have her in my arms and all but basically I'm just lying there without doing anything else, making any sort of a move, which is something she expects I suppose, I mean what else would she expect, and it isn't that she's not attractive, desirable or whatever, because as a matter of fact she most definitely is, but the thing is I don't even have the beginnings of a hard-on, I just don't, and that's really not like me, not at all, I mean put me in just a four or five foot proximity of a woman and I'll get the stirrings, the beginnings of a hard-on most of the time I'm saying, or five, seven, even nine times out of ten, but not now, no, I mean go figure, and it isn't like I've been screwing my head off these last couple of days or weeks or months or even years if you know what I mean, I mean it's more like this dry spell, this Sahara Desert as far as my sex life is concerned, and here, I suppose, here's the perfect opportunity, I mean what more can a guy ask for, but something's not working, something's just not right.

And then here, here's what I do. As hard as it is to relate, to believe.

I disentangle myself, just sort of slip out and away from her, leave the bed, and then I say something like, "Sorry, I'm really sorry but I've got to go," like I've got this pressing appointment or something which not even a child of three or four would believe, he just wouldn't, and then what else can she do but to just look, to stare at me like I'm this creature from another planet or something, which I guess in a way I am, but then she does walk me to the door and all, and all the time we're walking, me up front and she trailing behind, but all the time we're walking I'm thinking, "What, just what the fuck is going on, Bingo?' I mean I haven't a clue, nothing I can sink my teeth into, and then when I'm out the door I just turn around a give her this kiss on the cheek, I mean I don't want her thinking I don't like her, which is not the case, really, not at all, and she just kind of looks at me like,

Now I've seen everything,' and says, "Wow, a kiss. How exciting," and I just kind of try to smile and all, I don't succeed or succeed just a bit, and then she just shuts the door in my face, I mean that's what she does.

And then I just walk to the bus stop and all. You know. That's what I'm doing.

And all the while I'm walking, and this is stupid and curious, both curious and stupid at the same time, but all the while I'm walking I'm singing this idiotic song about an old dog and all, start somewhere in the middle and just keep singing, "'.. and Bingo was his name. Bee, eye, en- gee-oh, bee, eye, en-gee-oh,'" and on and on like that until I'm good and sick of the song, the old dog and me I guess, but the thing is I just can't stop, and it's "'Bee, eye, en-gee-oh, bee, eye, en-gee-oh,'" all the way to the bus stop. Like I can't think of anything else, just this stupid song that goes round and round in my head and out my lips.

And then when the bus comes, which isn't right away of course, but even when the bus comes I'm still singing this stupid song, "'Bee, eye, en-gee-oh, bee, eye, en-gee-oh,'" even as I'm ascending the stairs.

Like I just can't stop.

And the handwriting's on the wall I guess. You know. As far as my surveying job goes.

And it isn't like Bruce hasn't warned me, I mean he's been warning me for quite a while I guess, about this and a number of other things besides, like, "This is the time of life when a kid like you has to grab a hold of himself or become lost forever," things like that, but mostly it's about the job and all, I mean once we're done in the Everglades he doesn't know where the next job's to come from, I really don't think he does, and then he's been talking about Kuwait again, like he's got Kuwait on his mind, you know, just can't seem to shake it, but the more he talks the more appealing the prospect, I mean I don't know shit about Kuwait and neither does Bruce I suspect, but I guess he feels he's got nothing to lose and everything to gain by moving off into the great unknown as he puts it, and neither do I maybe, although I don't, really, I just don't know.

But it doesn't hurt to think, to plan a little in advance. Just a bit I guess.

So I'm thinking of other possibilities, different lines of work I guess, which I haven't done in quite a while, perhaps never in my entire life. And I run them past Frank, which is really a total, an absolute waste of time, I mean all he does is sit there, stare and nod and all the way he usually does but at least it helps me clear my mind a bit, talking, just thinking out loud like that.

And then I'm just thinking, you know, thinking and talking, just considering these possible jobs and all. And Frank just sitting there and nodding, like I don't expect him to say anything, I really don't, but it helps just to have him sitting there nodding, I don't know why, it just does.

And I'm thinking hospitals, you know. Hospitals.

I mean there are about as many hospitals down here as there are fast food joints, not really I guess, but close enough, some a bit more intimate and others the size of small cities, but I really have no preference, I don't think I do, and I don't even know why I start with hospitals unless it's because of my recent experience with my mother, I mean that sort of thing just stays and stays on your mind whether you want it to or not, but the thing is basically, and I mean really basically I'm this caring sort of individual, like if I see someone in trouble or suffering or whatever I'm usually ready to help, you know, whatever that may mean, and what better place to do this, you know, to make use of this trait or whatever than in a hospital I guess, I mean I have no training to speak of, absolutely none, but I could certainly empty bedpans or help patients to the bathroom and all, I mean if they're what they call ambulatory, able to rise and move just a bit, and maybe even clean them, you know, sponge them down and all, or clean up their vomit, their shit, whatever, I mean I'm not squeamish, not at all, "You remember, Frank," I ask, "you remember when I cleaned up your vomit the other night?" but he's just sitting and nodding, I mean you can't tell whether he actually does or doesn't remember, or I could just go around with this cart of books or magazines, whatever, and distribute them to the patients or read, just read to them I suppose, I mean you wouldn't know it from just looking at me but I'm a pretty good reader and all, or just to sit with them, you know, sit with the patients for a spell, hold their hands, talk, listen, whatever, I mean there's a need I think, really, a need for that sort of thing in most hospitals, about the only problem I think I'd run into would be having to deal with kids and all, I think I'd have a hard time, these six, seven or eight year old cancer patients with their bald heads and all, but I guess I could make that clear from the outset, ask not to be assigned to any children's ward I guess, but for the rest I'd be all right I think, handle just about anything I would come across.

Or.

Something else. Something entirely different if this hospital thing should fall through, not even materialize I guess.

"What do you think?" I ask Frank.

Just to pretend, you know, to make believe I'm including him in all this. Pest control.

And here, yes, here I really think I'm on to something.

I mean just about every house, building, whatever needs their monthly pest control, I mean even here, even in this place there's this guy that comes around pretty regularly, this Billy Shaw with his 'Billy Shaw Pest Control' truck parked right outside, this three hundred pound guy and all that I think will drop dead any second as he's climbing the stairs, I mean one day it's bound to happen, but this really nice, this personable guy, I mean he really doesn't do a hell of a lot of talking but then he does, you know, when you initiate, when you ask him something, you know, anything at all and not just about pests and all, I mean he's like this natural philosopher, I mean ask, just ask him anything at all and he'll have some kind of answer, some kind of response, makes sense I guess when all you do is just walk around these apartments and spray this concoction into the corners and crevices from this cylinder on your back, I mean that's the outside job I guess which isn't all that complicated, and inside, once inside you're free to meditate and shit, I mean in some ways that's right up my alley I think, and I'm not saying you don't have to know something about bugs and pests, the different kinds of pests and then mix and use just the right kind of concoction, but I bet I could learn that in a day, two at the most, I'm a pretty quick learner when I put my mind to it, and the rest just automatic, just a stroll in these apartments, and I'd start on the bottom of course, work as an assistant to someone like Billy Shaw I guess, but soon, I guess, I mean who knows, but soon I'd have my own business and all, 'Bingo Sherman's

Pest Control,' I mean there's plenty of room for competition in this town, I just bet there is.

And, "'Bingo Sherman's Pest Control,'" I say out loud.

And then Frank looks up, he really does and asks, "What?" and I just repeat, "'Bingo Sherman's Pest Control,'" and that's all right with him, I really think it is. And then here's something else. You know. Something entirely different yet again.

And this time it comes from Frank, believe it or not, I mean it looks like he's been listening all this time, although, really, by the looks of him there was no way to tell, but, "A pilot," he says, "what about becoming a pilot?" like that, out of the clear blue, and I don't know what sort of a pilot he's thinking about, you know, one of those crop dusting guys or something a lot grander, some guy in a spiffy uniform and flying one of those jumbo jets that sail across the skies of the Atlantic or something, and I just bet he's seen something on TV to make him think of that, but either way there's quite a bit of training required, no question, of which I haven't got any, not a bit, but I don't want to just shoot him down, you know, tell him what an asinine idea that is, I mean at least he's participating and all, thinking about possible occupations, and if you knew Frank even just a bit you'd realize what a big, what a tremendous deal that is, so I just nod and smile I guess and tell him, "Yeah, it's certainly worth considering," I mean the guy's trying, give him that much, at least he's trying.

But the thing is, pilot or no pilot, I have to give the matter some serious thought, I mean the last, the very last thing I want to do is to go into business with Frank, you know, there's always that possibility, when all else fails I guess, but, no, not even then, I mean working with Frank is about the very last thing I want to do.

So.

I'm walking down this street and all, just another of my endless attempts to clear my head, and I pass this outdoor cafe and all, although cafe the wrong word, it gives the wrong impression, just this outdoor joint I guess, and I see this guy, just this ageless guy in this army uniform, you know, at least this army jacket, unbuttoned with all these medals and all, the rest of him really not worth talking about, I mean the rest of his attire, but that jacket, you know, that army jacket sort of fascinates me, and I don't know if it's because my old man was once in the army and all, you know, once upon a time and well before I was born, I mean he's got the photographs to prove it, all these stupid looking photographs he'd now and again fish out from somewhere to show me, not that that's any sort of recommendation, just the opposite I guess, but for some reason this guy with his jacket and medals just sort of fascinates me, I mean, 'What about the army, Bingo,' I ask myself, 'what about that?' I mean it's not really a serious thought but the beginning, yes, certainly the beginning of one, and I just kind of stop by his table and all, which is something I never, practically never do, stop by anyone's table and all, and I just say something like, "Mind if I join you?" you know, like that, and he's drinking this bottle of beer, Forster's, this Australian beer, and, "It's a goddamn free country," he says, which I guess means that it's okay, really, okay by him.

So, we just sit there for a spell, I buy his next beer and all along with my own, I mean why not, and pretty soon I'm asking him all these questions about the army and all, and in reply what he does, I mean here's what he does, he just pulls up the pants on this one leg and all and shows me this really awful wound, I mean it's not festering or anything but still it's this really gruesome wound, and, "Afghanistan," he says, "my ticket out of hell," and that's about it I guess, I mean I was after something else, something more I guess but all he does is show me this wound, and we just kind of stare at it for a while, you know, like everything I need to know about the army is right there in that wound, I mean I don't know what I expected but it's pretty obvious he's not one of these talkative types, more like this let-me-show-you types I guess, and we drink a couple of more beers is all, but I've not yet given up, no, not entirely, but, "Fuck the army, fuck the war, fuck this country," he finally says, which is kind of strange seeing how he's sitting there in this army jacket with all these medals, but I let it go after that, what else, I mean my idea about joining the army was just this one idea among others, and not even a full fledged idea, just this one possibility among others I guess.

So, I just get up and leave after a while, I mean I shake his hand and all but still I just get up and leave, and while I resume my walk and all I say things like, 'Christ, Jesus Christ, Bingo,' to myself, stuff like that, and I'm also thinking, 'Looked at a certain way, Bingo, I mean not in all ways, but in a certain way your life is nothing but this gigantic failure,' and it's not that I'm depressed or anything, no, factual, just factual, and then I start thinking of all the people I know and see all around me, I bet, I just bet that at times they think their lives nothing but this gigantic failure, certain exceptions of course, your millionaires, stars, politicians, what have you, but, no, even there, even with them if you dig deep enough I bet you'll find them thinking that their lives are nothing but these gigantic failures, and that should make me feel all right I suppose but, no, it really doesn't, I mean your own failure is still your own failure no matter what, so then what do I do, you know, what do I do but head for the nearest McDonald's, I mean it's this thing with me, I don't know what but it just is, and when I get there I order this Big Breakfast as usual, I mean that's what I really do, and then I can swear, I can really swear that this young, this perky young woman behind the counter asks, "Do you want jellyfish with that?" I mean that's what I hear, so I just ask, "Christ, when did you start serving jellyfish around here?" you know, like that, I mean I wouldn't put it past McDonald's, not with the way they've got their eyes on the market and all, but, still, jellyfish, and then this young woman looks at me like I'm out of my mind or something, that is before she cracks up and all and says, "Jelly, I said, jelly," and of course I'm cracking up as well, and that's great, that's just what I need, and then I start thinking how life is nothing but a series of misunderstandings, you know, just one misunderstanding on top of another, and that's all right I guess, it really is, I mean if life is nothing but series of misunderstandings you can't, you shouldn't take it as seriously as you sometimes do, and then just one thing leads to another, you know, the way it usually does, and pretty soon I'm thinking of Yolanda and of the misunderstanding with her, which I'm pretty sure is what it was, and, 'Maybe,' I tell myself, 'maybe, Bingo, you should give it another shot,' you know, call her, I guess, 'and even though you don't know what you'll say to her it's worth a try,' and then I just concentrate on my Big Breakfast and all, I mean I'm glad I've got this thing out of the way.

And then this guy walks in, you know, this fairly ordinary looking guy but wearing this purple wig and all, and of course I stare at him, what else, but stare at him for a while at any rate, I mean here is this fairly ordinary looking guy, from the neck down at any rate, but then from the neck up, I mean I really don't know what to think, but then it just comes to me, like in a flash or something, 'Christ, Bingo, he's this wannabe Ronald McDonald,' I say to myself, I mean that's the key I think, and I'm the type of guy who's always looking for keys to things, I really am, so, 'Christ, Ronald McDonald,' I say to myself, and although I've only seen Ronald McDonald, in photographs I've never seen him in a purple wig, you know, red, I guess, or red with some yellow or blue in it but, no, never just, never entirely purple, but still, you know, this is something like creative freedom I suppose, or maybe, just maybe this guy couldn't find any other wig but purple, you know, the stores all out or something, but, 'Damn if it isn't Ronald McDonald,' I say to myself, and then the thing is I almost go up to him, I really don't but I almost do, I mean just to shake his hand or something, whatever, I mean it isn't every day you see some guy trying to impersonate Ronald McDonald, I mean not that he really is, he's just this goofy guy in this purple wig and all, but let's just say for the sake of argument, and I'm kind of glad you know, I mean people are forever going around trying to look like someone famous, you know, copy their dress, their walk, their whatever, right, but then here, here's this guy who only wants to look like Ronald McDonald, and it occurs to me then, it just does, that for all or much or even some of my life I had this kind of hero worship of Ronald McDonald, then why, really, why did I never try to look like him, I mean why not just look at times about as ridiculous as I feel, and then I'm back, yeah, back to thinking about Yolanda once more, and then what, yes, what if I just showed up at her place in this Ronald McDonald outfit, I mean what have I got to lose, and then maybe, just maybe that sort of appearance would cancel our misunderstanding, I mean who could resist a Ronald McDonald standing at the door.

And it's funny.

Yeah, I guess it really is how at times just one thought leads to another, just one ridiculous thought to another, and it cracks me up I guess, it really does.

And then I can't, you know, but I just can't shake this idea of becoming Ronald McDonald.

I mean not the real thing of course, I mean as a line of work I would never even consider it, but just a spoof you know, strictly for laughs, I mean if Yolanda wouldn't see the humor in it then the hell, really, to hell with her, but something tells me she would, she just might, and then I just can't wait to get home to Frank and all to share this with him, I mean even if he should think it the most stupid idea in the world, I still can't wait to share it with him.

And then as I'm walking up the stairs and through the door I'm already feeling like Ronald McDonald, just a bit I guess, but feeling idiotically cheerful the way the real Ronald McDonald does I guess, and I don't mean the guy, the poor slob in the outfit but just the image you know, the appearance, I mean that's all I really have to go by, but then when I walk through the door, as soon as I walk through the door Frank greets me with, "Fuck, the polar ice caps are melting," and this without even looking at me, you know, and the thing is the polar ice caps have been melting for years, for decades perhaps, but it's like it's news to him, no doubt he's seen something on one of his stupid TV shows, and it's like he's suddenly interested in the environment and all, and this from a guy who leaves his garbage all over the place, never recycles and makes his so-called living selling junk to these underage kids and all, but under or over age, it really doesn't matter, I mean it makes me laugh, but again he says, "The fucking polar ice caps are fucking melting, did you know?" and this whole Ronald McDonald thing flies right out the window, it does as far as Frank is concerned, I mean how can you discuss Ronald McDonald with a guy who's got polar ice caps on his mind, which is only temporary of course, I mean I bet if I mention polar ice caps to him in a half hour or even ten minutes he won't know what on earth I'm talking about, but that doesn't matter, it really doesn't, what matters is that for now Ronald McDonald is right out the window.

But, "They've been melting for years," I just tell him, just to maintain, to continue with this conversation, if that's what it is, I mean conversations with Frank are few and far between and I don't, I really don't want to miss my chance at one no matter the topic.

And, "What," he asks, "what?" And, "They've been melting for years," I repeat.

And, "Jesus Christ, holy fucking shit," he says, like why wasn't he informed or something, you know, like these melting polar ice caps were bound to change his life, make him reevaluate his whole life and all, which, frankly, I can't see him doing, I mean the thing about Frank, the good and the bad, is that he always was, is and will be Frank and all, I mean whenever I think of Frank I think of this one type of person and no other, to think of Frank in any other way, even slightly changed I mean, would be like thinking of the Statue of Liberty as this other kind of statue or the Freedom Tower down here as this other kind of tower, I mean it can't be done, so, where are we, I mean, really, just where the hell are we, we're back with the melting polar ice caps is where, I mean for now I can no more disregard or veer from this topic any more than I can disregard or veer from who Frank really is and always will be, so, "The thing with these melting ice caps and all is that they're just one, you know, just one of the really awful things going on all around us," I tell him, and maybe he's listening, maybe not, it's difficult to tell, "I mean you've got your earthquakes, your tsunamis, your hurricanes and shit," I go on, "your droughts, your floods, your freezing and boiling temperatures and all," I go on, "and maybe they're connected, maybe not, I mean who's to say for sure," and the thing is I can see I'm sort of losing him, maybe, just maybe I'm throwing too much shit at him all at once, but the last, really, the last thing I want is for Frank to be focusing, worrying about just this one thing, you know, the melting ice caps and all, I mean I know how he gets when he focuses on and worries about just one thing, it just starts eating him up alive, I mean he's difficult enough to deal with when he's not thinking of anything at all but when he starts focusing on just one thing he's practically impossible, "And, anyway, what about your comets, your meteors," I tell him, "all this shit from outer space, I mean we could be wiped out, all of life, in an instant, in a flash," and I can see this has an effect, not much perhaps but still something of an effect, "Just look at your dinosaurs," I go on, "how they were wiped out in a flash some eighty or seventy million years ago," and I can see by his glassy stare that he's thinking, picturing all these dinosaurs, and that's a good thing I guess, let him just start thinking, worrying about something other than the melting polar ice caps, and, "All of life?" he says, and, "Yeah, practically," I tell him, but, "All of life?" he repeats, and, "No," I tell him, "maybe not, your roaches and shit, your bacteria, they'll survive I guess, I mean there's a pretty good chance," and then I just start thinking about, seeing this dying roach on my mother's hospital room floor, I mean that's how it works, it can't be helped, and then Frank just looks at me, he really does this time, and, "So, what's the point," he asks, "really, what's the fucking point?" and I'm sort of surprised, I really am, I mean that's pretty deep for Frank or for just about anybody I guess, I mean the most serious, the deepest question anyone can ask is, you know, what's the fucking point, and I have no answer, I really don't, about all I can say is, "We're alive, I guess, you know, you and me, we're alive right now," and I can see he really isn't buying it, not really, and I don't blame him, no, not one bit, but at least we've gotten off the subject of the melting polar ice caps, I think we really have.

So. Here we are then.

Out in the Everglades and putting on the last touches on this last surveying job, I mean as far as anyone can tell, and the thing is, it's curious, but the thing is I don't really mind, and it's got nothing to do with the Everglades, not at all, I mean I like being out here in spite of your mosquitoes and shit, your river of grass and all the rest of that, I mean there are people, not that many I guess, but still, some people who fall in love with this endless vastness or whatever, I mean some people who can't see themselves living, existing anywhere else, and I'm not saying I'm one of those, no, but I can certainly see how that might happen, your Indians, your Native Americans and shit and some of your hunters, trappers I guess, I mean the place just teeming with life, and I'm not just talking your exotic creatures, your gators, cottonmouths, whatever, but all kinds of birds, bear, boar, deer and shit, and even your panthers I guess, and except for the birds it's not that you see these creatures, animals, whatever, all or even some of the time, but the thing is they're really there, I mean you really have to have patience to look, to see, to wait I guess, sometimes for days and nights I suppose, the thing is one time Frank and I actually discussed having some kind of hut and all, on stilts I suppose but right out in the middle of the Everglades, and I don't even recall who brought it up, it doesn't matter, but for some reason both Frank and I thought it was this terrific idea at the time, I mean the two of us out there day and night in the middle of nowhere, you know, just doing our thing, whatever, I mean I guess we could get our food and all by fishing and hunting, even though neither one of us knows shit about either, that's a fact, I mean the people who live, who survive out here have been doing it for years, all their lives perhaps, so we'd be starting with this handicap I guess, no matter, and the thing about fishing and hunting is that you could do some real damage, harm if you don't know what you're doing, and I don't mean to the critters, the animals, I mean there was the case of this guy, this diver mistaking his buddy for a barracuda and spearing him in the guts, that was the open ocean I guess but, really, the same difference, but anyway, here, right here in the Everglades this guy, this hunter mistook his friend for a bear or a deer or something and shot him clean through the head, that's a fact, and out here there's no telling what Frank might mistake me for or I him, and that's just during the day, I'm not even considering the middle of the night, but still, you know, in spite of all this we seriously talked about getting this hut and all, I mean about as seriously as we talk about anything at all, and the attractive, yeah, I guess the really attractive thing about this was this idea of getting away from it all, just leaving so-called civilization behind, "Just you and me and the gators," Frank even joked, I mean we'd make sure to have enough beer and all, you know, arrive with a supply to last us weeks, maybe even months, but maybe, just maybe Frank wouldn't need his stupid drugs, I mean nature,

I guess, nature enough of a drug for him, although I wasn't sure, no, not entirely sure on this score.

And, "Hey, Bungo, you asleep? or awake?" Bruce yells at me, and, "Awake," I yell back, "I'm awake," I mean he's at this distance a and holding up this measuring stick and I'm supposed to be looking through this instrument which I wasn't, not just then, looking off into the vastness and all and then above, you know, just above to see the buzzards circling and all, and, "We're not out here for our health," Bruce yells, and, "No, I guess not," I yell back and then just go back to what I'm supposed to be doing, but I just start thinking as well, I can't help myself, but I just start thinking about these Native Americans they used in building this so-called Tamiami Trail, and a bunch, yeah, I guess a whole bunch of them dying in the process, you know, your various diseases, snake bites and shit, and I guess that's what happens when you start building a road in the middle of nowhere, a road that's not even supposed to be there in the first place perhaps, I mean someone, you know, someone always pays the price, and then first it's a road and then pretty soon these look-alike houses and all, malls and gas stations, you know, your so-called trappings of civilization, or signs or whatever and· then pretty soon it's like, 'Christ, what the fuck happened to the Everglades?' and then suddenly I realize that I'm playing my role, you know, this kind of idiotic role in this process, and I just wonder if there is a job, a profession, an occupation, whatever that doesn't adversely affect anything else, and I'm back to thinking about hospitals again where all the doctors, nurses and shit, where all they do is pretty much take care of the sick and all, but, no, even there, I mean I bet there are any number of people just dying to die and these doctors and shit, I mean what they do is keep them alive and suffering for as long as possible, I mean that too is part of their job, their oath and all, and what's that but a crock of shit as far as the patients are concerned, and then I'm just glad, really glad my mother died when and how she did, I mean not too much pain and none of these extreme measures to keep her heart beating for another week, day or even hour, I mean what would have been the point, and then I'm just signaling to Bruce, getting him to move a little to the right or the left, I mean that's still my fucking job and all, but let me tell you something, I'm fed up, I'm just about fed up with everything all around me, and this sort of thing comes over me every now and again, but there's nothing, short of stopping to think and all, really nothing to be done about it.

So.

How does one become Ronald McDonald? Just temporarily, just for kicks, to accomplish this task. Which is to square things with Yolanda I suppose. And I make the mistake, always a mistake, but, anyway, I make the mistake of running it past Frank and all, and not just this Ronald McDonald thing but this whole affair with Yolanda and all, all except for her pouch of course, I mean the last thing I want is to introduce the topic of drugs into any conversation with Frank, other than to lecture him from time to time I guess which becomes really tedious after a while and at any rate has absolutely no effect on him as far as I can tell, but I run this thing past him, and "Yolanda who?" he asks, like all serious and shit, like this were the gist of my problems, and, "Just Yolanda," I tell him, and then, "I used to know a Yolanda once," he says with this kind of far away or meaningful or just stupid look, I mean I don't even know whether he did or not but at any rate what possible difference does that make to what I'm trying to tell him, but, "Was she a model?" I ask just to be on the safe side, to eliminate any connection, and, "No," he says all dreamy like, "no, this one a stripper, danced naked on a pole," which figures, I guess, it really does, and, "her hands all calloused and shit," he adds, and I can just see Frank with this stripper and all with her calloused hands, although at times I have a hard time seeing him with just about anyone of the opposite sex, but that's neither here nor there, and, "Called herself an exotic dancer," he smiles, which again is totally irrelevant to my story, so, "Can you just shut up and listen," I tell him, "just for a minute or two?" and then I try, I really try to explain to him not just about Yolanda and all but Ronald McDonald, you know, my ideas concerning Ronald McDonald as well, which is really the hard part, you know, practically impossible, and his reaction is, "What's this shit about Ronald McDonald? I mean who gives a fuck about Ronald McDonald?" and I really don't want to go into my childhood experience and all, I mean it isn't at all necessary to the story, I mean all I want him to grasp, to comprehend is that I want to do something pretty bizarre, outrageous to reestablish this link with Yolanda, but, "I don't get it," he just shakes his head, "why didn't you fuck her when you had the chance?" but he's missing the point, whatever point there is Frank's missing it by a mile or so, and by now I'm sorry, truly sorry that I didn't resist the urge to confide in him, I mean if that's what I'm doing, so I just stop talking after a while and stare at this stupid basketball game or whatever on TV, you know, it's really not basketball season but once in awhile they'll have these so- called great games of the past, and other than his idiotic nature shows Frank loves nothing better than watching these so-called great games of the past, but I can tell he's still mulling over this Yolanda thing and all, and I bet, I just bet that in his mind and all my Yolanda and his are one and the same, like he really can't tell the difference, and, "So, what do you think?" he asks, "You think it's all right to fuck her as Ronald McDonald but not as Bingo Sherman?" like he just doesn't get it, "I mean if every time you wanted to fuck someone,. he goes on, "you had to get dressed up as this clown that would be a really bad..," and I can tell he's searching for the word, the right word which is pretty unusual with Frank, but, "imposition," he finally says, which is pretty impressive I guess, I mean it may or may not be the right word but it's pretty impressive as far as Frank is concerned, "I mean then you'd be seeing nothing but these clowns and all," he goes on, "all these horny guys dressed up as clowns and shit," and I must admit that's a pretty funny image, these hundreds, these thousands of Ronald McDonalds trying to get laid and all, but, again, that's not the point, not at all, so I just wait for him to get this whole thing out of his system, this thing about Yolanda and the clown, and it takes a while I guess, just a while longer, and I regret I put it there in the first place, I mean I'm really sorry I opened my mouth and all.

And I don't even know where to start, how to begin.

I mean my temporary transformation into Ronald McDonald and all. But I guess the first, the very first thing I have to do is to really visualize him, the way he appeared the last time I actually saw him, which was like ages ago, but something, you know, something does come to me after a while, the best I can manage, and I see him in this flaming red wig, nose and lips, like the guy's on fire or something, you know, and his tie, even his tie is red, his tie in flames as well, but he's wearing it against this yellow sleeveless jumpsuit, I mean that's the way I see him, but under the jumpsuit, for sleeves I mean, this red and white striped T-shirt or sweater or something, and that's not bad, you know, that's pretty good for starters. I mean it's something to work with at any rate.

And then the thing, yeah, the thing is to get a hold of these things, but this is Miami after all, and somewhere, sooner or later you're bound to find just what you're looking for, and as a matter of fact I think I will, this party store up on Biscayne called 'Notions and Lotions,' meaning paint for your face and other parts I guess, but then just before going in this is what I think, what I realize, this is Grace's neighborhood, and what kind of a friend was, am I, I mean I haven't thought about her in weeks, granted there was this so-called death in the family, you know, but the fact is I felt or feel closer to Grace than I ever have to my mother, I mean the least I can do is to look for her again, you know, take a bit of time out from this Yolanda and clown affair and look for Grace, and it's not that I'm going to spend all afternoon doing it like the last time but a bit of time at the very least, a man, I guess, any man but me I'm thinking with certain obligations, you, me I guess can't just let people, certain people disappear from my life without at least trying to look for them, and, 'Maybe, Bingo,' I even tell myself, 'maybe that's what's wrong with you, that you let people disappear from your life without even bothering to look for them,' and I guess I'll just add this to the list, I mean now and again or when the mood strikes I just go through this litany of what's right and wrong with me, but mostly wrong I guess, but it's really not a litany so much as just focusing on now one thing, now another depending on the circumstances, now, just now it happens to be letting people disappear from my life, and that's pretty much tied in with one's, I mean my own various disappearances as well, and what I mean, the only thing I mean by that is that I'm more or less in the habit of losing my way in life, just flit from one thing to another without any sort of a way or plan worth talking about, 'Clueless, I guess,' I even tell myself, but then, 'Christ, Jesus Christ, Bingo,' I tell myself, 'here you are looking for Grace and what you do is start thinking, worrying about your own problems and all,' so I just head up the boulevard and I want nothing, but nothing but Grace on my mind, whether I am lost or not is really secondary to my looking for Grace now, I mean finding myself, my own way I guess an entirely different issue, it really is.

And then I'm visualizing, practically seeing Grace in her wheelchair and all, I mean whenever you're looking for something or someone it helps to picture that in your mind, I mean it can't hurt, but pretty soon I'm just walking without knowing where, about all I have is this picture of Grace in her wheelchair in my mind.

So, I just stop, you know, I do, and just go up to this hooker I guess, this pretty decent looking redhead, and I just ask, "Have you seen Grace?" like that, and what she does is just give me this hooker look and all, like, 'Who the fuck are you?' or, 'What is it you really want?' and she even says, "Whatever Grace can do I can do better," you know, but, "No, No," I tell her, "Grace, I'm just looking for Grace, the woman in the wheelchair," and then she, the hooker I mean, looks like she thinks it's some kind of joke or something, you know, that I'm teasing, having a bit of fun and all at her expense, which is understandable I guess, it might be, and she just kind of stares at me and all and makes this sucking sound with her lips, and then she just turns, she actually just turns and walks away.

Like what has she got to do with Grace or with me for that matter.

And then, or maybe not exactly then but a short time afterwards, but pretty soon let's just say this feeling of helplessness or hopelessness comes over me like it did the last time I tried to look for Grace, I mean for all I know Grace could be in some hospital or even dead, I mean what's the life span of a hooker in a wheelchair out on the street, and Grace no spring chicken, you know, as the saying goes, and there's really no way to find out, I mean you tell me if there is, all I know is her first name and all.

So. So.

It takes me quite a while to get back on track, to start thinking about Yolanda instead of Grace once more, and, 'Ah, the resiliency of the human spirit,' I'm thinking to myself, which is kind of like a laugh, it really is.

But anyway.

I make my way back to this store ,this ,'Notions and Lotions' once more, and in a way it's a good thing, I mean there's nothing like a store of this sort to take your mind off things.

And this bell, this little bell rings as I enter.

And this old, this really ancient woman comes out from somewhere in the back, I mean she's like this witch in some fairy tale, and she gives me this look, like, 'Christ, here's another one for you,' and she's like the last person in the world you'd think of as selling this sex paraphernalia, standing guard over these magazines, dildos, blow-up dolls in addition to your so-called party accessories, but what kind of a choice do I really have, so after a while I just sort of tell her what I'm after, more or less, so she just leads me to another room in the back, kind of like a dungeon with all this more serious, this S&M type of equipment, but she does find me some body paint although blood not flame red, no matter, but I'm grateful, you know,

I let her know that I'm grateful for that at least, but as for clothes, you know, nothing doing, and I try to describe to her what I'm after without mentioning Ronald McDonald by name or even clowns for that matter, and she appears to give the matter some serious thought, or some thought at any rate, and then, finally, you know, "What you need is a thrift shop, a Goodwill store," she tells me, like why didn't I think of that, and I pay for the body paint, and, "How about a nice dildo?" she asks as I exit and holds up this great big black thing that can be made to vibrate and all, just kidding I suppose, but, "No, thanks," I tell her, "some other time perhaps," and just exit the store.

Like mission aborted, I suppose. Or slightly, just slightly accomplished. So.

After all that.

And I won't go into the details, it isn't necessary.

But after all that I'm standing in front of Yolanda's door, the gate open like she's expecting someone, not me necessarily but someone I guess, and I'm this likeness or what I think of as this likeness of Ronald McDonald and all, and I have no idea how she'll react or whether she's even aware of Ronald McDonald, no matter, and the thing is I have no idea what I'll say to her, assuming she's home and all, no, not a clue, but, 'Looking good, looking good, Bingo,' I tell myself as I catch a glimpse of myself in this small window, this glass on the door, I mean as far as Ronald McDonald goes I'm a fairly decent if not entirely believable duplicate, but the whole thing's just a joke I keep reminding myself, you know, just this goddamn joke, and pretty soon or after a while or soon enough I guess Yolanda appears, and she says or all she says is, "What the fuck?" I mean it's pretty clear she can't or doesn't want to put two and two together to come up with this link between Ronald McDonald and me, but the thing is she does smile after a while, you know, in a manner of speaking, and I just step back and open my arms, a gesture meant to be reminiscent of one of Ronald McDonald's although I don't recall ever having seen him actually do it, and I just say, "Ta-dah," like that, which does have a certain effect, whether desired or not I can't really say, but at least a certain effect on Yolanda, and, "I'm collecting for the needy," I tell her, "please, give what you can, what's in your heart," like that, and finally, yes, finally she does say, "Well, come in then, come in and let's talk this over," and she can't, she doesn't realize what that means to me, I mean all I want, basically I guess, but all I want is to have this really long, this meaningful conversation with her and then just to take it from there, see what we'll see I guess, and "Come on, come on, clown," she says, "follow me," and then I'm both comfortable and uncomfortable in this role of Ronald McDonald, but, still, that's an improvement over the last time when I was just uncomfortable and all.

And then things happen, they actually do between me and Yolanda, or between Yolanda and Ronald McDonald, but I don't want to go into it just now, maybe later, but not just now.

And Frank's just giving me this look.

And sometimes I think Frank does nothing but go through life just giving people these looks, I mean that's about it, and then he says, "Ah, the clown, I guess the clown was successful," and that's even though I'm no longer wearing the wig and all and the paint too, you know, the paint pretty much washed off my face, I mean I'm still in this clown outfit and all but minus the wig and most of the paint, and then he just comes close to touch me all over and say, "Ah, the Bingo boy got laid, long live the Bingo boy," I mean he's got no idea what he's talking about, his ideas, if he has any, but his ideas about sex and love entirely, but radically different from mine, that's pretty much it, I mean his idea about sex and love is to have this kind of orgy in the apartment which he has on several occasions in the past, but just this bunch of men and women with booze and drugs and all, the whole thing like a scene out of some really bad Hollywood movie produced by Bob Guccione or someone, you know, the decline and fall of the Roman Empire or something, like, 'You are there,' you know, or at least he is or was, like it's nothing but limbs and tits and cocks and asses, you know, the works, I mean you really can't tell just who is doing what to whom or even where anyone ends and another begins, it's just this gigantic mess, this mindless free-for-all, I mean basically I don't care, I really don't, but it's like this rutting season at the zoo or something, and the morning after no one seems to remember a thing, what they've done with whom let alone who they are and all, I mean everyone just moving around in a fog and all, but the thing is no one remembers a thing, and what's the point if you don't remember a thing, I even asked him once, I actually did but he just kind of smiled and shrugged his shoulders, and right now the very last thing I want to do is to discuss Yolanda with him, I mean a part of me does but the other no, not at all, and I just hate the way he keeps looking at me and all and making these occasional comments, and after a while he just keeps repeating, "The Bingo boy got laid, the Bingo boy got laid," like the refrain from this really stupid song and all, I mean I can't stop him, you know, I don't even try, about all I do is just wait for him to get it out of his system, and that's the thing about Frank, from time to time he'll just get one thing or another into his head, his system but then after a while he'll be over it, gone pretty much the way it came, I mean Frank doesn't have this terribly long attention span, not even close, I mean he'll still keep saying, "The Bingo boy got laid, the Bingo boy got laid," but I can tell he's no longer thinking about it, just mouthing the words is all, I mean if I asked him, 'What do you mean?' you know, like that, I bet he couldn't say, but, still, he keeps it up for a spell, "The Bingo boy got laid," even after I go into my room and shut the door.

Let me tell you, really, let me tell you something about Yolanda. I mean the sex was pretty good, or maybe even great, yes, let's just say it was great, although what's great sex for someone may be just adequate for someone else, no matter, and this after a bit of fumbling let me just add, mostly on my part I guess and a bit, maybe just a bit on hers, but the thing is I don't recall ever having had sex without a bit of fumbling leading up to it, almost like a necessary part I guess, I mean I'm not this great or smooth lover or anything, which is not to say I don't do all right on occasion, I mean Yolanda the perfect example, once we got going, you know, really going, it was like, 'Whoa, where's this coming from?' I mean I forgot all about Ronald McDonald and all and I guess Yolanda did as well, the thing is I dare anyone to picture Ronald McDonald making love and all, it's pretty hard and maybe even impossible, but I was all Bingo once we got going, and Yolanda, no, I don't exactly know who she was but if she was someone other than Yolanda it was impossible to tell, I mean the whole thing just a combination of screwing, fucking I guess, but with something, yes, definitely something else as well, you know, don't hold me to this but I could swear it was, and now and again, you know, not for the entire time, but now and again I even said, "Yolanda, Yolanda," out loud, and she, "Bingo, Bingo," like that, I mean we didn't have to, we just did, and it was like we weren't even fucking for the first time but for like the tenth or the twentieth, you know, give or take, what I mean is it just felt kind of natural, like, 'Ah, so there you are, and we just fucked, and that may or may not be unusual but it is with me, I mean with nearly all the women I've ever been with I fucked them a lot better in the imagination than I ever did for real, that's a fact, but not with Yolanda, no, I mean I don't think I ever imagined

fucking her, thought about it I suppose but not really imagined, not in any sort of detail at any rate until we actually did it, and that's something, you know, it really is, and then afterwards, and here's the thing, but afterwards we just sat around all naked and just talked a bit, nothing special you know, just talk I guess, but when was the last time I sat around and talked like that with someone, after sex I mean, I mean I really can't recall, and it wasn't just the kind of talk where I'm saying my thing and she hers, you know, these separate monologues and all, but more like a real, an honest to goodness conversation, I mean that's rare, you'd have to admit that's pretty rare, I mean I'm asking her all these questions and she me, like we're filling in all these gaps, and, "Tell me, tell me," she said or the other way around, "Tell me, tell me," I said to her, and it was just one question and reply after another, and it was then, I hate to admit it, but only then I realized that we hadn't taken any precautions, about the sex I mean, I mean, 'That's just like you, Bingo,' I even said to myself, 'I mean you go out of your way to dress up as Ronald McDonald and all but then you forget your rubbers,' and I even said something to that effect to Yolanda, you know, no longer a precaution or even a caution because it was after the fact and all, but, "Nah, nah," she just smiled and shook her head, "we're all right," and it turned out she had had this hysterectomy, I mean on top of her pouch and all this hysterectomy as well, and I know I should have felt pretty good about this but I'm not sure I did, I both did and didn't I guess, and then I just started to think how one goes through life, you know, anyone at all, but how one just goes through life losing this or that part of one's body, I mean looked at a certain way life nothing but this series of subtractions until the very last subtraction of life itself, and that should have upset me I guess, I mean you can see where it might have, but all I could think of was how precious everything was that remained, how precious life itself while anything of it remained.

And the thing is I don't even know how long we sat naked and talked like that, I mean I can't even estimate, but then after a while we just had another go at it, the sex I mean, I mean it seemed like the most natural thing in the world, or like one good fuck deserves another, although I don't mean to make light of it, not at all, and then I just left I guess, and for now that's all I'm prepared to tell you, really, that's it I guess.

Funny, I guess. How things work out at times. Or don't. Either or. But really funny, I guess. I mean at times I'm tempted to think that if not everything then at least most things really accidental in life, and that's from the get-go, I mean just think how you're born this Bingo Sherman and all, and what's that if not this gigantic, this mind blowing accident, I mean given the choice, any kind of a choice I don't think I would have opted to be Bingo Sherman, no, not in a million years, although that's hard, really impossible to say now that I'm actually Bingo Sherman, still, or take this thing with Yolanda, I mean what else but an accidental meeting on this bus and all, the whole thing as if dependent on my mother's dying, my traveling on that particular bus at that particular time and I don't know what else, and that's without even considering all the accidental events in Yolanda's life, I mean it would be tempting, perhaps even terrific to say she for me and I for her, you know, like there's this one Bingo Sherman in the world and this one Yolanda Zimmerman, Christ, what a name, no matter, but that we were somehow destined, meant for each other from something like eternity, like Romeo and Juliet or Angelina and Brad I guess, but even so, look, just look at the problems they've encountered, you know, I mean, I mean to make neither too much nor too little of this except to say that most if not all things in life are accidental and all, but, no, all, really, all things in life are the results of accidents.

Which means what? You know. What? Which leaves you, the individual, I mean where does it leave you in the end? And I'm tempted I guess, you know, sorely tempted to bring this up with Yolanda the next time I see her, I mean why not, why not just share everything that goes on in one's mind no matter how off the wall and all, I mean as far as I'm concerned a relationship is more than just this great sex, it's sharing all these crazy ideas, whatever, but the thing is it never comes up, I mean the circumstances, the timing just not right, the next time I go to see her I just walk into this bizarre scene and all, and try, just try to picture this if you can, Yolanda, you know, but Yolanda stark naked and lying flat on her back on this elaborate dining room table, all dark with its carved legs, the table I mean, like it's from the Spanish Golden Age or something, and her eyes shut, Yolanda's I mean, and all around her these lit candles like the ones you see in Catholic churches and all, these votive candles I guess, and, "Hi, there, Bingo," she says to me but without opening her eyes or moving even a single muscle except for her lips and, "Sit," she says, "why don't you just sit down?" and I guess she means the floor, the carpeted floor because she's removed all the chairs from around the table, and I guess in some universe, I don't know which, but in some universe this makes perfect sense, but, no, not in mine, and, 'Christ, Bingo,' I say to myself, 'like what have you gotten yourself into this time?' I mean it never fails, I once dated, if that's the right word, but I once had a relationship with this young woman who went around dressed up as a priest and all, I mean that was her everyday mode of dress, 'Father Lisa' she insisted on being called, other than that she was perfectly or nearly perfectly all right, and I'm not saying that this 'Father Lisa' business didn't make the sex interesting because it did, but once, just once I'd like to run into a woman who's perfectly all right without any exceptions, I mean no priests and no naked women on tables like altars, and maybe I'm asking too much, it's possible, and maybe, just maybe I attract these types of women or they me, I mean who's to say, but right now I'm just sitting on this carpeted floor and all and staring up at Yolanda on this table like some kind of dish, you know, but like some kind of sacred dish displayed but not yet served, I mean, really, what else am I supposed to do, and then, still without moving, she asks, "How you doing?" and, "Fine," I tell her, "just fine," I mean what else can I say, and then she just takes her time, she really does before sitting up and looking at me, and, "Care to join me?" she asks, and then, again, what else can I do, so I climb up the table, carefully, you know, so as not to knock off any of the candles, I mean god only knows what would happen if I did, and I'm not saying the sex isn't good or even better than good, and this in spite of the limited space and all and the very hardness of the wood, but you'd be amazed what can be accomplished when one concentrates, puts one's whole mind and body into the thing, but still, once, just once I'd like to run into someone who isn't a priest, a sacrificial virgin or whatever, you know, and it isn't that I'm complaining, no, not at all, just hoping I guess, kind of hoping is all.

Something else now.

Yeah, something else to worry about.

I come home and find Frank foaming at the mouth, just flat on the floor and foaming at the mouth, but not exactly flat I guess but in this kind of fetal position and foaming at the mouth" and, "Christ," I just say out loud, "Jesus fucking Christ," which is not something I normally do, I mean combine Christ with fuck and all, but there are times when nothing less than such a combination will do, I mean no sooner do I say "Christ," than it's followed by, "Jesus fucking Christ," but Frank is like this infant, embryo even just all curled up and foaming at the mouth, I mean god only knows what combination of drugs or drugs and liquor he's got in his system, I mean leave it to Frank to come up with just the right or wrong combination of drugs to have him foaming at the mouth, and his eyes, you know, his eyes just half, just semi-open but the pupils way up in the sockets so you can barely see them, and, "Frank," I yell at him, "Frank, do you know where you are?" which doesn't help of course, not at all, but it just seems to me that so long as one knows where one is there's something of a fighting chance, but at any rate in a situation like this it's hard to know what to do, I mean right away, and then for some reason, don't ask me why, but for some reason I figure it's best to get him up and have him move about, which is what I do, I mean it isn't easy but this is what I manage in the end, with his arm, his limp arm about my shoulder and mine about his waist and just trying to drag him along and all, and, "Frank," I yell at him, "goddamn it, Frank, move!" which I'm not even sure he's doing, you know, just letting himself be dragged along and all, and then, thank god, I spot his cell phone on the floor, I mean maybe he was trying to use it but maybe not, at this point it really doesn't matter, but thank god I spot it, and laying him back down on the floor I make this call to nine one one, and I don't even know what I'm saying other than to give the address and all, I mean I get that right at least, and then the thing, you know, the thing is the paramedics arrive in practically no time at all, at least that's what it seems like, these two hefty guys and this short but pretty hefty young woman as well, and the next thing I know is they're yelling at me, "Step away, just step away from him!" because I'm still sort of hovering over Frank, and then I just quickly move to some far corner of the room, I mean practically up against the wall, and let them, you know, just let them do whatever it is they're doing, and then one of them just yells out without even looking at me, "You know what he's taken?" and I could take some guesses but, really, you know, it could be like everything under the sun, so, "No, no!" I yell back, and then I just can't help but admire the way they're doing whatever it is they're doing, I mean it's nice, really nice to come across people who seem to know exactly what they're doing, most people don't, they haven't got a clue, but these guys, these two young men and this woman seem to be on top of things, I mean one-two-three and Frank's on this stretcher and all with this oxygen mask like he's being readied for a launch into outer space, you know, and I can't help thinking, you know, saying to myself, 'Here, now here's a job for you, Bingo,' being a paramedic and all and, yeah, I'd have to put on some weight and be properly trained and all but what a hell of a job or profession if you will, and then I just follow them down the stairs, and it's pretty amazing how smoothly, how quickly even that goes, and the thing is they let me ride to the hospital with them, I mean I don't know what the policy is or even if there is a policy for such a thing but I just hop on and no one says a word to me, you know, they're busy with Frank and all, and then it's just sirens all the way like it's the end of the world or something, which it may well be for Frank but I'm guessing, hoping not, and then, 'Here we go, here we go, Bingo,' I say to myself, meaning I'm not sure what, but, 'Here we go,' I say to myself, meaning everything and nothing at all.

Shit.

I mean sooner or later it does hit the fan, shit I mean, that's been my experience, I mean no matter the situation or the people involved sooner or later the shit is bound to hit the fan, and with Frank it's either sooner or later, later I guess, because I'm surprised, I really am it hasn't happened any sooner than this, I mean Frank like this crazy character living on the very edge of things, the edge of life and death I suppose, and this in spite of the fact that Frank's this death dodger or something, I mean I often imagine him on this high wire and all and then falling, taking the inevitable fall without a net underneath, and then with every bone broken in his body until I see him get up and all, brush himself off, and I know it doesn't make any sense but that's just how I see him, but maybe not this time, you know, I mean who knows, but maybe not this time I guess.

And in the hospital it's like this death watch or something.

I mean he goes in and out of consciousness, and I'm talking days as well as nights, like one minute he's Frank and the next someone or something else, like he's already dead or something, but he really isn't, you know, that's the thing, I mean he always seems to rally or something, and, "They're out to get me," he whispers to me this one time, which is okay I guess because that's kind of like a theme with him, you know, certain people or even the entire world out to get Frank Sherman, and when he says, you know, whispers that to me I know he's back on track, more or less, and, "Who's out to get you?" I ask, which is my usual response, "who?" and he just smiles and shakes his head, so he's coming around I'm thinking, he'll be all right I guess. And, "Changes," I tell him, "we'll have to make some changes." And you can say that just about anything or anyone at all, I mean take any situation or any person and you can bet there's room for change and all, it's just that in Frank's case it's a little more obvious than in others', and I don't even know what sort of changes I'm talking about, I mean in general I do but not in any of the particulars, and unless one gets down to the particulars, I mean, really, what the hell good is it, but still I tell him, "We'll have to make some changes, Frank," and I can tell he's listening from this great big distance or something, I mean both hearing and not hearing me, and this may not be the right time or place, but it hardly ever is when it comes to changes, and you might be thinking, and I wouldn't blame you, no, not one bit, but you might be thinking, 'Just who the hell is he,' I mean Bingo Sherman, but, 'just who the hell is he to talk about changes?' I mean all you have to do is look at my life and all to realize whatever changes there have been have been usually for the worse and not the better, sometimes for the better I suppose but, no, usually for the worse, but that's not the point, really, right now that's not the point at all, the thing is even a death dodger like Frank can come too close at times and just how often can he come this close you know, without crossing over, ceasing to be a death dodger and all, but, "You know where you are, Frank?" I just ask instead, put any talk of changes on hold for the time being, and I don't know whether to be grateful or not when he gives me this blank, this typical Frank look, I mean I'm glad the look is back but at the same time I really don't think he knows where he is, so, "Take it easy, take it easy, Frank," I just tell him, I mean it'll take time I guess, you know, just one step at a time as far as Frank is concerned.

And then.

'Where, just where are all his so-called friends, his associates?' I start to think, and that's another thing about my theory of the shit hitting the fan, I mean when it does you can be pretty sure there'll be no one, practically no one else around, each one, you know, just busy with his own fan and his own shit I suppose, but who else does Frank have but me is what I'm trying to say I guess, and, "Bingo," I tell him, "Bingo's here," like it's this great big deal or something, which it really isn't, like if I were Frank and all I'm not sure I'd feel all comfy-cozy knowing that Bingo and only Bingo Sherman was by my side, but things are what they are, that's the thing, things are always what they are, and at least he's got me, you know, at least he's got Bingo Sherman by his side.

And I'm trying not to make too much of this. Really. I'm not. I mean the last thing Frank needs right now is someone, anyone making too much of anything at all, really, that's the last thing he needs.

And then I just fall asleep. And it's high time I guess.

I mean with Frank going in and out of consciousness and me keeping this death or life watch I guess, it's high time, at any rate I have little or nothing to say about it. I really don't.

And then I have this great, these really great dreams and all, and even though I couldn't tell you the specifics, the particulars, the feel of them is really terrific, like suddenly I have no burdens, no problems, I mean in the dreams I'm just this guy, this Bingo Sherman with no burdens or problems at all, I mean I can't for the life of me recall a single day, hour or even a moment in my life without burdens or problems, except now, except in these dreams, I mean in these dreams my whole body as if tremendously alive, you know, the brain, the heart, the nerves, take your pick, and, "Bee, eye, en-gee-oh," I start to hum in the dream the way I occasionally do in actual life I guess, but that's not the important thing, it really isn't, the important thing is the feel, just the feel of this dream or dreams, I mean it's like I'm out for a walk on this incredible day or something, and the feeling remains, stays with me after I wake and all, and I'm not saying for a long time, nothing like that, but for a spell let's just say, and I feel like telling Frank about it, I mean why not, but the only thing I manage is, "Listen, listen, Frank, the only misfortune is never to have been born at all," or something like that, and he doesn't get it, of course not under the circumstances, but anyway this is Frank we're talking about, so regardless of the circumstances I don't think he'd ever get it, and even though I say what I say, I myself am not entirely sure what I mean by it, I just say what I say without any certainty as to what I really mean by it.

Now, don't laugh.

But after Frank returns from the hospital and all, and he's somewhat changed I guess, I mean how could he not be after an experience like that, but in others no, I mean basically he's still the same Frank and all, but for several days, perhaps even weeks all he does is talk about this fish tank, about getting this aquarium and all, I mean you can't beat him for peculiar, for bizarre ideas, he's the original bizarro kid all right, like who starts talking about fish and all after a brush with death, but it's like he's got nothing but fish, these tropical fish on his mind, I mean first the guy practically ODs and then it's just fish, you know, nothing but fish on his mind, and, "What the fuck do we want a bunch of fish for?" I even ask, but it's like he doesn't even hear me, and you can just about see the fish, these tropical fish swimming in his eyes, figuratively speaking, like his whole head's become this fish tank and all but the eyes, you know, only the eyes the glassy part where you can actually see the fish, and the thing is he's still pretty weak, you know, weak as a kitten, and if I were a fish, one of these tropical fish I certainly wouldn't want to depend on someone in his condition to feed me, let alone take care of the entire tank, you know, do whatever has to be done, and that's another thing I guess, I mean it's one thing to think, to dream about this tank but quite another to take care of it, I mean guess, just guess who would wind up with the job, yours truly, Bingo Sherman, that's who, and it's not that I have anything against fish and all or any of god's creatures, you know, I mean did I or did I not spend a good half hour or even an hour talking to this fish guy off the highway, and I know that's a different matter, a different kettle of fish but I guess you know what I mean, but I have this theory about everything in its proper place, you know, tropical fish in the ocean, pigs, horses, cows, what have you on the farm, the only exceptions are your dogs, cats and some of your larger parrots, I mean they belong just about anywhere I guess, but if Frank's got this thing about tropical fish and all why not just go down to the ocean like I occasionally beg him to and put on one of these goggles so he can dive by some reefs and all, that'll be the day, no, what he really wants is just to stare at these fish the way he stares at the TV, like his very own Nature Channel I guess, you know, broadcasting day and night, but for now I'm in no mood to argue with him, I'm really not, I'm just glad he's alive and all, but I'll be damned if I'll set up this fish tank and all, do all the work just so he can sit and stare at it day and night, but for now I'm just glad he's alive, you know, that's the bottom line, I mean close, he was this close to checking out for good, and that's a fact, it really is.

Gainfully unemployed. I guess you might say.

I mean the Everglades job is over and done with, and in some ways, you know, in some ways good riddance I say, and Bruce made sure I'd be collecting unemployment for a spell, "A Bingo needs to live," he smiled at me, but the last few days out all he did was talk some more about Kuwait and all, I mean it was like he was practically there and me along with him, and, "Smell the air," he even said, "take in the sights," but for some reason I have my doubts about clean, fresh air in Kuwait as much as about these so-called amazing sights, you know, these skyscrapers or mosques with their minarets, whatever, I mean my guess is as good as his, the only difference is that he's looked at these brochures and all and been in touch with this guy who, by the way he tells it, is just desperate to get him over there, I mean all Kuwait needs is this bunch of surveyors from the States to make it a living paradise, but I have my doubts, I mean I've never given that part of the world any serious thought, the Middle East I guess, I mean what else have they got there but a lot of oil wells and a bunch of fat cats riding around in their caddies and flogging people left and right for some minor religious infraction, and that's the one thing about this place, the States I mean, at least they don't flog you to within an inch of your life, not in most places at any rate and certainly not for some minor religious infraction, but, "Think, Bungo," Bruce told me, "picture all these veiled beauties," but the thing about veiled beauties is that they may not be beauties at all, just these plain or even ugly looking women, and at any rate what on earth would they want with this lanky kid in his black T-shirt and cap, you know, I bet that even talking to me, saying hello or something and they'd be flogged and I along with them, but, "There's a great tradition of hospitality in a place like Kuwait," Bruce told me, but what the hell good is hospitality if you can't even talk to one of these veiled women without being flogged and you have to wonder about Bruce, you really do, I mean he's after something all right but I doubt if he himself knows just what, I mean Kuwait's like this land of milk and honey as far as he's concerned, I really think he believes that, and the thing is I'm after things as well but at least I don't fool myself into thinking I have to go to the Middle East to find them.

"So, what do you think," Bruce asked, "what do you think, Bungo?" Like my opinion really mattered, like he just had to have it or something.

But the thing is I don't. Know about the Middle East. I just don't. "What do you say we saddle up?" he persisted. "You and me, kid, just you and me. Ride off into the sunset." Pulling this Butch Cassidy and the Sundance Kid on me. I guess. But I don't know. I just don't.

'Bingo Sherman Landscaping.' That's what I think. It just comes to me like a revelation.

What I'm doing, all I'm doing is sitting by the pool, smoking my fags, my fags, just one after the other the way they do in those gangster films of the thirties and forties I guess, I mean I'm not thinking of any particular movie just now, just gangster flicks in general, and then it just comes to me, and I don't know if it's the sight of that filmy water and all, I mean that pool could sure use a bit of cleaning, or if it's something else, I mean I don't know where one's ideas come from, at least some of one's ideas, but, 'Bingo

Sherman Landscaping' I just see on the side of this truck, whatever, the truck all blue, sky blue and the lettering in gold, I mean that's how specific the vision is, and then plants, whatever, just a bunch of green plants all around the lettering, and then there I am up in the driver's seat, and I'm wearing this green jump-suit, that's how I see myself, and my black cap, of course, my 'Chicago Bears' cap of course, and, 'Way to go,' I say to myself, to the vision, 'way to go, Bingo,' and I'm just cruising up and down Ocean Drive, Collins, Biscayne Boulevard, you name it, and then farther inland, Kendall, whatever, and right up to the edge of the Everglades, I mean I'm like this Good Humor man of plants, trees, shrubs, what have you, and I'm making all these calls, you know, just one house, one property after another, and out come all these housewives in their negligees, house coats, short shorts, whatever, and, 'Thank god you've come, thank god you're here,' they all say, their front and back yards overgrown with weeds and dying trees and bushes, and, 'Not to worry,' I tell them, 'come, let's just go inside and talk this over,' and that's just what we do, sit at their large, natural wood kitchen tables and talk things over, I mean I have several, quite a few ideas I run past them, I mean the choice is theirs of course but I throw out all these options, and talk about being grateful, I mean I'm doing nothing less than restructuring, relandscaping their lives, and, 'How about a cup of coffee, a glass of wine or something stronger?' they ask, and, 'Sure, don't mind if I do,' I reply, and then, one thing just leads to another, and pretty soon the green jump-suit comes off, but not the cap, no, I don't think so, and the negligees, the house coats, the short shorts, whatever, and there we are up in their bedrooms on their truly amazing beds, I mean they stretch from wall to wall, practically, the mattress all foamy yet firm, and no sheets, no, I mean that's my preference, and I concentrate on the landscapes of their bodies, head to toe, shoulder to shoulder and breast to breast, and, 'Yes, ah, yes,' I tell them, 'there's a lot we can do with these,' and I go to work, of course I do, 'Bingo Sherman Landscaping,' and the women blossom, of course they do, and afterwards their gardens, their front and back yards, their gardens a cinch after that.

is.

What do you think? A hell of a way to make a living. It most decidedly

"So, what are we doing here?" I ask Yolanda.

Not the time and the place, the specific time and place, I mean we're sitting outdoors at one of the hotel restaurants on Ocean Drive, Yolanda with a penchant for seeing and being seen, waiting, I guess, you know, just waiting to be discovered or something, although as far as I can tell she's been discovered and rediscovered any number of times already, and we're just talking, drinking of course but basically just talking, I mean Yolanda's going on about one thing then another, for example, how there's this one, this last trip she has to make to Bogota, the very last of her life, she swears, I mean how she owes this doctor and all, "Christ, Bingo," she smiles, "he's been good to me, you can't imagine how good," and she's got me there of course, I mean for the life of me I can't imagine how anyone in the business of slicing open another's belly can be said to be good to that person, but that's just me I guess, but on she goes, and the thing about Yolanda is that she's a pretty slow starter when it comes to conversations but once she gets going she's good to go for an hour, maybe more, I mean whatever comes into her head and wherever it comes from, and it's just the opposite with sex, where she starts out hard and then finishes kind of slow, you know, just kind of slows down as we go, but that's neither here nor there, and the thing is I don't mind listening to her, not a bit, especially when I can listen and look at the same time, I mean she's got this really amazing figure and all and the face to go with it, the only thing I can compare it to, her face I mean, are those Virgin Mary paintings from the thirteenth or the fourteenth century, and the reason I know is that I once dragged Frank downtown to this museum and all where they had this special exhibit of Virgin Marys through the ages I guess, a big mistake in retrospect, I mean all Frank did was keep saying, "Fuck the Virgin," and all, meaning no disrespect I guess but just smiling and saying, "Fuck the Virgin," as we moved from one picture to the next, no matter, but the thing is Yolanda really looks great in this orange tank-top and white shorts, I mean after all she was or is or will be a model, one can never tell about those things, but that's just when I say, "So, what are we doing here?" meaning, you know, not just us and not just here but everyone alive or whoever lived on this planet, in life I guess, and Yolanda just kind of looks at me, I love it when she does that, but she just kind of looks at me and asks, "What? What?"

and then I just go on to explain, I mean I give it a shot, and I can tell she's sort of listening and sort of not, I mean she's just sort of staring at me with these great big dark eyes, brown I guess, and kind of alternating between looking at and looking right through me, and the more I talk the more she stares, it just happens that way, and for some reason it's important, really important for me to get this right, to tell her exactly what I mean even if I'm not quite sure of it myself, and the thing with me, you know, sometimes I guess, but the thing with me is that I'm a pretty good talker myself once I get going, I mean just one word, one sentence after another like that without my even having to think about them, I mean that's the feeling I have, and when I'm done, although not really, because one is never done with that sort of thing, but when I stop Yolanda just says, "Whoa, where's all this coming from?" and I can't tell her, I really couldn't, so I just say, "Didn't you know? Back in the Middle Ages I was this philosopher and all," which is a stupid thing to say but it just cracks her up, it really does.

And then back home, back at her place we just go at it like it's the first or the last time, sometimes it happens that way, I mean we're doing it all sorts of different ways to these crazy images on the TV and all, no sound, just images, and it's like this marathon or something to see who'll outlast the other, and that's the thing about Yolanda, now and again she's like this Energizer Rabbit, she really is, but the thing is I keep thinking about this doctor and all, this mythical doctor whose place, whose mansion this really is, I mean he could just walk in out of nowhere like that, and I picture this ogre or something with immense hands and feet and a shock of white hair, I just do but Yolanda doesn't seem the least bit worried,.like this guy is forever out of town or even the country, I just don't know, but if she's not worried then why am I, but still, I think it would be better if we did our thing in Frank's place or even some motel, because this place, this mansion gives me the creeps after a while, it really does.

And I'm just thinking. I am. What if, you know.

But what if I got this job at one of the fancier hotels on the beach, it doesn't matter what, but just one of the dozens, hundreds of menial jobs they have at places like that, waiter, busboy, pool attendant, bellhop, whatever, and the more menial the better I sometimes think, the less time to think, to worry, and anyway I've always believed in starting at the bottom, sort of, and then working my way up, you know, from pool boy to lifeguard to bartender to manning the front desk, I'm just using these as examples, but working at one of these large hotels with the definite possibility of upward mobility, not to mention steady hours and pay, more or less, and who knows but that I could get a room in the basement or some shack on the beach belonging to the hotel as my temporary or even permanent residence, be done with this Frank business once and for all, I mean, 'Bingo Sherman, Fountainebleau Hotel, Collins Avenue, Miami Beach,' how would that be for an address, I'm just thinking, have some business cards made while I'm at it, I mean why not, just the name, 'Bingo Sherman,' followed by the address, I mean the best, the most impressive business cards I've ever seen were ones with just a name with an address underneath, like nothing else was needed, the name and the address alone entirely sufficient, just 'Bingo Sherman' and all the rest, and even if I don't know to whom I would give these, that's something of a question in my mind, still, I'd keep a bunch of these on me at all times, ready to hand them out whenever the occasion called for them, like, 'And who are you?' someone might ask, or, 'Just who might you be?' and I'd just give him one of these cards, or her, either or, and it wouldn't matter what I'd do, you know, wash dishes, park cars, whatever, so long as I'd have my name and address on these cards, I mean let them think what they would, that'd be entirely up to them.

'Bingo Sherman, Fountainebleau Hotel, Collins Avenue, Miami Beach.' I guess that's what I'm talking about. That's it, I guess.

Something, yeah, I guess, something has to be done. Whatever. But something has to be done.

Like I walk in on Frank the other day, this man returned from the dead, and what is he doing but sitting there glassy-eyed the same as always, and what else but watching this dumb show about Antarctica, about this search for life beneath the permanent sheets of ice of Antarctica, and they find it I guess, they do, I mean there's life just about everywhere, but it's nothing but these bacteria, you know, the lowest form of life imaginable, and he really doesn't get it, not at all, I mean Frank does all this staring, this looking about but without any sort of capacity for drawing conclusions, for putting two and two together, I mean it's fairly obvious that his life, I mean right now, the way he's living it is about at the level of these bacteria and all, and maybe that's what life is after all, I'm just saying, that we're basically nothing but these bacteria living beneath these sheets of ice and all and the rest just window or salad dressing, whatever, but still, you know, still we have it in us to rebel, I guess we do, but in spite of what he calls his 'exotic lifestyle' Frank hasn't got a rebellious bone in his body, not really, so I just sit down next to him, put my arm around his shoulders and say, "Frank, Frank, what the fuck are you doing now?" like that, but he's just mesmerized, I can tell by the way he looks at me, there's no difference between the way he looks at me and the way he was looking at the TV just now, I mean I'm about as real to him as those bacteria living on the bottom of the Antarctic Ocean and all, but then he says, "Hey, there, Bingo boy, how come you're not out there getting laid?" like that, and that's about all he can think of, getting laid or high or staring at the TV, and there's not much anyone can do, that's fairly obvious, so I just sit there with him for a spell and watch these guys in their dry wet suits dive to the bottom of the Antarctic Ocean to collect these specimen of bacteria.

Like whoopteedo, I guess.

And then I just start thinking. You know.

The way I always or usually or sometimes do.

And even though Frank isn't the perfect or even an adequate audience I just ask, "So, when does a culture die?" just thinking out loud I guess, just out of the clear blue like that.

And I don't expect an answer, not even close, just a puzzled look and a shrug of the shoulders is all, but that's not the point, not at all, right now I'm just in the mood to take on the Antarctic, the bacteria and Frank combined.

I just am.

And then this commercial comes on, you know, but this stupid commercial about this housewife I guess and her kid, and I don't even know where they get these really fine, these healthy looking people for these stupid commercials and all, no matter, but this housewife or whoever is saying to herself, just thinking out loud, "Can a little bowl of cereal change your life?" you know, like that, and the thing is both funny and sad, I mean it both amuses and pisses me off I guess, and then she answers her own question, you know, after they show this box of stupid cereal and all, and she says, "I think it can," and that just about takes the cake, it really cracks me up, and Frank's just sitting there repeating the housewife's words, "I think it can, like there's no hope for him, there really isn't.

So, I just launch into this monologue or tirade or something, I just do, and begin by saying something truly idiotic, truly out of left field or

something, like, "Frank, Frank, when does a culture die?" I mean I know as much or as little about cultures as Frank does, that's a fact, but still I just ask him, "When does a culture die?" and go on from there, I mean I'm not even sure what I'm getting at, only that I need to get at something I suppose, and Frank's just looking at me like I'm from another planet or something, which I guess I am, but no more and no less than he, the only difference is that we're from different planets and all, and he's paying about as much attention to me as he is to those bacteria living under the sheets of ice, or less, yes, maybe less, but I go on to explain to him that cultures come into being, thrive and then just die the same as everything else, I mean that's the general gist of it, and what we've got here, I mean Miami, the States, all over I guess, is just a dead culture and all, I mean people just going through the motions, whatever, and hanging on to dead things, I mean nothing and no one is truly alive any more, things like that, and I'm just getting started, at least I feel I am when he interrupts, when he says, "You know, I've never seen a person die," like that, and I'm close, this close to saying, 'Well, just look around you,' or even, 'Just look at yourself in the mirror, Frank,' but then I realize that he's probably talking about one thing while I'm trying to discuss another, and it often happens like that, nine times out of ten I'd say, and he's probably got my mother's death on his mind or his own near brush with death, I mean Frank is forever reducing general topics to specific ones that concern him directly, more or less, but the one thing I don't feel like discussing is my mother's death or even Frank's near brush with death, I just don't, so I just lead the conversation, and that's a laugh, it really is, but I just lead it back to more general ideas and say, "When you think of it, I mean when you really think of it, we start dying the moment we're born, every hour, every minute of every day," and what I mean is the body of course, the sheer physical process, the very act of living sooner or later exhausting itself, "but we never face it of course, I mean we never look at life and death directly," and here again, of course, my old idea of life within death or death within life, you know, but I don't want to start that up again, I really don't, so, "and because we look at neither life nor death directly, the very preciousness of life escapes us," I just tell him, "and we wind up clinging to dead things, you know, like boxes of cereal or images of bacteria on the bottom of the ocean," and he just nods and says, "Yeah, yeah, that's it I guess," like he really comprehends, gets what I'm talking about, but he really doesn't, because all the while I'm talking he continues to watch this stupid show about bacteria in the Antarctic, like that's really going to tell him about life or life and death together, I mean the whole thing's pretty pointless after a while, and sooner or later I get good and tired of hearing myself talking to myself, I mean that's the last thing I wanted to do, it really is.

And that night I have this dream of Ronald McDonald and all. You know.

About this guy, this poor slob whose job is being Ronald McDonald during the day, you know, just putting on all this paint and dressing up in this outfit just to make kids happy and all, and he does that by pretending to be happy himself, or happy and sad at the same time I guess, but my dream is really about this guy when he gets horny and all, I mean it's really more like a nightmare than just this ordinary dream, because when he gets horny and undresses this guy's just a miserable slob with nothing going for him, and the place, his place looks a lot like Frank's apartment, it really does, I mean not in every detail but in some I guess, and he just sits there in this dark apartment like it's the end of the world or something, I mean this whole Ronald McDonald thing was just an act, this miserable piece of fakery, you know, and in the dream this just about breaks my heart, I mean if there's one thing this guy wants, in the dream I mean, it's to be Ronald McDonald for real, I mean to go through life, all of his life as this real Ronald McDonald, but of course it isn't possible, being Ronald McDonald is just this stupid job and all, I mean once you get dressed up and smear on all that makeup anybody, just about anybody could do it, I mean there's no one, no real Ronald McDonald, just all these fakes, these imitators, and in the dream this just about breaks this guy's heart, mine I guess, and I wake suddenly, you know, like someone just shook me, and I just stare into the darkness, that's all I do, just stare into the darkness like that.

Something else, though. After a while I guess. But something else as well.

I turn on the light, and next, and next, and this surprises the hell out of me, but then I just fish out this old pocket watch from the drawer of my dresser, I mean I've had it for years, hang on to it and take it with me wherever I go, but all this without ever thinking about it let alone winding it, like it's really useless for telling time and all, it doesn't matter, like I simply need to see whatever time it says, whatever time it's stuck on and that'll do just fine for my purposes, but this old pocket watch given to me by my father, no inscription, nothing, he just simply handed it to me one day, and not a word, nothing, not even, 'Here you go, Bingo,' he just simply handed it to me, and it's brass, not gold, not even gold plated, I mean it's this really cheap, this worthless watch, but the thing is he got it in the army, from his days as a glorious warrior or something, it's got the emblem of his unit on the back, I mean can you beat that, and the thing is he must have gotten it for a song and a dance, a pack or two of cigarettes perhaps, and why I'm looking at it now is totally beyond me, except it kind of goes with my nightmare about Ronald McDonald, don't ask me how, it just does, the time it says is six thirty, night or day, there's no telling, but it's like it's forever six thirty on this watch, I don't bother winding it, I never have, and then I just slip it back into the drawer, it'll be months or even years perhaps before I'll look at it again, or maybe just leave it behind this time, I mean who knows, but just leave it behind when I'll finally move from this place.

"Man affecting his environment," Yolanda says to me as I'm pushing the sand about on the beach at South Beach, smiling, kind of smirking I suppose, and I'm not even trying to build anything, just kind of digging and shoving the sand aside, and all around us these gorgeous, these beautiful people, or most if not all, and Yolanda, yeah, Yolanda definitely one of them, I mean there's nothing she likes better than to see and be seen, occasionally she strikes these poses and all, just shuts her eyes and strikes these poses, and all around us this army, I mean it, this regular army of skaters, joggers or just people lying around on their blankets, I mean what the hell can you make of such a scene, I sure as hell don't bother attempting anything at all, but, "The good life Bingo," Yolanda says to me, "the good life," and I don't even know what she means by that, but after a while we start drinking a couple of beers, Yolanda on her blanket and me in this hole I've dug for myself, and watching, you know, we're basically just watching everything around us, and then she starts, Yolanda just starts in, "The thing is I'm screwed up, Bingo," she says, 'I always was and always will be," and I say nothing, not a blessed thing because I'm really curious where she's going with this, "Like you think I'm this one kind of person but I'm really not," she goes on, and that's really funny because I never told her what kind of a person I thought she was, so how would she know, but, "I mean I'm out for the good things in life," she says, "and I don't, I really don't care how I get them," and, "That's great," I tell her, "that's really great," but that can only mean one thing, at least as far as I can figure, that can only mean that her upcoming trip to Bogota won't be her last, and not only that, you know, not only that, but that her doctor, her ogre is probably back in town, I mean what else, why else insist on meeting me on the beach instead of me picking her up the way I usually do, and, "You're this sweet, this really great kid but one has to be realistic in life," she says, "I mean I am," and so on and so forth, I mean it isn't that I stop listening, not quite, but only a part of me is listening by now while the other continues digging this hole, I mean digging this hole is suddenly terribly important, I mean to make it as wide and deep as I can, "I mean I'd like for us to remain friends," she says, "you're really this terrific friend, Bingo," and that irks me, it really does, I mean there's nothing worse than some woman telling you you're this terrific friend and all, so I just stop digging for a spell and look up, and then this, this is what I say to her, "Don't kid yourself, Yolanda, all we did was fuck around a bit," like that, and the thing is it comes out meaner and cheaper than I meant it to be, but once you say something it's said and there's really no use trying to take it back, I mean with certain words you slip into this role and all and then you have to play that role to the end I suppose, and, "How cheap, how shallow," she just kind of looks at me, and that's good, really good corning from her, so I just return to digging my hole, I mean what else can I do, and I don't even see when she gets up to leave and all, you know, folds up her blanket and just leaves, and I'm trying hard not to think of anything at all, just concentrating on digging this tremendous hole.

And, 'Thank god for your Chicago Bears cap, Bingo, I tell myself, like that, 'just thank god for your cap. But I still go on digging this tremendous hole.

And the thing, right now the thing is to keep from thinking, concentrate on just digging this hole, I mean the way I'm going at it you'd think I was tunneling my way to China or Kuwait, and that's a laugh, I mean I'm filled with this kind of negative energy or something, like I could dig from now till sunset and into the night and even sunrise the following morning, and several people stop to look, they actually do, like they're trying to figure out what I'm up to, but I just go on digging, like I don't even bother looking up, like I've got this tremendous task or something, 'Dig, Bingo, dig, like someone said to me, and I've got sand all over my legs, my shorts, my torso, face, hair, you name it, but China's still along way off and so is Kuwait and then the water just starts seeping in, and I found this out during my surveying job, you start digging just about anywhere in South Florida and pretty soon the water starts seeping in, I mean this whole place was nothing but ocean one time, and I don't know if that was a good thing or bad, I mean how can you say in retrospect, but the thing is I still continue digging for a while, which is no longer digging I guess but just splashing about in this dirty water, and then I'm done, I mean don't ask just when or how I know, but I'm done, and I take this swim in the ocean to wash the crud off my body and all.

It would be nice I guess. You know. It really would.

But it would be nice if there were such a thing as true love, and that's like saying wouldn't it be nice if there were such a thing as god or even a real, an authentic Ronald McDonald, and I guess now and again you encounter couples where you say, 'Yeah, that's it,' or, perhaps, 'That's close enough,' but, no, all the couples I've ever known wound up fighting and breaking up in the end, I mean if there are exceptions I've never met them, I really haven't, and after a while all you want is to say, 'Give me a break, just give me a fucking break,' and let me tell you something else, Frank's stupid orgies no longer appear as stupid as they once did, I mean I don't think I'd ever join in, but the thing is they no longer appear as stupid as they once did.

But the thing is Yolanda and me could have, should have lasted longer than we did, and I'm not saying we had something real, something genuine, I mean I'm not this romantic type with stars in his eyes and all, but we should have lasted longer than we did.

But then, 'Give me a break,' I say to myself, 'just give me a fucking break, Bingo.' But then I can't help myself. You know.

I just can't.

I start thinking of all the ways people hurt each other, I mean if you look at the whole history of the human race what else do you find but all these different ways of people hurting each other, and maybe, and I'm just saying maybe, but maybe they don't start out that way, but sooner or later that's exactly what happens, and that's a fact, sooner or later people wind up just hurting each other.

And Frank's at home, surprise, surprise, but he's at home just watching this incredibly stupid show and all, I mean if it's not one incredibly stupid show, it's another, Miss South Beach or Miss South Beach Teen or something, and, "The way to Miss U.S.A.," this guy in this ridiculous suit announces, and he's as serious as hell but this kind of mock or fake seriousness, and Frank's pretty serious as well in the way he's watching it, I mean about as serious as Frank can get about anything, and, "Bingo, Bingo boy, look at all these girls," he says like he is some goddamn commercial, and I don't even bother sitting down, just kind of stand around for a spell, and then these girls, these young women, whatever, parade up and down in front of the camera, you know, wearing these one piece but really thin bathing suits, just exhibiting their legs, their asses, their tits, whatever, and I'm not saying the sights are displeasing in any way because they're not, but, "They're fake, Frankie," I tell him, "they're all fake," and, "What," he asks, "what?" like he has no idea what I'm talking about, and I don't mean their tits or asses which probably aren't, I mean it doesn't matter, but just the girls, the women themselves, the whole damn show in fact, and once in a while there are close-ups of their faces when they're answering all these stupid questions, like, "If you could change one, just one thing in the world, what would it be?" and you can tell they haven't a clue in the world, they're just trying to remember and parrot back some answer fed to them by their coaches or keepers or whatever, I mean anyone with half a brain can see, you don't have to be this flaming intellectual or whatever, and it just kills me the way Frank can just sit there and swallow this hook, line and sinker, and he's already picked his favorite and all, the most attractive as well as the least intelligent, and that's always the way with these contests, if they've got it downstairs you can bet your life they haven't got it upstairs, but Frankie's just dreaming, just going with the flow, I mean I almost prefer him on this chemical high or something than on this visual one, and, "Frankie, Frankie," I just shake him a bit like I'm trying to snap him out of it, but that's the thing with most people, when they're gone they're gone and you have a hell of a time trying to snap them out of it, I mean most people I know have a hell of a time just trying to tell the time of day let alone comprehend what it is they're actually doing, for most of them there is really no escaping the inanities all around, and, "Frank, Frank," I try again but it's no dice, and, "How would you like to have that sitting on your lap?" he smiles at me, and I have a good mind to stand in front of the TV and all or to just shut the damn thing, but that's not in my nature, it really isn't, I mean if people want to clutter their minds with garbage that's their affair, and, anyway, why should Frank be different from nearly everyone else around.

And here's something else.

Later that night Frank is dancing with the stars, and I don't mean the ones up in the sky which would be all right with me, no, but all these personalities, these have-beens on TV who waltz or polka or just hop across the screen on the arms of some out of work professional, I mean that's a hell of a way to make a living if you ask me and how is that any different from some deprived kids dancing on street corners for loose change and all, I mean you don't see that so much down here but you do in some of your larger cities, and once again Frank picks his favorites, it never fails, this woman with her fairly large butt and fake smile dancing with this skinny guy with the seriousness of a bullfighter or something, but I'd rather not go on with this, I mean what's the point, but Frank is tapping the rhythm on this table like he's this ghetto Lawrence Welk or something, and the thing is he hasn't got a clue, he really hasn't.

'Green Acres Funeral Service. Now hiring.' Just this sign on the corner of this building, this yellow building that looks like a bank but is really a funeral parlor I guess, and I'm tempted to go in, I mean why not, but instead I just stand there and stare at the sign for a spell, maybe I'm just trying to get into the mood, and, 'Bingo Sherman Funeral Service' I'm thinking, you know, once again this idea of starting on the bottom and working my way up, the American way I guess, and talk about your steady work, your predictable flow of customers, I mean if the living then the dead, it stands to reason, and even though all that embalming and dealing with bereaved family members doesn't appeal to me, no, not in the least, I can just about picture myself in this dark suit and all, mind you, just about, the cap I guess, the 'Chicago Bears' cap about the only problem, and, 'So sorry about your loss,' I say to myself, then, "So sorry about your loss," out loud, and I shake the men's hands and embrace the women I guess, I mean I'm not exactly sure about the proprieties, the financial aspects something of a stumbling block in the beginning, no doubt the owner would insist on handling those himself, and, 'Let's make a deal,' I say to myself, no rhyme or reason, I just do, but then it would be down to work I guess, picking up the body at the hospital, the morgue, wherever and setting out to prepare it, 'Bingo,' I can just hear the owner say, 'let me see how you go about this thing,' and the thing, I guess, the thing to keep in mind is that you're trying to make the dead resemble the living as much as possible, like they're not even dead but just fast asleep or something, makeup for the women and some for the men as well I suppose, and that's in addition to all the other concoctions, and, 'God,' I can just hear the friends, the relatives say, 'he never looked better,' and that's it I guess, that's just what you're aiming for, and then of course the service, the funeral itself, but the more I think of it the less appealing the entire business, I mean one is just cut out for somethings but not for others, I mean I can fake things with the best of them if I absolutely have to but this kind of full time fakery would get under my skin after a while, and can I tell you something, I will, Frank would be a lot better at this than I, I mean he's half out of it most of the time and that's just the right attitude, demeanor, whatever for a job like this, I mean he could be as high or as low as he wanted to be and still carry on to everyone's full satisfaction, fooling everyone I guess including himself, the only thing is Frank's got this thing about dying and death, he really does, I mean first he'd have to come to terms with it before even thinking about applying for a job like this, and I don't see that happening, I really don't.

'Green Acres Funeral Service. Now hiring.' And it's too bad, it really is, given the steady work and all, but I think I'll pass, you know, what else, I mean just picture Ronald McDonald at a funeral service and you'll get my point, but I think I'll just pass on this.

How time flies.

I guess it does.

But how time flies.

I mean it's nearing Easter and all, and the resurrection of the body is neither here nor there as far as I'm concerned, it's the resurrection of the spirit I'm after, never mind, but Frank comes home with this flier and all, I mean I don't know where he finds these things let alone why he bothers bringing them home, but he comes home with this pink and gray flier that says, 'The Gay Choir Easter Celebration,' I mean talk about your Easter egg hunts, but I just tell him, "Yeah, that's great, just what we need," and I don't know about Frank, I really don't, like I don't even know if he seriously intends to go or just likes this poster, likes the idea of bringing it home to show it to me, and I can tell he is thinking about pinning it to the wall or something, I mean Frank's a great one for pinning things to the wall, all these advertisements for events he never attended, the walls just filled with them, and as far as I'm concerned there's nothing worse than having all these posters of events you've never attended, I mean good or bad, it makes no difference, but they're just these dead reminders of all the things you've missed out on, personally, yeah, I guess personally I'd just as soon go and get the damn thing over and done with and not have this poster up there on the wall, I mean I can't tell you the number of things already up there, flamenco dancers, Hungarian orchestras, revival meetings, you name it, I mean you'd look at these things and think, 'Man, like this guy is living this rich life and nothing, but nothing could be further from the truth, so I just take the poster from his hand like I need to study it or something, give the event, the place and the time some serious thought, and, "Yeah," I tell him, "we'll go, I think we'll go," and I can tell by the look on his face that's about the last thing he had on his mind, but the main thing is I'm hanging on to the poster as if for future reference, I mean the last thing we need is another damn poster up on the wall.

And, who knows? A bunch of gays singing about the resurrection or whatever might do him some good, I doubt it but it just might, at least it'll get him out of the apartment for something other than his lunatic sales, like, 'There's a great big world out there, Frank,' I often mean to tell him, I don't though, in the beginning yes but not any more, I mean why bother wasting your breath.

And the thing is this church, whatever, is in a kind of a ritzy part of town, the Gables I guess, and why a bunch of gays would want to gather there to sing about Christ and all is beyond me, no matter, but on the day of the concert Frank and I have to take two buses, I mean good luck, you know, something of an adventure in itself which I don't care to go into, let me just say that I've got to keep my eyes on Frank which I always do when we're out of the apartment, like except when he's selling his crappy drugs he really has no idea where he is or what's going on around him, like he's this contestant on this survival show or something but out, I mean really out of it, put in there for laughs I guess and the first one to be voted off the island or out of the jungle or something, like, "Sit, sit down, Frank," I even have to tell him on the bus to keep him from standing in the middle of nowhere like that, it doesn't matter, and then we walk this short distance to this church and all that looks like one of those Christian Science places, I'm just guessing, but a place that both does and doesn't look like a church is what I'm trying to say, and that's pretty much the way I feel about Christian Science itself, you know, I mean you can either have Christ or science, I don't particularly care, but why, why on earth would anyone want to combine the two, no matter, and while I'm trying to keep an eye on Frank I'm looking around to see the types going to this gay choir fest or something, I mean I'm just naturally curious about things like that, and the thing is they're not at all what I expected, I mean I'm not entirely sure what I expected but in the audience they're not these swishy guys and butchy women, some are I guess but on the whole, no, just these regular people, young, old, male, female, whatever, and we get settled in our seats, pews, whatever, and I let Frank slide in first because otherwise he'd just stand around and gape and all, "In, in you go," I tell him, and it could be worse I guess, the place, the audience, the entire setting, and then after what seems like an eternity but is only five minutes I guess, these guys start walking down the aisle, single file in their black suits, whatever, the gay choir I guess, and they're these really terrific looking guys and all with even one or two blacks among the group, I mean they wouldn't be out of place at some stately funeral or diplomatic reception, they'd blend right in, and the thing is they don't just look straight ahead which is what you'd expect I guess but they sort of glance around and nod and smile as they pass, I mean if they were used car salesmen I'd sure as hell buy, I would, and, 'Sales, Bingo, sales,' I say to myself, and that's something I never considered, never even thought of, no matter, but then they line up in front of the altar, whatever, in a kind of a semicircle, and I'm looking around for the orchestra, I mean I'm curious where they'll come from and how they'll position themselves, but after a while it becomes obvious that, no, there won't be any orchestra, and I don't care either way but singing a cappella like that is taking a chance, you know, it's harder to fudge or fake whatever you're singing without an orchestra in the background, and then this guy, the leader, director or whatever steps out from semi-circle to discuss Handel's 'Messiah,' not the real messiah of course, which is fine by me, but just the music, just Handel's 'Messiah' and how they've had to make certain alterations, deletions to adapt it to nothing but voices, and by this time Frank's dozing off, just a bit, but that's all right because I'm perfectly capable of nudging him, which I do, and then this guy steps back into the group and they start in, like that, I mean they really start singing.

And the thing is even Frank is paying attention now, I mean I don't think he can help himself, the voices really terrific, you know, modulated but clear, really pure I guess, and it makes you realize there was really no need for an orchestra, not for these guys at any rate, I mean they do just fine, really terrific I guess.

And while I'm listening, which I am, no question, but while I'm listening I sort of look around the place, I mean the last thing I want to do is just stare dead ahead the way Frank is doing, and it isn't that the music isn't getting to me because it is, especially in certain places, and that's the thing about Christianity, it's entirely off the wall but at certain times in certain places it did produce this really great art and all, no matter, but while listening I just look around, like, 'Let's see, Bingo, let's just see what we can see,' and then, you know, lo and behold or something, but what do I see but this really terrific looking woman in this white hat and all, and for my money I guess there is nothing more terrific than some terrific looking woman in a terrific hat, and, 'Yeah, right,' I tell myself, 'keep dreaming, Bingo, keep dreaming,' and the thing is I only see her profile and all, I mean she's sitting way off on the other side and one or two rows ahead, but she turns you know, now and again she does turn just slightly to her right when I see her profile and all, and it's this strong, really strong face with very pronounced features, and, 'Oh, shit, Bingo,' I'm thinking, 'oh, shit,' I mean it never fails, I'm nearly always attracted to these really soft or really tough looking women, either or, and both, I guess, both types turn out to be nothing but ball busters in the end, or she's wearing this dark dress, and you wouldn't think dark and white go together, you know, this dark dress with the white hat, and most of the time they don't, but this time, you know, this time the combination seems just about perfect, and she's got this really great posture to boot, sitting up perfectly straight with her square shoulders squarely back, I mean if I had to pick someone in this place with the best posture this woman would be the hands down winner, no question, and the thing is I'm already planning what I'll say to her afterwards, which is not something I normally do, hardly ever I'd say, I mean I don't make it a habit to go up to perfect strangers let alone plan in advance what I'll say to them, but the thing is nothing comes to me, an absolute blank, so, 'Wait, Bingo,' I say to myself, 'just wait for her outside and then just say whatever comes to mind at the moment,' and it may be something great or totally idiotic, you can't tell in advance, but for now just wait and then leave the thing up to chance.

And that's it, I guess.

That's it.

And for now I just concentrate on these gay singers, I mean they're really terrific, but it's becoming harder and harder, I mean I just can't keep from glancing over to this woman and all, but that's just me I guess, I mean I'm like this idiotic crow in this fairy tale, whatever, that drops its cheese because the fox below is telling it what a beautiful voice it's got, and in the end it, the crow that is, winds up with no cheese and certainly no beautiful voice, I mean that's not a perfect comparison, far from it, but I think you get my drift, I think you do.

And.

"That Handel sure is something," I tell her when she finally exits. I do.

And she exits by herself, I make sure, and Frank and I just standing around and waiting, and even though he doesn't know what we're waiting for it really doesn't matter to him, I mean he just as soon stand around for no reason than start walking to the bus and all, that's the way he is, but then she does come out, and by herself, and that's when I say, "That Handel sure is something," like that.

You know.

And then she stops and gives me this look, I mean people are forever giving me these looks that are hard if not impossible to figure, mixtures of curiosity and disdain for the most part, but sometimes, you know, just sometimes with something else there as well, like now perhaps, although, no, I wouldn't swear to it, "So, you and your partner enjoyed the concert?" she asks in this clear voice with this beautiful pronunciation, it really is, and I can tell even Frank is paying attention, kind of, I mean he sort of looks up and all, but I just say, "What? What?" before I realize her mistake, her misunderstanding, and, "No, no," I say, this is Frank, my cousin and I'm Bingo, Bingo Sherman," and once again I curse the day I was named, christened Bingo but still it's a pretty good recovery I guess, I mean introductions are bound to move things along, and, "Ah, I see," she smiles, "I'm Susan Duino," Italian I guess, I mean her name at any rate, and then I say this really stupid, thing, "Like that church in Florence," like where the hell do I come off talking about things I know next to nothing about, but the thing is now and again I just do, like I can't help myself, but she just smiles and says, "You mean the Duomo," like that, I mean nothing mean, just correcting me is all, but then I say this next stupid thing, blurt it out I guess like one stupid thing is bound to follow another, but, "Do you like Chinese food?" I ask out of the clear blue, like that, and the thing is I don't even know of any good or even decent Chinese places except this one hole in the wall place, this Chung's Chinese Restaurant up on Biscayne where I once took Grace, but it's a good thing she's got a sense of humor, I mean, thank god, because she smiles and says, "Well, yes and no, it all depends I guess," and, "Good," I tell her, "good," and it goes on like that for a while, mean from one blunder to the next, but in the end what does she do but give me this card and all, real professional, with her name and two phone numbers and 'Speech Therapist' underneath, like who would have guessed, and then, "Call the second number, not the first," she says, "the second's the home and the first the school I work at." And then we just stand around a bit more, you know, I mean there isn't a hell of a lot more to be said and basically we're just kind of in the way of the rest of the audience piling out, so, "Well, I guess I'll see you fellows," she just says, I mean what else did I expect, and then as she turns and walks away, once again that white hat and that dark dress just pierce my heart, and I guess there must be better ways of putting it but for the moment I can't think of any, but that white hat, especially that white hat just about kills me, and I just turn to Frank and say, "There goes the woman of my dreams," which is a mistake of course, a huge one, but the words are out before I can stop them, and Frank's just standing there looking at me like, 'What the fuck, Bingo?' but by then it's too late to take back those words or to think of new ones to say.

And all the way on the ride back home Frank just keeps it up, his staring at me that is, I mean it's like he's trying to figure things out or something, and if there's anything he's really bad at it's figuring things out, and now and again I'm close, I mean just this close to saying something like, 'Just kidding, Frank,' or, 'Don't you know bullshit when you hear it?' but I just can't, I mean I could say the words all right but even someone as obtuse as Frank would recognize my comment about bullshit as nothing but bullshit itself, I mean I can fake just about anything but sincerity I guess, from the time I was a kid I just learned to keep my mouth shut about certain things because I knew that as soon as I'd say something it would be nothing but trouble, and I guess that's exactly what I should have done this time as well, just kept my mouth shut, and the thing is, you know, Frank has a point, I mean who goes around saying, "There goes the woman of my dreams," about someone he just barely met, and based on what, you know, basically just this apparition and all, the white hat, the dark dress plus the profile, the posture, I mean someone like that should have his head examined, no question, but the thing is even after an examination and all I'd still say the same thing, I mean an examination wouldn't solve the problem, not one bit.

And then. After a while.

Frank just asks, "What's this thing with Chinese food?" like that's all he can think to ask, I mean I know there's all this other stuff going on in his mind but all he can think to ask is, "What's this thing with Chinese food?" And by then I've just about had it, with him, with me, with the whole damn thing, I mean even if one were to take my statement, "There goes the woman of my dreams," seriously, is there anything, I mean anything at all to suggest that I am or could possibly become the man of hers, I mean here's where a little insight, a little honesty is bound to do me a hell of a lot of good, but the thing is it doesn't, not really, I mean even if I haven't a shot in hell of becoming the man of her dreams, and let's face it, I really don't, but even then my comment still stands, I mean I don't necessarily have to be the man of her dreams for her to be the woman of mine, and it's just too bad that sometimes it works like that, and unless one lies to oneself, which I'm not in the habit of doing, not really, but unless one lies to oneself one is simply screwed, you know, and, really, that's all there is to it.

And, "You don't even like Chinese food," Frank says to me, and the thing is he's doing, saying this just to annoy me, I mean you can be pretty sure that from now until we get home the topic of conversation will be Chinese food, I mean once Frank gets a hold of something he thinks this clever thing and all he won't let go, he'll just run it to the ground, run it to death I guess until he gets good and tired of it himself or simply forgets the original reference, which happens you know, more often than you'd think, but the thing is by now I don't give a damn, I really don't.

So I get this letter and all.

And the return address is this prison with my old man's name followed by this number, and I'm not surprised, not in the least. And his writing is nothing but this scrawl, I mean here's a guy who supposedly fought for his country but his handwriting is like this six or seven-year old's, I mean I can just see him struggling with these separate letters and all, the poor slob, the poor bastard.

And all it says is this.

"I'm in jail. Come when you can." I mean that's it. No salutation, whatever, and no, 'Love, Dad,' or just, 'Dad,' or even 'Your Old Man.' Nothing like that.

And what did I expect, you know. I mean, really. What? And the thing about my old man is that being in jail is nothing new to him, just the

opposite if you want to know the truth, all the while I was growing up jail like his second home or something, I mean they'd lock him up for all sorts of reasons for his own or the so-called community's good, but mostly, I guess, mostly for being drunk and disorderly, which meant anything, you know, but just about anything under the sun, but ever since I've had the pleasure of knowing my old man he had just about as hard a time with himself as he did with the rest of the world, I mean he'd lash out at himself as much as he would at everyone else, I mean whenever he'd beat me, which was like his favorite pastime or something, but whenever he'd beat me I would get the feeling that he was like beating himself, I mean don't get me wrong, I hated the bastard, I really did, but at the same time I couldn't help feeling this thing, you know, whatever this thing was, and the thing is I survived, it's incredible what a kid can survive, but now this letter, if you can call it that, and I don't even know how he found out where I was living and all. I suppose he had someone make some inquiries or something, I mean he can be pretty gentle and persuasive when he's sober, you know, get people, some people to do just about anything for him, but the thing is what does he expect of me, you know, just drop everything I may or may not be doing, which granted, isn't a hell of a lot, but still, just rush to his aid, bail him out, whatever, and then, you know, what, I mean really, what then, I mean I've had it with this guy a long time ago, and now this so-called letter, this letter out of the clear blue.

To hell with the guy. Really.

But the thing is it isn't as simple as that, I mean this sort of thing settles on your mind, it does on mine, and you have to sort of grapple, struggle with it for a while, I know I do, and it isn't like I'm tempted to go up there to do I really don't know what, but still I have to think about it for a spell, clear my head or something before I can get on with things, you know, whatever those things might be.

So.

Without saying anything to Frank,I mean what would be the point, but without saying anything to him I just hit the streets, walking's always been my best way of clearing my head of things, I mean I don't care where I am, it always has, even as a kid I'd go for these long, but really long walks, I mean nothing for miles around and I really had nowhere to go but I'd just walk and walk, like I tried to put a distance between me and all those things in my head, and if that sounds crazy I don't care, I mean some things may sound crazy on the surface but underneath it all they make a lot of sense, they actually do.

So I just head up Collins and all. I mean where else am I going to go? I could head for the beach I guess, walk up to the very edge of the ocean I suppose, I mean the ocean's supposed to be this immense thing and all whose very sight is supposed to put things into perspective, you know, one's own insignificance along with one's problems, whatever, but for some reason I want to have nothing to do with the ocean just now, just walk the streets, stay on Collins and all.

And then what happens? I see this guy from the back, you know, just this guy up ahead who's like the spitting image of this guy, this kid I grew up with, and, 'Shit, holy shit,' I say to myself, like I take this for a sign of something, I mean if this guy is really who I think he is , then maybe, just maybe I should seriously consider heading back to the Panhandle, I mean that's how my mind works, it really does, but when I catch up with him this guy turns out to be a total stranger, I mean from the back I could have sworn it was this kid I used to know but from up front he's this complete stranger, and I take this for a sign as well, what else, and, 'No, Bingo, no, the last thing you want is to go back home,' and I'm relieved I guess, I really am.

And what next? And this may or may not have anything to do with my old man but in my present state of mind nearly everything does, but I see this swastika on the sidewalk and all, this black swastika drawn with a magic marker and all, so what do I do but keep walking until I get to this CVS where I go in to purchase a black magic marker, I actually do, and then I head back, I actually head back to this swastika on the sidewalk, and what do I do but start turning this swastika into this stick figure, I mean I draw a head, hands and shoes on him, the head a bit on the small side but the hands and the shoes really big, I mean oversize, and damn if it isn't this Ronald McDonald figure just walking or stumbling along, and I'm pleased, really pleased with myself, and damn if this isn't another sign for my not going back home, I mean it really is.

One more thing.

When I get back to Frank's place he's watching another of his idiotic tv shows, like these shows just keep multiplying, like god forbid we should ever run out of them, and this one is about some biologists or whoever setting up this automatic camera in the middle of the Amazon, because life, I guess, there's all this life there no one knows about let alone gets to see, and what this camera does, and this is in the middle of the night, but what it does is snap these pictures whenever something moves in front of it, a kind of infrared camera I guess, and later when the photographs are developed you get to see all these hazy images of creatures no one's ever seen before, a bunch of ordinary, well known ones as well, I guess, but, really, a few that no one's ever seen before, and seeing these hazy images Frank's just about ready to jump out of his skin, and, "Shit!" he yells, "Holy Shit!" I mean he doesn't even know what he's looking at, but, "Shit," he just keeps saying, "holy shit," the thing is it's like he's forever looking for the key or maybe just some clues to explain everything that's going on around him, but maybe looking is the wrong word, I mean if he were truly looking he'd find it soon enough in just about everything around, but, no, he just wants this thing handed to him or something, I think that's right, but here's the funny thing, you know, I mean who do these hazy images remind me of except my old man, my father like this hazy image of a creature that one gets to see only in the middle of the night, that's about right I guess, I mean this unknown and even unknowable creature that can only be photographed by this automatic camera in the middle of the night, and this is like the very last sign I need to tell me that going to see him would not only be a waste of effort but probably the biggest mistake of my life up till now, I mean I wish him all the best that remains of the rest of his life, which at the rate he's going can't be very much, but I'll be damned if I re-enter his life again, what for, to be pulled down, sucked under, I mean my mind's made up and for awhile I don't even move from my spot, just keep sitting next to Frank and listening to him saying, "Holy shit, holy shit," over and over again, and that's just fine for now, it really is, I just don't want to have to think about my father at all.

'Bob's Barricades.' I mean you see these things all over the place, up and down Collins and even on the beach, Ocean Drive I guess, but really, just about everywhere you go in Miami, I mean this is a place where they're forever digging, laying down new pipes or just widening the roads I guess, and you can't do this without putting up all these barricades and all, 'Bob's Barricades,' and I'm just thinking, this Bob, whoever he is, has got this sweet deal going, I mean you never see any barricades but his, 'Bob's Barricades,' and, 'How would it be,' I ask myself, but, 'just how would it be, Bingo, if you got into something like this,' you know, 'Bingo's Barricades' and all, but the truth is I haven't the foggiest of how one starts in this line of business, although not without some capital and not without some connections I suppose, and the thing is it would be nice, I mean really nice to sit down and have a chat with this Bob whoever he is, I mean it certainly wouldn't hurt, and maybe, just maybe in the end it's all who you know and who you talk to, you can never tell where your next idea for making a living is going to come from, that's a fact, like the other day I dragged Frank way into Kendall, just this little excursion we took because I was getting so fed up with the beach, and it was like this different world, still Miami and all but this different world with these mini ranches or whatever, I mean you'd think you were out west or something, and then what do we see, what do we pass but this store that says, 'Cowboy Boots, Hats & Clothing,' and, 'Equestrian Equipment, Apparel & Riding Equipment,' and I wasn't even sure Frank knew what equestrian meant, but I think he got the idea with this picture of the face of a horse and all, and, 'Pet & Livestock Feed & Supplies,' and here, I mean there was something, and, "Frank, Frank," I heard myself saying, "can you picture yourself on a horse?" like that, I mean I certainly couldn't, picture myself well enough but, no, not Frank, not exactly, but then, "How would it be if we became cowboys, Frank?" I just asked, mostly in jest I guess but with a touch, you know, just a touch of seriousness, I mean the age of cowboys is dead and gone as far as I can figure, all you have are these fake, these make-believe ones on the screen, especially these black-and-whites of the thirties and forties which come pretty damn close for my money, but maybe, you know, just maybe there are still a handful left somewhere way out west, these Randolph Scott types, you never know, and then, "I think you'd look pretty good in this leather hat and vest with this red bandana about your neck," I say to Frank, who just gives me this blank stare the way he usually does, but the thing is I'm picturing Frank as Randolph Scott or the other way around, and myself as well I guess, but all I'm saying, all I'm trying to say is that you never know where your next ideas for making a living are going to come from, and granted most of them are fairly far fetched or even impossible, but you're okay I think, you really are so long as you leave yourself open to them, I mean just let the ideas come from wherever, and sooner or later something's bound to click, bound to be just right.

And that's all I'm saying.

And then where? Just where do I take this Susan Duino, or rather she me, because she does the driving after I somehow make it to her place, but where except to this place called 'Tropical Chinese,' which is way out on Bird or somewhere but is according to her just about the best Chinese restaurant around, "But not like the ones in New York," she has to add because she's been around and all, which I don't mind, not one bit, but the thing is it's funny how you lock yourself into a situation by just some idle, some thoughtless question like, "Do you like Chinese food?" which is what I asked her when we first met, and Frank is right I guess, I don't much care for Chinese, eat it when I have to I suppose but my preference is plain old American or even Cuban food, no matter, but the thing is after I show up at her place in the Gables with this bunch of flowers and all, not roses, you know, anything but roses, but just this bunch of wild flowers, she just smiles and says, "Hey, there Bingo," and then right after that, "You'll lose that hat, I guess," and I didn't even realize I had it on, my 'Chicago Bears' cap and all, I mean I wear it just about all the time but I didn't realize I had it on just then, and, "Yeah, sure," I tell her, but this is before she takes the flowers, which she does of course after I take the cap off, but it's a peculiar way to start the evening, you know, I think it is.

But she's this really terrific looking woman and all, I mean no hat this time, which is really a shame, but even without the hat she's this real knockout, I mean she's wearing this really loose, this almost shimmering dress, all in folds or something but light, you know, light as a feather, I mean you see a dress like that and you really have to keep yourself from touching, from stroking it, and then what she does is show me around her place, her apartment, I mean she does ask if I want a drink or something, but, "No, no, thanks," I say, "I think I'll hold off," but then I feel like I'm on this guided tour or something, you know, I mean her apartment is like this mini museum or something with all these paintings and photographs, and it's a good thing she only pauses at some of them to explain their significance to her life, whatever, I mean if she paused at every single one I bet I'd be here most of the evening just taking this tour and all, and then I'm just thinking what it'd be like if I gave her this tour of Frank's place and especially my room, I mean we'd be done in something like five seconds flat, but then, "Come, come along, Bingo," she says, "we mustn't keep the Chinese waiting," like that, and then off, off we go, and she's got this white Volvo with leather seats and all, I'm just remarking, I mean it's the kind of car you'd think twice about farting in or even picking or just scratching your nose, I'm just saying, and then she puts on this disc of something by Bach, and, "Do you like Bach?" she asks, and I'm nodding like a fool, like who doesn't, and you can hardly feel the car moving, it's this really smooth ride and all, and all you can hear is this organ music by Bach, it fills the entire car, I mean there seems to be no space for anything else, not even for thinking.

And I won't say much about the meal, this Chinese restaurant and all, except that it's like this show and all, all these chefs working behind this glass window, and, "What do you think?" she asks, and, no, I really don't know what to think, I just don't, and she insists on ordering, you know, and the food may be really good or even outstanding, but as I'm not this particular fan of Chinese food it's hard for me to say, but I do manage to drink a lot of rice wine, she does as well, and that's really Japanese not Chinese but I guess that doesn't matter, but the thing is it gives you this really fine warmth, this glow both inside and out, and as I'm just sitting and looking at her once again I think, 'There sits the woman of my life,' but, no, not with the same intensity or even spontaneity as when I said, "There goes the woman of my life," to Frank, but just the same I'm still thinking it, and then I just can't wait to get back to her place, I mean museum or no museum, I just can't.

And I don't know if I want to go on with the rest of this. I do and I don't. Some highlights sufficient perhaps.

And it's not that this Susan Duino plays hard to get, which happens now and again, you know, it's just that she sort of takes over I guess, which may or may not be a bad thing, you know, it all depends. Disorienting, let's just say, you know, just a bit.

Like we're just standing there and all, you know, already in the bedroom but still just standing there, and she's sort of examining or studying me, you know, I mean like I could be one of those exotic animals caught in the lens of this automatic camera, and, "Look at your eyes," she says, "both dreamy and penetrating," like that, and we're not even touching, no, not yet, and then "Your nose, straight but kind of drooping," and, "What? What?" I have to ask and smile, but she goes on, "And this smile, this kind of half-smile on your lips," and I'm starting to feel like one of her art works on the wall, I can't help it, but then she does back off a bit, and, "Take your clothes off," like that, "go ahead, undress," and that's pretty unusual to say the least, it is in my experience, which is not to say that in my opinion men and women have these assigned roles and all, far from it, but still, it is a bit unusual, I'd say so, but I do as I'm told, I mean why not or what have I got to lose, and when I'm buck naked what does she do but back up and study me like I'm one of her so-called works of art, I mean this woman strikes me as something of a collector if you ask me, you know, this combination of the pleasures of ownership and appreciation, I'm just saying, and then, "Lie down, go ahead, lie down on your back," and even though I'm not sure what I had in mind, I rarely am, this probably wasn't it, she being the woman of my dreams and all, and, "Relax," she says, "take it easy, just shut your eyes and enjoy," and about the last thing I want to do is shut my eyes again, she being the woman of my dreams and all, but, still, once more I do as I'm told, and, 'The trouble with you, Bingo,' I'm thinking, but, 'the trouble with you is you let just about anybody tell you anything at all and you'll go along with it, at least at first,' and I don't know whether this is out of sheer curiosity or because I'm this easy going guy and all who doesn't mind being told what to do from time to time, so I'm just lying there with my eyes shut and this pretty impressive hard-on, I mean it doesn't take much, and the next thing is she just starts stroking me all over but eventually, you know, sooner or later down there, and the thing is I don't exactly mind, I mean why should I, but she being the woman of my dreams I would sure love to see, to watch her as she's doing it, but the thing is, you know, nothing doing, I'm still keeping my eyes shut, and, "No peeking," she even pauses to remark, and I don't think she even bothered to undress, unless she did it remarkably fast, you know, like in five seconds flat, but I don't think so, and then it's like I'm in this tunnel or something, the tunnel of her mouth I guess, and, 'What's the difference between this and having a wet dream, Bingo?' I ask myself, I mean talk about the woman of my life, of my dreams, but for some reason I'm not even supposed to see her, and then, you know, I just shoot off, I mean what else, and, "There, there," I hear her saying, "that's good boy, that's a good Bingo," like that, and when I open my eyes I see her kneeling on the floor and wiping her mouth and smiling, but this really lovely, this incredible smile, and I can't help smiling myself, you know, but when I sit up and move towards her what does she do but hold up her hand like some cop stopping the traffic, and, "No, no," she says, "that's enough, I'm really tired now," and, "How about a nice cup of coffee before you're on your way?" and what else can I say, and all that rice wine and Chinese food is just repeating on me, and, 'So much for hats and Chinese food, Bingo,' I tell myself, I mean what else, and then afterwards on the bus I feel like I'm riding not only through the dark but right into the very heart of darkness itself, and I promise myself I won't say a word about this to Frank, that's the last thing I need, if anything I'll just say I had a nice evening and all but this woman, you know, she's not really the one of my life, and I can just see him make a face and all followed by one of his stupid comments, but that's Frank I guess, I mean no big surprise there, but the main thing is not to go into any details about the evening, I mean I don't see the point, I really don't.

So.

Back at Frank's place and throughout the rest of the night what do I do but picture Ronald McDonald and all, I mean this poor slob dressed up as Ronald McDonald and somehow, I don't know how, but somehow getting this blow job in the back of McDonald's, maybe by the garbage bins, I'm not entirely sure, but just getting this blow job and then having to go back to work, I mean what else, and his heart, I guess his heart is breaking, what else, and I don't care if you are Ronald McDonald you're entitled to more than just the occasional blow job, I mean clowns have dreams the same as everyone else, that's a fact, and no matter how hard I try I just can't shake this image of Ronald McDonald getting a blow job and then having to go back to work, and it isn't until I start singing, "Bee, eye, en gee-oh," that Ronald McDonald starts to fade to eventually disappear, and then that's how I finally fall asleep, just singing this stupid song and all, but not before Frank comes in to ask, "You all right, Bingo boy?" and, "Fine," I tell him, "just singing is all," and that doesn't faze him, I mean very little does, and, "Well, all right then," is all he says and shuts the door, and that's when or shortly after that is when I finally manage to fall asleep.

Who knows, I guess. Really.

Who knows? I mean things happen or they don't, or certain things some of the time and others at others, or nothing, you know, nothing at all for a spell, but things with a way of evening, of balancing out in the end, or maybe not, or maybe it's all just a question of what one's after, which is not always easy to figure, to pin down in the end.

So, what do I do but come across this sign on this building and all, 'Attention: Sabbath Services. Lectures, Important Information About

Judaism,' like that, and I really don't bother with the where and the when, I just don't, but the sign itself intrigues me, and, 'Bingo,' I say to myself, 'you really know shit about Judaism or anything else for that matter,' but for now it's just Judaism, and it's not about religion I guess which leaves me absolutely cold, I mean I've met all sorts of religious types and they never once struck me as any more enlightened than anyone else, just the opposite in fact, but I mean just the history of things in general and now Judaism in particular, and then I just start thinking about getting my G.E.D. and all, you know, just a way of filling in certain gaps, but that's neither here nor there for the moment, but like Judaism is this cradle of western and a number of eastern civilizations, I mean the Arabs and all, and here I am knowing next to nothing, knowing just shit about it, I mean I know a bit about Abraham and Moses and all, like Abraham the father of a host of nations and Moses just leading them out of one captivity right smack into another, you know, leading them right smack into the wilderness, and I must say something about that appeals to me, this whole idea of being lost in the wilderness and all, I mean I can certainly relate to that, I mean right now what else am I doing than wandering in the wilderness on the edge of this park and all, but other than that, what, see what I mean, what else do I really know.

And it's a good thing there's this bench and all where I can sit and gaze around for a spell, forget about Judaism and everything else.

And the thing is there's always something to see, the here and now I mean, the immediate present.

Like right now there's this guy on this other bench feeding the pigeons and all, and the pigeons, those birds are all over him, I mean on his head, his shoulders, his arms, his lap, and as some fly off new ones arrive to land on him, and think, just think what it's taken for those birds to trust him like that, that guy's been coming daily for years I bet, maybe even rain or shine although I'm not entirely sure of that, but let's just say, I mean whatever else that guy does to make his living and all he's here every day to feed the pigeons and all, and that's something, it really is, and I'm not exactly saying that's the purpose of his life although if you have to have a purpose that's about as good as anything else I can think of, and I really envy him I guess,

I actually do, I mean, 'How would it be, Bingo, if you had those birds all over you?' I even ask myself, pretty terrific I bet, really satisfying.

And then something else. On this other bench there are these two young women, one of them slightly overweight, not much, just a bit I guess, but these two young women making out, and if there's anything I love to watch it's people making out, men, women, it doesn't much matter, and these two women are really going at it, touching, stroking, kissing and now and again grabbing, then pausing, you know, just a bit, talking and smiling before starting up again, and like, 'Wow,' I'm thinking, 'wow,' I mean that's what life's all about I guess, I mean isn't it, and then, 'How come, Bingo, you've never had this?' I mean I guess I've come close on a number of occasions but, no, never or never exactly this, and maybe I should have been born a lesbian, I'm just saying, but women with women a lot more caring and even playful than women with men or men with men or women, and again I'm just saying, but the thing is I could just watch these two forever I guess, and it's not that they're doing anything new, it's pretty much the same thing over and over again, but it just makes me feel good just watching them, and anyway they're oblivious to the rest of the world, they pretty much are.

But back to Judaism. You know.

But, no, I'm no longer interested, all I want now is to watch these two women and all, I mean I hope they never stop, never tire of doing what they're doing, because all I want is to watch them for a spell, forever if at all possible.

"You hear about this crazy guy?" Frank asks.

Like all of a sudden he's informed, or at least knows something about something that doesn't have to do with his stupid TV shows or his idiotic drug deals, but, "This crazy guy shot up McDonald's down the block," he says, and my first reaction is just to look at him, you know, like Frank's hallucinating or something, I mean it's not like it hasn't happened before, but his gaze is steady and his eyes relatively clear, not exactly signs of hallucination, and at any rate why would Frank hallucinate about McDonald's of all things, so, "Say that again," I just tell him, "go ahead," and he does, "This crazy guy shot up McDonald's," he says, and then I'm like in shock or something, I mean if he had told me about the imminent destruction of the world, you know, through a collision with a monster comet it couldn't have been worse, and I'm just standing there, unable to move or even think, and all I'm seeing are these images of Ronald McDonald lying face down in a pool of blood, and, "It even made the national news," he adds, "you wanna see?" but, "Hell, no, shit, no," I tell him, I mean the last thing I want is to see this as another, as one more item on the news, and then when I'm finally able to move, which is I don't when, not exactly, but when I am I just head for the door, I don't even say good bye to Frank but just head for the door and then down the stairs and up the block, because I can't be anywhere but on the scene where this crazy thing happened, no rhyme or reason, but I just have to be there and nowhere else, that's all I know.

And I'm actually running. You know.

Which I almost never do, hardly ever, I mean a couple of times in the past when I was chased and all, when it was unavoidable, but other than that never, hardly ever.

And while I'm running I'm picturing not just Ronald McDonald but this crazy gunman whoever he is, but just this guy with his automatic or semi-automatic walking into the place and starting to spray it with bullets, and the thing is in slo-mo or something the way you often see on TV or the movies, and no sound, I mean the thing happens in absolute silence in my head, and the workers and customers just ducking or dropping as this guy just stands there and sprays away, and whether it happened this way or some other that is just the way I picture it, and after a while, a few seconds I guess, there's no one left standing in the place except this crazy guy, this crazy gunman and all, and then what does he do but turn the gun on himself and just blast away, I mean that's how I see it, and the guy is faceless I guess, all the rest with recognizable features, I mean I know all the workers and most of the regular customers in that place, except every now and again, and don't ask me why, but just now and then this guy, this crazy with my father's features and all, really, it makes no sense, but for the most part he's just this faceless, this unknown character.

And talk about your convention, your gathering of cops.

I mean they're all over the place and their cop cars with their flashing lights, I mean they've got the place pretty much blocked off, and that's not to mention all the others, the medics, the newscasters and a bunch of gapers all along the way, and the thing is they're all like too late, all of them after the fact, and, 'Shit, if that isn't the way it always is,' I tell myself, but I sort of keep my distance, I mean the last thing I want is to be a part of any sort of a crowd, but, 'At least you're here, Bingo,' I tell myself, no reason, I just do, and I half expect to see Ronald McDonald carried out on a stretcher, clinging, just clinging to life I guess or dead, maybe even dead by then, but I don't of course, a number of others but not Ronald McDonald, but still I get this sinking feeling in my stomach like, 'They've finally got Ronald McDonald,' and of course I feel for all the others, wounded or even shot dead, but what I'm thinking is, 'They've finally got Ronald McDonald,' I just am.

And later.

Not much or much later, I don't even know, but later when I'm walking home I'm thinking, 'There's nothing and no one safe in this world,' I mean no matter who you are and what you'll do this isn't the kind of world for anyone to be safe in, and maybe that's always been the case, you know for eons of human existence, but maybe not, maybe it's just now with the world gone crazy and all, and then, and not for the first and probably not the last time, but I'm just thinking maybe it would be best to be done with this whole scene and all, and I don't just mean Miami or any place specific but with life, with all of life I guess, and it's not that I'm suicidal, nothing like that, I mean that's the one thing about me, in all my life no matter how bad things got I've never been what you'd call truly suicidal, I've known a few who have but not me, not the type I guess, I mean it's one thing to think you want to be done with this whole damn mess and quite another to be truly suicidal, at least I think it is.

And then.

The way I wanted, had to be at the scene of this crime or whatever, that's exactly the way I now want or have to be away from it, I mean it's like reality is on its way to becoming unreal, just another happening or media event, and, 'The vultures are taking over, Bingo,' I even tell myself, and by those I mean just about everybody including the cops, and the way I feel about it is that shooting up McDonald's is like shooting up Frank's place, there's really little or no difference, and I just have to get out of there, I mean anywhere but here as far as I'm concerned.

And then life, I'm thinking, all of life is just this giant disaster waiting to happen, I mean I don't care who or where you are but sooner or later your life is nothing but this giant disaster waiting to happen, or, 'As in the beginning, so in the end, Bingo,' I tell myself, I mean if your life started through this accident and all you can be pretty sure it'll end the same way, and I don't even know if that makes all the intervening time precious or ridiculous, you know, I just don't.

So I just start walking down Collins and all, heading neither towards nor away from home, you know, just heading nowhere in particular, and then what do I see but this bus come driving down the avenue, this bus with this 'NO SERVICE' sign on it, and I'm thinking wouldn't it be great, really terrific to be on this bus with the 'NO SERVICE' sign, driving neither fast nor slow but just kind of rolling along without any specific destination, and I'd be the only passenger, just me and the driver, and the bus kind of dark inside, I mean you could see out but not in and just kind of riding, heading nowhere at all, I mean there'd be this movement and all but the movement directionless, heading neither towards nor away from anything, just this movement is all and me just sitting there absolutely still in the dark.

And then these other, all these other crazy images in my head. It's like I'm dreaming or something while walking on Collins and heading nowhere in particular.

And the images are in fast forward I guess, unlike the ones I had about the shooting in McDonald's which were more or less in slo-mo.

I'll just name them I guess without going into any sort of details, because as I said the details were sketchy, just one image after the next.

And time, I guess, time screwed up as well. About the images I mean. I mean some from the recent and others from the distant past, but not in any sort of order, you know, the distant first and then the more recent, no, the images just all over the place as if independent of time.

I'm standing by my mother's bed in the hospital, and she's neither living nor dead or both living and dead, and I'm gazing down at her and she up at me, but she's gazing at me with her eyes closed.

My father's drunk. And I don't even know where we are but he's drunk with this wild look in his eyes and he's coming at me with his tight fists, but it both is and isn't me, I mean my father just going at this kid who both is and isn't me, and I both do and don't feel the pain as he connects, I mean one second I do but the next it's like I'm immune or something.

I'm making love to this woman. And she's definitely the woman of my dreams although, no, I have no idea who she is, but we're making love in some kind of field and all the while she's whispering, 'Ah, Bingo, I knew you'd come, I knew you were out there somewhere.' Frank is foaming at the mouth. But it's not because of an overdose of drugs or anything like that, in fact he's laughing while he's foaming at the mouth and saying, 'Ah, Bingo, you mustn't take everything so seriously, it's all just a joke after all. Then I'm with this fish guy on the highway, and we're having this terrific talk, this discussion, but no words, I mean neither one of us actually talking, but we're having this terrific exchange of opinions, of ideas, and then we just sort of levitate, both of us as light as feathers as we rise above the highway.

Grace gets out of her wheelchair. And once again I don't know where we are or how I found her, but as soon as I see her and she me she just gets out of her wheelchair and walks towards me, and she's this amazing looking woman, practically ageless, 'Ah, Bingo, don't look so surprised, there's so much you don't know,' and then we just dance, I mean this music coming from somewhere or everywhere at once, but we just dance in ever widening circles around Biscayne Boulevard.

Bruce and I finishing our last job in the Everglades. But as we're surveying it's more like a beginning than an ending, I mean we're starting this incredible surveying job that's all about the reversal of time, I mean we're not surveying for this new mall that's to replace this river of grass, just the opposite, we're surveying to re-establish the old, the original boundaries of the Everglades, to push back the malls, the buildings, the roads, whatever, and Bruce is just smiling and saying, 'I never thought I'd live to see the day, Bingo, you and I surveying in reverse, returning things to the way they once were instead of the way they had become,1 and we're both hurrying and taking our time, I mean this is one hell of a job, we mustn't waste any time but still take our time to do it just right.

I meet up with Ronald McDonald. I don't know where. But he's holding this crazy gunman, whoever, by the scruff of the neck, and this crazy, this gunman is like this spent, this helpless creature now, and Ronald McDonald just holding him practically effortlessly now, and he smiles as he says, 'There will always be crazies in this world, Bingo, but so long as there are a couple of Ronald McDonalds left to handle them I don't think we need to worry, and then we just carry him off, this crazy gunman, carry him to the edge of the ocean somewhere.

And so on and so forth. A bunch of more images like that after that.

And then it's late, pretty late I guess by the time I get home to Frank, and he's in this time warp of his own, which he pretty much is practically all the time, but he's in this time warp as he listens to his digitally remastered recordings of pop tunes from the sixties and seventies, I mean he's got this amazing collection, and the thing is he was never around when they were first released, but now, every once in a while, he does his best to pretend he's this child of the sixties or seventies, which he really isn't of course, but for once I don't mind, I mean most of the time any sort of pretending like that just gets under my skin, especially from Frank, but just now I don't mind, and we just sit around listening to these hits by the Everly Brothers and the Shirelles, stuff like that, and the thing is it keeps me from thinking, it really does, and we spend about half the night just listening to these old hits without either of us talking, you know, without either of us saying a single word to each other.

And that's fine. Really. That's just fine with me. And then here's the thing.

The next afternoon or evening, whatever, who should show up but Bruce, I mean I haven't seen him in several weeks I guess and it's pretty obvious he's come to say good bye, you know, next stop Kuwait or something, and he finds me by the pool where I'm just sitting around and thinking about all sorts of crazy things, most of them stemming from the McDonald's shooting and all, you know, like this remnant of the Big Bang or something, but Bruce finds me, comes up from behind and just grabs me as if to keep me from falling, and, "Hey, there, Bungo," he says, "watch out you don't crack your brain," and that's funny because that's more or less what I was doing, just cracking my brain with all these crazy thoughts, and it's pretty amazing, at least to me, how glad I am to see Bruce, but maybe I would have been just as glad to see anyone at all to interrupt my crazy thoughts, and, "Hey, there, how's it going?" I look up, and Bruce just pulls up a chair facing mine, and he's brought a six-pack and all, I mean it's pretty obvious he's come for this heart-to-heart before pulling out for part or parts unknown, for Kuwait I guess, which to me is just about the end of the world.

And, "It's next week, Bungo," he says, "I'm leaving for Kuwait next Wednesday, and it's not too late for you to change your mind." And the thing is he's serious and all. He really is.

I mean here's this guy with a legitimate family and all, fairly settled I mean, but he's ready to chuck it all, pull up roots or whatever the expression may be, and there's something at once admirable as well as crazy about it all, at least I think there is, I mean compared to him I'm just this blade of grass or leaf in the wind, I mean if anyone should be ready for a fresh start it should be me and not Bruce, I mean what's holding me to this place, Miami and all the rest of it except maybe Frank perhaps, and it isn't like I'm doing a hell of a lot of good even with Frank, maybe sometimes I guess, just once in a while, but, no, not on the whole, I wouldn't say so, so what's keeping me here, you know, I mean really, and I'm thinking of all the explorers, adventurers, what have you who just walked away from one life in search of another, and sometimes I guess, yeah, sometimes without even knowing what that other life might be, and the thing is all my life I pictured myself as this explorer or adventurer or whatever, more or less, and now here's the perfect chance, the perfect opportunity and I just can't is what, I just don't see myself doing it.

But, "What about this McDonald's thing?" I just ask Bruce, both to change the topic I guess but also because it's what's been on mind, just mulling it over as I was sitting here.

And, "This country's had it," Bruce looks at me, "the crazies, you know, all the crazies taking over," and, "You owe nothing to this place," he says, "you stick around here long enough and you'll become a crazy yourself, it's practically inevitable." And that's pretty funny I guess.

Because what was I thinking about before as I was sitting here but this notion of inevitability I guess, how some or even most things in life have this feeling of inevitability about them even if it's only after they happen, which is not to say the whole damn thing isn't dependent on chance, but it's chance and inevitability both I guess, if that makes any sense, and I'm not sure it does, but it's chance and inevitability both.

And Bruce moves his chair closer and all and opens two more cans of beer.

And, "You've got your whole life ahead of you, Bungo," he says, "you bet you do, and while it's true you've got this crummy start and all, you know, not too many breaks as far as I can tell, still, which of us hasn't, really, very few of us haven't," and for a second I think he's about to tell me some stories from his own childhood, you know, but luckily he doesn't, "but the thing is,

Bungo," he continues, "you've got a certain something, you actually do, I mean in a lot of ways you remind me of myself when I was your age, you know, bright, defiant but not knowing which way was up and which down," and then he, Bruce, just reaches over and and puts his hand on top of mine, just a friendly gesture I guess, "and it would be too bad, really, just too bad if you had no one to guide you along, I mean I never did, so I do, I actually know what I'm talking about," and then he like gives my hand this little squeeze, noting special, just a squeeze, "and these are crucial years, Bungo," he goes on, "and a friend, a true friend is about the only thing you can depend on," and suddenly he withdraws his hand, just backs off a bit, "I mean this country's going to the dogs, and really, this is a hell of a time and place for a kid like you to try to find his way. And then, "A fresh start, Bungo," he stares at me, "that's what you need, a fresh start for you and me both."

And then I don't know what to think. I really don't.

I mean I'm the last guy to jump to any conclusions, I really am, 'Take it easy, Bingo,' I often tell myself, 'just take it easy,' but I can't help feeling a bit uncomfortable and all, and Bruce, yeah, I guess Bruce as well, so we just sit there sipping beer without saying anything at all for spell, you know, just sitting there and staring at this crappy water with all the leaves and bugs floating on top. I mean the guy who's supposed to take care of this pretty much comes and goes as he pleases, I even doubt he really knows what he's doing, but he pretty much comes and goes as he pleases.

And then, "I don't get it," I just say, "I don't get it about this guy shooting up McDonald's." And Bruce is just nodding and staring, I mean that's pretty much all he does, and then, "Well, maybe you'll think it over," he says, "there's still time," and, "Yeah, maybe I will," I tell him but without much conviction, and then he just gets up and sort of waits for me to get up as well, which I do, and then he gives me this great big hug, you know, and I hug him back, I mean what else, and then, "Wherever I am I'll be thinking of you, Bungo," he says, "don't forget, I'll always be thinking of you," and, "Yeah," I tell him, "yeah," because, really, what else can I say.

And I just stay by the pool and continue staring at that crappy water and all.

And I don't even bother turning around to see Bruce leaving, which I'm pretty sure he himself has, turning around for this one last look I mean, but I don't, I just go on staring at this crappy water.

And, And, 'Christ, Jesus Christ,' I'm thinking.

'The thing,' I tell myself, 'the thing about life, Bingo boy, is that nothing is what it seems,' I mean you may think you've got something, just anything figured out, more or less, but then, bam, something unforeseen or unexpected happens, and the thing is so entirely out of left field or whatever that it just doesn't fit, I mean there's no way, but it just doesn't fit into any sort of picture you may have had of it, whatever that thing was before, and I'm not just talking of Bruce now, I mean Bruce is just this one, this single example, but you can take just about anything at all, the shooting at McDonald's for example, and it'll be the same I bet, I mean before this shooting and all you, I, would have thought that if there's any one place safe in this world it was this stupid McDonald's, you know, the once and future home of Ronald McDonald, but, no, not even close, and, 'Think again, Bingo boy,' I tell myself, so, any and all images you may have of the world, and I don't care what they are, I really don't, but any and all images are only temporary, you know, good or valid or whatever only for a while, up to a point, and then, bam, you know, all these new images start rushing in, and then you have to re-evaluate like crazy, I mean if you expect to survive and all, but all the time you just have to keep re-evaluating now one thing, now another, I mean it never ends, and not once, I mean not one single time do you get this whole, this entire picture of what's going on, and I'm not just talking about me I guess, I'm really not, but no one I've ever known or even heard of has ever gotten this whole, this entire picture of what's going on.

And if there's just this one, this single person who ever did or does I sure as hell would like to meet him, I mean I'd give my life just to meet a person like that.

And then the longer I stare at this crappy water and all the crappier it becomes, I mean even that doesn't make any sense, I mean I guess I could stare at just a single dead leaf or bug, which I do, and eventually that might make some sort of sense, although I doubt it, but as for the entire picture, you know, of how one thing fits in with all the rest, not a chance, and the worst, about the worst thing you can do is just to fake it and all, you know, just tell yourself, 'Ah, but it must fit, it's only that I'm incapable of discovering just how,' I mean that doesn't help, not one bit, but worse, maybe even worse than that is just to give up and all, you know, turn to booze, drugs, whatever, like my old man I guess or even Frank up to a point, but maybe, you know, maybe it's just thinking about all these things that gets us all screwed up in the end, but the thing is I can't stop thinking and all, I just can't without becoming this goddamn vegetable or something, I just can't.

So.

I see this sign and all, on this passing van in the street, 'Cat Network.

Meowmobile. Spay/Neuter. Now $15.00,' and I'm thinking, 'Damn, damn if that doesn't make some sense,' you know working at this small, this specific thing in life like spaying and neutering cats and all, I mean forget about the big picture, just let it go, and focus on the small, the specific things that do a bit of good, like spaying and neutering cats I guess, I mean the damn things are all over the place, the strays as well as the pets, they're just about everywhere you go, and what's going to happen if there's no one to spay and neuter them at a reasonable price I guess, and I can just see it, 'Bingo's Meowmobile. Spay/Neuter. Now $10.00,' to undercut the competition and all, and I bet I could make a decent or perhaps an adequate living just working with animals and all, I mean forget people, just forget about them for the time being and focus on animals, one could certainly do worse, and for some reason the sight of that van makes me feel pretty good about things, I mean as good as they can be under the circumstances, and when I finally get upstairs to Frank and all I just ask, "You ever think about going into the cat business?" like that, and he gives me his usual uncomprehending look, I mean what else, but I don't bother to explain, just not in the mood I guess, and, "Cats," I repeat, "just think about it, Frank," and leave it at that, just go into my room and shut the door.

And that's it I guess. You know. That's it for the time being.

So.

Who turns up at our door, you know, who but this exotic dancer Frank used to know, this Linda Affable, which I can tell right off the bat isn't her real name at all, I mean how could it be, although Linda Affable is no worse than Bingo Sherman when you think of it, it really isn't, but she just shows, pops up out of nowhere like that, and, "Holy shit," Frank says, "holy shit," who's just watching this special about whales in the Pacific or something, how they migrate and all, and, "That's a fine way to greet an old friend," this Linda Affable just smiles, and if she can do anything at all she can sure as hell smile, and I read somewhere, I don't know where, but just somewhere that these exotic dancers, performers, whatever put vaseline on their teeth to make it easier to break into smiles and all, but then Frank just gets up and hugs her, whatever, like they're these old friends or something, and the thing is you never know about a guy like Frank, or anyone else for that matter, I mean for all I know this Linda Affable could have been the love of his life one time, I'm not saying she was, just that she could have been, I mean there's no accounting for these things, there really isn't, and then this Linda Affable just stands there like that as they're looking at each other, I mean you half expect her to take a bow or something, but then Frank says, "This is my cousin, my cousin and my best friend Bingo," like that, and Linda says, "Well, hello there, Bingo," and just holds out her hand like she's this grand dame or something, but I just shake it, you know, the way one guy just shakes another's, and she just stands there in these really tight shorts and this see-through, this practically see-through blouse and all, and on the floor next to her this ratty little suitcase that not even Goodwill would bother to try to sell, and the three of us just standing around like that for a spell, I mean what else are we supposed to do, but then, "I hope you don't mind my just dropping in on you like this," she says, and Frank with his usual, his idiotic grin on his face, I mean he can grin at just about anything at all, and then, "Mi casa tu casa," he says, like he's this goddamn linguist or something, which he really isn't, I mean all he's got are these few phrases and most of them for selling his drugs and all, but then after a while, you know, long or short I really can't say because we're just standing around and all, but after a while he says, "We've got plenty of room, I mean if you want to stay over or something," and I don't know what room he's talking about except for this windowless space in the back where we keep all the junk we never use or don't know what to do with, I mean Frank's like this hoarder and all, I've never seen him throw away anything at all, not even an empty carton or paper bag, I mean if I didn't start tossing things out once in a while this place would be nothing but junk from wall to wall and floor to ceiling, but, "God, you're an angel," Linda smiles, and, "you can't believe what a tough time I've been having," and, "Tell me about it," Frank just says, "things are tough all over," like suddenly he's this worldly philosopher or something.

I mean the guy's just amazing. You know.

Once in a while and in more or less unpredictable ways. He just is.

And then Linda just says, "You think I might freshen up a bit?" like she's just booked into this five star hotel or something, and, "Absolutely," Frank says and shows her the bathroom and all.

And then she's in there showering, whatever, and the thing is that shower's the best thing about the place, I mean the water just cascades and all like it's Niagara Falls or something, and once you get under it, and I don't care who you are, but once you get under it especially on a hot day like today you'll just stay and stay, and that's exactly what Linda does, she just stays and stays, and outside we can hear this gushing water and all like it's flooding the apartment or something.

And then Frank and I are just sitting there. You know. Just waiting.

Just watching these whales migrate. Up along the California and Oregon coast or wherever.

And I know Frank's just waiting for me to ask him things, and that's the thing about Frank, I mean he'll never start talking about something, about anything at all unless he's asked these questions and all, but I'm just like biding my time, you know, because when you have all these questions to ask the best thing is just to bide your time, not rush anything, just take your time considering which question you're going to ask first.

And I don't know. I just don't.

I mean it's his place and all and he can pretty much do as he damn pleases, but nice, I guess, yeah, it would have been, to have talked this thing over a bit, just a bit, before letting this woman invade our lives or whatever it is she's doing.

But I just take my time.

And maybe just a bit too much, because after a while Frank's already absorbed by the sight of these whales, and he even kind of smacks his lips and whistles through his teeth the way he sometimes does, and he even says, "You know, Bingo, one day we've got to go out there, see these whales up close," and he hasn't an inkling, I mean not a clue of what that would involve, you know; the preparations, the money, the time of year and all the rest of it, but Frank's a great one for planning things without actually planning to do them, I mean he once even mentioned going up to Alaska and all to spend the winter as though that were the simplest thing in the world, and this from a guy who starts shivering when the temperature drops below sixty and all, but the thing is he's got the attention span of a gnat or something, so if I don't start asking him about this Linda Affable soon it'll be a lost cause or a done deal or whatever it's going to be.

So, "How'd you meet this woman?" I just ask. You know, to start at the beginning. To get some kind of a grasp on this situation.

And he gives me this look. This Frank look and all. And, "At the Club," he says, "the Kit-Kat Club," like I'm supposed to know all about this place and know that Frank was this regular or whatever he was.

So, "The Kit-Kat Club?" I just repeat.

And I can tell that he's thinking, that at least the wheels are starting to turn and all, and that's a pretty rare sight whenever you're talking to Frank, but, "Yeah," he says, "closed, out of business now," and, "You know, like everything gone bust around here," he adds, which is not to the point, it really isn't, I mean getting into a conversation with Frank you've got to watch he doesn't go off on some tangent or other, I mean it's practically inevitable, so, "What were you doing at this Kit-Kat Club and all?" I ask and, "Just hanging out I guess," he smiles like he's this king of the enigmatic smiles, which, if you know Frank, is pretty hard to swallow, but I sort of let it go, I just do, even though I have a hell of a time picturing Frank with all these horny middle-aged drunks and all, but maybe he was peddling his drugs, you know, that's halfway believable, "And then you met her?" I prompt, and, "Yeah, I guess I did," he smiles again, and it's like pulling teeth or something, getting anything other than these five or six-word sentences out of him, so I try another approach, you know, just making light of the whole thing, and, "So, she stole your heart?" I ask, but, "Man, oh, man," he replies, which could mean anything, just about anything at all.

And, "Right," I tell him, "yeah, right," like that. And then we just watch the whales migrate some more.

But after a while, "And? And?" I ask, and he, "What?" and I,· "Now what?" and he just kind of shrugs his shoulders and all, "I mean is she here to stay?" and I'm just thinking about that ratty suitcase in the middle of the floor, but, "Damned if I know," he just smiles, like it's neither his business nor mine, which just about takes the cake, it really does.

But then, "Let me tell you, Bingo, can I, just let me tell you something.

She's this great, this terrific kid, which you'll discover as soon as you get to know her, and anyway, what am I supposed to do, I mean I took you in when you had nowhere else to go and I don't see how it's any different with her, I mean you're supposed to do for friends, you really are, I mean if you don't, I don't see how anything makes sense, I really don't." And that's about the most I've heard Frank say anything about anything at all, I mean just stringing all those sentences together, and forget for the moment whether this Linda Affable is this terrific kid or not, I mean I've got my own ideas I guess, but it's truly amazing that Frank said all that he said, I mean I've got a hard time just coming to terms with it and all, and then there's nothing, really, nothing I can say after that.

Life is just full of the unpredictable, of unpredictables I guess. I mean it's one thing now and then in the space of a moment, a second it's something entirely different, I mean in some ways still the same, but in others, no, entirely different.

And that very first night Linda sleeps in her storage room or whatever, I have this strange, this really bizarre dream, I mean most of the time I don't even remember my dreams, I just don't, and I even used to think, 'Yeah, Bingo, you're not the type, you just don't dream at all,' but I know that's not the case, I mean sleep experts, whoever are forever telling you that all of us dream practically all the time and it's just that we don't recall, whatever, but this time I do, you know, this crazy dream about Ronald McDonald and Linda whom I don't even know.

I mean, can you beat that? But in this dream, set on this deserted island or something, I mean it sure felt like this deserted island, there's Ronald McDonald just wandering around, like this beachcomber or castaway, whatever, but Ronald McDonald like this last human being in the entire world, which made sense I guess, it did in the dream, and I was like dreaming this dream without being in it, you know, just like this pair of eyes to see but nothing else, which is pretty rare I guess, it just might be, but there's Ronald McDonald and all, just looking for shells or coconuts or whatever, I mean he's really in a bad state, just skin and bones but still Ronald McDonald and all, and then out of nowhere, suddenly by a palm tree or something there's Linda Affable, and she looks exactly the way she did when she first walked into the apartment, red shorts, see-through blouse and all, and what does she do but dance around the trunk of this palm tree like it's this pole in some sleazy girlie club, and to say that Ronald McDonald is surprised is putting it mildly, I mean he just sits down in the sand and all and stares at her like she's this apparition or something, I mean he forgets about his thirst, his hunger, his whatever and just sits there staring at her, and Linda, I guess, just does her thing, I mean she slides up and down and all around that palm tree trunk, gyrates I guess even though there's no music, I mean how could there be, and then the palm tree trunk is really this pole and all, and maybe it was all along, I mean who knows, and the deserted island something like the Kit-Kat Club only with no people in it, don't ask, but it's just this Linda Affable and Ronald McDonald like they were destined to meet or something.

And then other stuff. You know.

I mean I don't exactly know what else happens in the dream because that's all I remember, but I'm pretty sure other things do, and later I'm just trying to get back to this dream and all to find out what, but nothing doing, you know, I mean it's about as hard to get back to some dream you were dreaming as it is to get back to some moment in the past, in real life I mean, just about as hard I guess.

"So, what's your problem?" Linda says to me.

Because I've been sort of keeping my distance I guess, you know, just keeping our conversations to the barest minimum, like, "Morning," "How you doing?" stuff like that, and if I've been watching her she's been watching me as well I guess, and it's like we're trying to make our minds up about things but having a tough time of it, so, "What do you mean problem?" I ask her, like I haven't a clue of what she's talking about, and she's like watching 'Dancing with the Stars,' which if not the stupidest show on TV it's pretty damn close as far as I'm concerned, and on this sofa and all she's making all these moves like she's one of the contestants or something, and, "I mean it's like I've got the plague or something the way you look at me sometimes," she says, and I just stand there, you know, and say, "No, no, I don't think you've got the plague," and the thing is she's not a bad looking woman at all, a bit large boned perhaps and on the skinny side but she's got this terrific blond hair which even if it isn't real is still pretty damn terrific, and, "Like what am I doing " she says, "coming between this male bonding like Butch and Sundance?" and Frank's just sitting there and all, I mean I can tell he wants no part of this, and, "I've known guys like you before," she says, "not an ounce of compassion for anyone but themselves," and, man, if she isn't barking up the wrong tree, she really is, and, "I guess I'm going out for a while," I just tell them, I mean what else, and, "Wait, wait," she says, "I'll tag along, unless that'll turn your stomach or something," but, "Suit yourself," I just tell her, "it's a free country." Like that.

And then where do we wind up, you know, and the thing is I had no specific place to go, I mean I didn't even know I was going out until I just stood there watching the two of them staring at 'Dancing with the Stars,' but where do we wind up but at McDonald's, and I've been keeping away

from the place for quite some time now, wanting to have nothing to do with the so-called scene of the crime I guess, and on the way we don't say much of anything at all, we just don't, but that's all right I guess, I mean the silence seems to suit both of us just fine, and, "Ah, fine dining," she smiles when we get there, to McDonald's I mean, and, "Nothing but the best," I tell her, but both of us smiling, so it's all right, you know, the whole thing's all right I guess.

And I don't know what I expect to find. I just don't.

I mean the whole place awash in blood or something, with chairs overturned and bullet holes in the walls, like I had this idea of time coming to a stop at least as far as this shooting at McDonald's was concerned, but the thing is the place is the way it's always been, I mean exactly the same, and I don't know if that's a good thing or bad, I just don't, and there are some new faces behind the counter, hired after the shooting I guess, but other than that the place is exactly the same.

And I don't know if that does or doesn't give me the creeps. You know. I just don't.

So, "What's your pleasure?" I ask, and, "Why don't you just surprise me?" she looks at me.

And I just get a couple of Big Macs and fries, I mean you can't go wrong with those, but, "You're not some kind of vegetarian?" it suddenly occurs to me, but, "No, I saw the light just out of puberty," she smiles, which is a pretty funny remark I guess, maybe not, but it's an okay remark at the very least.

And we sit in the booth I always sit in, I guess I can't imagine myself sitting anywhere else, like this is where I belong or something, and we just watch each other eat, I mean what else, and all that sauce, whatever, is just dripping down our face, I mean I just dare anyone to take a bite out of a Big Mac and not have some of that sauce dripping down her cheeks, I mean that's why a Big Mac is a Big Mac and like nothing else in the world, and then out of the clear blue, I don't exactly know why, but just out of the clear blue I say, "Look, look, Ronald McDonald," and she looks up and turns around, I mean quick, and asks, "Where, where?" and I don't even know whether she's playing along or thinks I'm serious, but then she says, "Now promise you won't laugh, Bingo, but as a kid I used to have this thing for Ronald McDonald," and like, 'Holy shit,' I'm thinking, but I just kind of smile at her without letting on, and then, "I was like both scared and fascinated," she goes on, "scared I guess because I never really trusted clowns, but fascinated because Ronald McDonald was this beautiful creature and the first guy I ever fell for, I mean he looked like he could really just love you to death if you really wanted him to, I mean I know it sounds stupid and it really is," and then what Linda does is just start talking about her life and all and how she had this fantasy that this Ronald McDonald character could take her out of one life and put her into another, and I'm just thinking, 'Man, if this doesn't sound familiar,' but I don't let on, I just keep on nodding and listening, I mean damn if her childhood isn't like a mirror image of mine, I mean not exactly but close enough, but I just go on nodding and listening and listening and nodding without saying anything at all, it's just the way I am I guess, but when she gets to this part where this man, her drunk father beats her with his fists, I finally say, "Hey, maybe you and I are brother and sister," like that, but she just smiles and goes on, "Other things too, Bingo, I mean he'd do other things to me as well," and then I'm not too sure I want to hear all this, it's pretty horrific stuff, but sometimes you really have no choice about whether you want to listen or not, and, "I can't tell you the number of times I thought of killing the bastard," she goes on, and then it's like I'm seeing Linda Affable, or whatever her real name is, in this new light, whatever, like it's the first time I'm taking this really good look at her, "but then I just ran away," she finishes, "I mean all that stuff stopped by the time I was fifteen but at sixteen I ran away just the same, and right now I don't even ask her for the rest of the story, what happened after sixteen and all, I mean there's only so much to tell and listen to in one sitting, so we just finish our Big Macs and sodas, but we both realize the change, that everything's different from the way it was before.

And then we just walk home. You know.

Taking our time and all, but we just walk home after that. And what's Frank doing, you know, but watching this really zany, this idiotic Japanese picture, 'Godzilla versus Mothra,' you know, 'the Battle for Earth,' I mean leave it to the Japanese to make these truly zany, these idiotic pictures, I mean it's like they're reliving their experiences with the atomic bombs or something, and leave it to Frank to watch them like they're the last word in art or something, and this Godzilla is about as fake as you can get, I mean his movements all stiff and his eyes really lifeless, but he's out to destroy the world or something and breathing fire at just about everything in sight including Mothra, this giant moth that's like the protector of earth, and this giant moth has this buddy and all, Batches or Patches, I can't quite make out the name, but this meaner, this uglier version of himself, and the two of them are just ganging up on Godzilla and zapping him with these bolts of electricity, and they win, you know, these moths finally win, and they carry this stunned Godzilla out over the ocean where they drop him, but the thing is Batches or Patches hangs on and plummets along with Godzilla, so now only Mothra is left, and on and on like that.

And Frank's just mesmerized. I mean he really is.

And, "Frank," I try to talk to him, "hey, Frank, it's just a fucking moth," but he's really absorbed and all, and all he wants is to see the end where Mothra is supposed to save earth yet again, this time from a corner or something.

And Linda and I just look at each other. You know.

Like Frank's just this kid and all, like the two of us are the adults and Frank's just this kid or something, but the feeling doesn't last, no feeling ever does, and then I just get some beers for us and watch the credits with Frank with this like Russian, really, Russian music in the background.

And it's this really great morning.

A nice breeze and low humidity, I mean you wouldn't think summer's just around the corner, which it is, and summer's just one more thing to worry about as far as I'm concerned, I mean is this or is this not the land of hurricanes, and even up in the Panhandle I used to think about hurricanes, you know, just once in a while, but fantasize, whatever about this killer hurricane wiping everything off the face of the earth, like the one in twenty- six or whenever, but I mean everything including people, houses, vegetation, the works, and as a kid there were times when I wouldn't have minded, and maybe I myself would have survived but maybe not, I mean even that didn't matter so much, different now I guess, I mean there are any number of people I wouldn't like to see get blown away, Frank, Grace, Bruce, Linda, whoever, but all I'm saying is that now there's at least a list of people I wouldn't like to see get blown away, but it's a bitch, it really is when one starts thinking and caring about certain people, I mean where does it end, if one starts caring about certain people then pretty soon there are others to be added to the list and then it might just be the whole world, the entire human race I mean, and that's like asking to have your heart broken because there's no way for everyone to be saved, I mean as far as I can tell most people are born losers and die pretty much the same, and I don't even know what it might mean to save someone, you know, other than from the obvious like a hurricane or something, but I'm talking in a bigger sense I guess, and, no, I really don't know what it might mean to save someone.

And the thing is I've never been the type. You know.

But thinking about saving this or that person, and this without even considering what that might mean, but I've never been the type to worry too much about the welfare of others, I mean who in this world looks out for others unless in some way it's connected to looking out for himself, and, 'Guess what, Bingo,' I even used to say to myself, 'looking out for yourself is like this full-time occupation,' I mean what else, but now I'm not so sure, I mean I'm not saying it is or it isn't, just that I'm no longer sure, but maybe, just maybe you can't look out for yourself unless you're looking out for others as well, but, again, I'm not sure, I'm really not.

But take Frank, just take Frank as an example.

I mean if anyone needs saving or looking after it's Frank for sure, I mean he hasn't the foggiest of what is or isn't in his best interest, and I'm not saying I do, but at least I give the matter some thought from time to time, but Frank just goes from one minute, hour or even year to the next with no apparent concern how any one of his actions might be connected to the next and the one after that, I mean just look at the way he practically odeed and all, I mean who couldn't have foretold that sooner or later something like that was bound to happen, but something like that might be news to him I guess, it really might, I mean the notion that he's got this one life and all is like this alien concept, I mean he seems perfectly content just watching these idiotic Japanese flicks or just selling his stupid drugs and all.

I mean, 'Just get a life, Frank,' I often mean to tell him, and do sometimes, but then again look who's talking, I mean I'm not exactly the Albert Einstein or the Joan of Arc type, I mean Bruce was right in a sense, I mean I have to forget about the all the why-s and just start focusing on all the how-s and when-s, it's just too bad that half the time I don't even know whether I'm coming or going, hanging out here with Frank is a perfect example, I mean at times I can just see my whole life passing by while I continue living here with Frank, win like loser of the month, year or even decade award, I wouldn't be surprised, and if something terrific or even just moderately good came my way I bet I wouldn't even recognize it, that's how losers are, and, really, it's high time I stopped dishing out advice and took a long look at my own life.

I mean have I ever been anything else other than a loser, and I'm talking right from the time, I mean practically from the time I was born, and, "I give you Bingo Sherman, loser," I even say out loud, I actually do, I mean what else have I ever been but this dreamy kid and all who incapable of turning his dreams, whatever they may be, into reality, I mean not a single one, and maybe I should just get one of these self-help books like 'How to Succeed in Life with or without Trying,' I mean I wouldn't even care which, and then just study it, memorize it from cover to cover I guess, but the problem with that is that I hate self-help books even more than I do Frank's silly TV shows, and as for succeeding in life I probably don't give a damn, I mean I want to succeed and all but not necessarily what they call succeed in life, and the thing is I don't, I mean I really don't even know what I'm talking about.

But never mind. Really. Just never mind.

And the thing is it's this really great morning and all, and, 'Why can't you just enjoy something just for what it is, Bingo?' I ask myself, I mean without thinking about a million and one things that have or are bound to go wrong in the future, I mean I'm walking along Ocean Drive and it's real early in the morning, too early for most people other than a few joggers and assorted sleepless types, and it's like the very start of creation or something or the Garden of Eden perhaps, and while it was probably nothing like this at the beginning, you know, just a lot of gas lava or whatever, still, you know, there's nothing to keep me from thinking this is the very beginning of time or maybe the Garden of Eden, whatever, and maybe I'm fooling myself, which I guess I am, still, there's nothing wrong with fooling oneself from time to time, so long as one realizes that that's just what one's doing, I mean basically there's nothing wrong with that.

And, "Bingo Sherman, success,' I just tell myself. But not out loud. Not this time.

But just, 'Bingo Sherman, success,' I tell myself.

And then I just stop thinking altogether, and it's not because I force myself to, nothing like that, I just do, and it comes from just staring at the deserted beach and the open ocean, the orange and purple sky, whatever, I mean that's enough, it really is to keep you from thinking and all, and then it's like I've disappeared or something without actually disappearing, it's hard to describe, but here I am just looking and all without any consciousness of who or what is doing the looking, and that's close I guess, I mean that's about as close as I can get to describing it.

And, "How do you feel about a dog?" Linda asks.

And like, "Give me a fucking break," I just smile at her.

And I guess she's seen this stray around the neighborhood, I have too, but this large spotted Dane or something, and I guess you don't see too many of those around, not as strays at any rate, and the thing is I don't even know if he ran away or was abandoned, I mean you can never tell, but if he had run away I bet there'd be these notices all over the place, you know, 'Killer, beloved pet..' etcetera with some photograph of the animal, but there were, there are none, and I tell Linda my theory, you know, that hi s owner was this dealer and all who suddenly disappeared and the animal was left to fend for himself, and. "What dealer?" she asks, but, "Just any dealer," I tell her, and, "A lot of dealers have these amazing pets and all, good for business I suppose," but what she's really interested in is the dog's future and not his past, I mean she's really got her heart set on this animal, and the thing is he's pretty friendly and all, it's quite amazing, I mean I've called him a couple of times and he just came bounding over like we've known each other for years or something, but the thing is he's about the size of a horse or a pony at any rate, I mean you could just about saddle him and ride him off into the sunset or something, and, "What about Frank?" I ask, but we both know that Frank would have like absolutely no opinion on the matter, I mean dog or no dog, it would be all the same to him, and then Linda says this really funny, perhaps even stupid thing, and I can't even tell whether she's kidding or not, but she says, "Don't you want to be a family, Bingo?" and like what, you know, just what am I supposed to say to that, and the thing is this building has a policy and all about not having any pets unless you can carry them in your arms or something, and I can just see one of us trying to budge this beast let alone carry him in our arms, but, "Since when were you worried about policies?" Linda asks, and I can see it's already a done deal or something with only the details to be worked out, but I'm beginning to realize Linda's pretty good at stuff like that, I mean when she really sets her mind t something she's pretty good at working out the details of how to go about getting it.

And, "We could call him Bingo," she even adds. As a joke or something.

And I don't, I really don't know how I feel about that.

But, "'Come here, Bingo,'" she smiles, "'sit, Bingo, go, fetch, Bingo,'" you know, stuff like that.

And it serves me right, I guess, for being called Bingo, but, "How am I supposed to know whether you're calling me or the dog?" I just look at her, and, "You'll know," she just smiles, "you'll know all right," and I guess maybe I will.

So.

We don't even tell Frank about it, I mean what would be the point, and one day we just put a leash around the dog, around Bingo and all, and he's happy as a lark, and we just bring him up into the apartment where we let him loose, and the next thing he's just all over Frank on the sofa and all, and Frank's just saying, "Shit, holy shit," but he really doesn't mind, you can tell, I mean Frank probably just imagines he's out in some jungle somewhere where he encounters this really friendly and amazing beast and all, I mean it's like we've brought one of these Nature shows right into the apartment, and Frank doesn't mind, he really doesn't.

And this dog, this Bingo is like in love with Frank or something.

Which really doesn't figure, I mean not at all, because it's Linda who does most of the work of taking care of the dog, "Bingo really loves his treats," she keeps telling him as she feeds him, takes him for his walks, whatever, and Frank just sits or lies around on the sofa most of the time, but the dog has this thing for Frank, I mean go figure, and he, Bingo I mean, barely leaves his side whenever he's in the apartment, like he, Bingo, the dog I mean has taken it into his head that Frank needs this guarding, this looking after, which in a way he does I guess.

And this dog is like a horse or a cow or something, and I know I said horse before but at times he's really more like a cow, it depends I guess, and he's neither bright nor particularly stupid, just kind of average I suppose, but he's got these lovely blue or lilac eyes that now and again have these intense, these curious looks to them, but at other times, no, just these blank looks that remind me of Frank's, I mean no wonder I guess, but, really, no wonder the two of them get along so well, but the thing is the presence of this horse or cow or whatever is playing havoc with the dynamics of our personal relationships, I mean it is at least as far as I'm concerned, and I'm not saying they were so smooth or great or whatever to begin with, I mean you get three people living together and this without even considering the kind of people they are, but just three people existing together and there are bound to be any number of ups and downs, and this dog, this Bingo seems to exploit, to take advantage of the ups as well as the downs, and what I mean is that both the ups as well as the downs seem to be magnified by his presence, and then to make matters worse Linda and Frank with this relationship in the past I know nothing about, I mean good luck trying to get anything out of Frank about it or even Linda for that matter, and I'm not the prying type, I'm really not, but being in the dark about something like that with its definite disadvantages, I mean who knows, really, just who knows, and if I start having certain feelings for Linda, and I'm not saying I will or won't, but just supposing, and if Frank is still sticking it to Linda, which I'm not saying he is but, again, just supposing, then what would that do to our relationship, Frank's and mine I mean, and then this dog that's in love with Frank and all but that Linda's taking care of just adding to the complications, I mean you can see where he would.

But.

All I'm saying, asking is how long can we go on like this, I mean I'm not exactly partial to complicated situations, even though all my life, I mean looked at a certain way, but practically all my life I've known nothing but.

You know.

And then Linda comes down with this urinary infection or something, I mean you might as well add that to the list.

And the thing is it may or may not be a urinary infection although she insists on calling it that, like, "I've had it before," she says, "this fucking urinary infection, it just comes and goes I guess," but I for one am not convinced, not entirely, and, "You sure, are you sure that's what it is?" I ask, but she just gives me this look and all, and, "What are you saying?" she asks, and, "I'm not saying anything at all," I tell her, "just wondering why you don't go to a doctor," but, "You're not listening to me, Bingo," she just looks at me, "I said just a fucking urinary infection," and, "Right, right," I tell her, but she's got this deathly fear of doctors or something, like what they'll tell her is that she's got a week or two to live at most, I mean she wants nothing and no one messing with her body, her symptoms, I mean she's one of these cure it yourself types, she really is.

Like, what's to be done? You know. Really. What's to be done? And lately, just lately, she and Bingo, the dog I mean, have been tagging along with Frank on his various selling jaunts, sort of staying in the background I guess but still tagging along with him, and I could just see where the three of them would be busted one day, it's practically inevitable, I mean Frank is anything but this slick salesman, this with it guy and all, and I don't think it helps, I really don't, that this tall skinny blond and this great spotted Dane are just standing alongside of him, you know, just calling attention to themselves.

And the thing is if and when that happens, but it's more like when than if, but when that happens I don't want to be around, I mean I'm sick and tired of other people's problems, I've got plenty of my own, thank you very much, and what I need is to start seriously thinking about my future and all, and I'm almost regretting not having gone to Kuwait with Bruce, not really I guess, but almost as I said.

And then here's the thing.

I mean as crazy as it sounds, you know, but this is how my mind works But here's the thing.

I just start thinking, asking myself, 'What would Ronald McDonald do in my place?' as though he were this real person and all, which he both is and isn't, I guess you know what I mean, but I just start having these fantasies about this all knowing, all wise Ronald McDonald in my shoes, and the one thing I never considered, I mean all the time I had this fixation or whatever on Ronald McDonald, was that he was all knowing or all wise, I mean not even close, I mean what was he but just this clown and all who had this skill I guess of taking the sting out of certain impossible situations, I mean for practical purposes that seemed entirely sufficient, but like all at once I mean to have him all knowing and all wise as well, but I can just picture sitting alongside of him, on some stupid bench or something, but just sitting there and telling him all my problems, confusions, whatever, and he, Ronald McDonald, just nodding and blinking and saying, 'Hmm, hmm,' like that, I mean that's all he would do, but already, you know, like already making me feel better and all because I could tell he was giving some serious thought to my problems.

And this is pretty fucked up, I know, and maybe even as fucked up as one can get, but once he's there, I mean the image of this Ronald McDonald sitting on this bench with me, I just can't shake it, him I mean, and I just go on telling him about all the weird stuff in my life, and fast I guess, real fast, because without having to actually speak the stuff just races through my mind and his as well I suppose, I mean it feels like the speeded up version of 'This is your life, Bingo Sherman,' and of course he's not doing anything but just sitting and listening and nodding, I mean what else, I mean he's just this figment of my imagination and having him say anything would be like having me say something, which I really can't, I mean all I can do is rattle on about my problems and confusions, it's about all I can manage.

And the thing is I don't even know how much time passes in this hallucination or mental exercise or whatever, I just don't, but then after a while I just start feeling better, and maybe not a whole lot, but, still, just better about things, and I even say, 'Just decide, Bingo, just make up your mind about things,' and I can't even tell whether I'm saying this or Ronald McDonald, but it's me, I guess, it's only me, I mean why should Ronald McDonald give a shit about my problems and confusions.

And then I know. I just do.

That sooner or later something will have to be done, and I'll just do it, when the time is right I guess, but I'll just do it when the time is right.

And we're just watching TV and all. All three or all four of us I guess.

Because Bingo the dog seems to be into the same silly shows that Frank is, I'm almost sure, and Linda and I just going along, I mean we're just watching to keep Frank company and all.

And we're watching this travel show and all, you know, like, "Welcome to Paris, the City of Light," or, "Welcome to Florence, the birthplace of the Renaissance," stuff like that, and I doubt that Frank even knows the difference, I mean it could just as well be, 'Welcome to Trenton, the armpit of the universe,' you know, and he'd watch it just because it happened to be on, but that's when it comes to me I guess, it just does, and the next thing I know, I mean the very next thing is I'm saying, "Well, I guess it's time," and the thing is they haven't a clue, I mean how could they when I haven't a clue myself, I mean the words are just out of my mouth and what will or won't follow is anybody's guess, but then, "It's time for me to be moving on," I add, and that's when I know, that's the first time I really know that I've been mulling this over all this time, and it's like hearing or overhearing yourself thinking or speaking out loud I guess, and then I give them this little speech or something like I've had it prepared all along, but this little speech how one, that is I, but how one can't just stay put in any one place for any length of time, and there are all kinds of people I guess but some, that is I, some just need to be on the move, and here is where I bring in a comparison to sharks and stuff, strictly for Frank's benefit who has this thing for whales and sharks and shit, but here's where I tell them that sharks have to be constantly on the move to be able to breathe, and even though that's more myth than fact as we both know from having watched all those Nature shows, it serves to illustrate my point, and Frank's like, "What's going on, Bingo?" and Linda, "Yeah, what the fuck is happening?" but for the life of me I can't go into any more details than that without babbling, rambling on for hours I guess, which I'm not even sure would do a hell of a lot of good, I'm really not, so I just more or less repeat what I said before but using different words this time, and, "Nothing but nothing's happening to my life here," I tell them, and, "What am I doing here but just marking time and being in the way I guess," I add, and Linda gives me this peculiar look, Frank as well I guess but Linda's more peculiar, and then we're on this boulevard in Paris or this piazza in Florence; but just standing around and having this pointless, this ridiculous argument, I mean I don't even know but that's what it feels like, and then Linda just gets up and walks to the set to shut the TV, I mean the remote is right next to Frank, but, no, I guess she feels the need to get up and walk to the set to shut it, to get rid of Paris or Florence or whatever, turns around, looks and says, "No, if anyone's going to bolt it's going to be me, me and Bingo," meaning the dog I guess, but, "No, my mind's made up," I tell them, "I'll pack and leave in the morning," and that's pretty funny I guess, seeing how I have practically nothing to pack and nowhere to go, I mean I haven't given it any thought, so, "Where will you go, what will you do?" Linda asks, I mean what else, but, "New York," I just tell her, them, "I'm going to New York." And that's like news not only to them but to me as well I guess. I mean it's like I just pulled this place out of a hat or my mind I guess, I mean I could just as easily have pulled out Antarctica or the Amazon to the same effect, as a matter of fact Frank probably would have been a little less surprised at those, I mean New York is like this last place on earth as far as all three of us are concerned, you know, like people basically go there to disappear and all, I mean what else, in fact the only one I've ever known from the Panhandle to have gone there was this kid called Tommy Ticks, we called him that because one summer he had these ticks and all, I mean worse than anybody else, and anyway there was something wrong with him besides, some kind of genetic mental disorder or something, and what did he do one day but just start talking about going to New York and all, and then he actually did, just packed up and left never to be heard of again, and, 'Welcome to the world of Tommy Ticks,' I just tell myself like I've just turned into this mentally defective kid I used to know, and, 'It could be worse, Bingo,' I'm thinking, but, no, I don't see how, but once it's out of my mouth, New York I mean, there's really no taking it back, that's just how I am, and pretty soon I just start making up stuff as I go along, I mean it's N.Y.C. this and N.Y.C. that like I really know what I'm talking about, and both Linda and Frank are just listening to me like I've lost my mind or something, which I guess is kind of debatable, it really is, and Linda's like,

"Where will you stay?" and, "At the Y," I just tell her without batting an eye, because I'm just assuming that every large city on earth has this Y or something, and, "On the West Side," I even add because for some reason the West Side sounds a bit more homey than the East, but, you know, like don't ask, but suddenly I'm just amazing myself, like out of nowhere I'm coming up with this plan and all, I mean if you can call it that, and, "What will you do?" Frank asks, and, "Whatever it takes," I tell him, "wait tables, wash dishes, park cars, whatever," and I can see he's not exactly buying it, I mean who would, but for every one of his questions and hers I seem to have some kind of answer, I mean I'm pretty good at making up stuff and all once I get going, there's really no stopping me, and, "Will you go up the Empire State Building?" he asks as though that were in any way relevant, but, "Bet your ass," I just tell him, and, "What about the terrorists? Linda asks, like New York is the only target, the only place where the terrorists are active and all, but, "I've got nothing to do with the terrorists and they've got nothing to do with me," I tell her.

And, "Boom!," like that.

I mean it's practically the middle of the night by then and it's funny how time flies when you start bullshitting and all, but, "Boom!" there's this explosion, and it's like the end of the world or something, it really is, I mean I can't tell you the number of times I imagined the end of the world but it was never like this, never just this single explosion, this ear splitting, "Boom!" and of course we're all like, "What the fuck?" because with the explosion comes this pitch black darkness, and I'm like, 'Yeah, that makes sense, I guess,' I mean what else at the end of the world but either blinding light or pitch black darkness, but it's like it's just this test run or something, I mean it's not the real end of the world, not just yet, Linda's already lit some candles and given each of us one, and they're like these Jewish candles for the dead or something that were on sale at the corner CVS, and like Linda can't resist anything on sale no matter what, no matter, but we're just walking around like we're in this ghost or mystery play or something, I mean all around the apartment first like we're looking for something, the source of this explosion or whatever, but then out the door and down the stairs to see how much the rest of the world is affected, I mean it's like, 'Is it the end of the world just for us or are others included as well?' but pretty soon we discover it's just our building and our side of the street, and I even overhear someone saying something about a transformer exploding and all, I mean that would make sense, so, 'The end of the world is selective,' I'm just thinking like I'm disappointed or something, but no special reason, but it's just funny or amazing, and I don't know which, but just funny or amazing how out of all the different apartments of our building all these people start appearing, I mean people you've seen maybe just once or even never before, I guess in the darkness it's difficult to tell, and later it's the same thing for people from some of the other buildings, I mean all these characters just start appearing as if out of nowhere, I mean it's like the darkness birthed them or something or I don't know what, but everyone just standing or milling around, you know, like no one's got a clue, and that's when I overhear someone say something about this transformer and all, and I guess that's the explanation but, really, no single explanation is enough, I mean it's like everyone wants to get to the bottom of the thing, they really do, but the bottom's so deep or something that no one's got a shot in hell, I mean even after all explanations have been exhausted there will still remain this something that will be basically inexplicable, I mean that's been my experience, that no matter how deep one goes or digs or whatever there's always this inexplicable one never gets to, no matter, but the thing is we're all just standing around and it's only after a while that someone who's been in touch with F.P.L. or something announces that it'll be a couple of hours before the power will come back on, and then the rest are like, 'Yeah, all right,' like the whole thing suddenly makes sense or something, which it really doesn't, I mean it does at one level but not at another, and then everyone starts drifting back to their separate buildings and apartments, but not right away, in time I guess, I mean some of them would just rather stand around in the darkness outside than return to the darkness of their apartments.

And I'm thinking this is a hell of a start. Whatever. But, 'This is a hell of a start, Bingo,' for my so-called escape, trip or whatever.

And then.

The power comes back on. Like that.

And it's already early morning or dawn or whatever, and none of us have slept a wink, we just kind of moved around in the dark for most of the night, but then the power does come back on, and I just throw a few things into this duffel bag and all, I mean I've had this duffel bag for ages and you can stuff just about anything you need into it, I highly recommend it to anyone who needs to be on the move and all, and I'm not even sure I'm still thinking about New York, you know, about the only thing I'm thinking about is being out of this place, you know, putting as much distance between Frank, Linda and me as I possibly can, and I almost, not quite, but I almost start humming, 'Bee, eye, en, gee-oh,' to myself as I'm packing, and Frank's just standing there and watching, and Linda, no, I really don't know where Linda is, no matter, and then Frank just says, "Christ, I hope you find a great shrink in New York to examine your head," like that, "because I guess there are nearly as many shrinks as crazies there, like the ratio is something like one to five or ten or something," I mean I guess it's his way of trying to make light of things, give the guy some credit I suppose, and then what he does is just pull out this wad of bills from his pocket, I mean I don't even know how much and I doubt he knows himself, but it's like this bunch of tissue papers stuck together, and Frank really has no concept of the worth of anything at all including money I guess, but now and again he can make just piles and piles of it in a week or month or whatever, and it's not like he's this keen businessman or something but just the law of supply and demand I suppose, and I hesitate before I take it, you know, and I don't know if it's for formality's sake or because I really don't feel like taking any of Frank's money, but, "Don't be an idiot," he just smiles, "take it," and I do of course, who wouldn't, and, "Maybe I'll come visit when you get settled," he says, which we both know is a lot of bullshit, I mean I don't even know where I'm going and Frank's like this miserable traveler and all, like put him down in any one place and he'll just stay there for as long as possible unless things start to get really out of control, impossible I guess, and then Linda shows up, you know, just out of nowhere to stand alongside of Frank, and, "You're a heart breaker, Bingo," she smiles, "you're the original heartbreak kid," and I don't know what she means or whether she's even kidding or not, I mean Linda has this way of saying serious things in a funny way or funny things with this mock seriousness, but I'm like, "Yeah, whatever," like the last thing I want is to get serious at a time like this or to just laugh it off, whatever, I mean I really don't know just how I want to face this thing, and then Bingo, the dog is just sitting there and all, just staring the way he sometimes does, and, human or animal, he's about the best starer I know, I mean he can just gaze into your eyes like he's about to climb inside you or something, and then I just leave, I mean Linda just calls this cab for me that neither Frank nor I would have thought of, we just wouldn't have, but, really, then I just leave, there's nothing more to it than that, nothing I care to discuss, to go into just now.

Finally Frank may be right, I mean he's rarely right about anything at all, for the life of me I can't think of a single thing just now, but, still, he may be right about this.

And, 'Bingo, you need to have your head examined,' I'm thinking. What else? I mean I'm at the airport and all, American, which is like the first terminal at M.I.A. and anyway I like the name, like, "Where we going?" the cabbie asked and I just said, "American," right off the bat, like I was this great patriot or something, which makes no sense at all, I know, but not everything has to make sense, but, "American," I just said, and then we just got here in no time, which is usually the way when you're leaving some place, I mean once you know where you're headed and all and pronounce some name, you just blink and there or here you are, and I really don't want to go into all the trouble I had with security after I finally managed to purchase a ticket, one-way I should add, like I'm this cockeyed optimist or something, but no doubt I fit some kind of profile with my duffel bag and 'Chicago Bears' cap although just what kind is anybody's guess, but I'm just pulled from the line and spend a bit of time in this room with these two serious types, but it's like they're the keepers of the gate or something and they're debating whether I'm one of the elect or not, and one of them is just firing all these questions while the other's going through all my junk in the duffel bag, and the questions aren't simple at all, I mean they are at one level but at another they're these serious, almost philosophical types, like who I am, where I'm coming from and going, and for a moment I'm tempted, really tempted to start kidding around with them the way I sometimes do with people who get serious on me for no particular reason at all, but then, 'No, Bingo, no,' I just tell myself, 'this is neither the time nor the place,' so

I just start making up stuff, which is another thing I do from time to time, it all depends, but just stuff about my background and reason for traveling, you know, just about anything that comes to mind, and I don't even care whether it sounds reasonable or not so long as it's half-way believable, and, "So you say this great aunt, this Priscilla Sherman will be waiting for you in New York?" this first serious type asks, and, "You bet," I tell him, "I mean I haven't seen her in ages," "And then you'll be living with her and attending..," and, "Columbia University," I tell him, I mean no sense lying small when you can lie big, why not, and the thing is I can almost picture this Aunt Priscilla and all, the only one of the Shermans to have escaped and made some kind of life for herself, and she and I, you know, like we always hit it off, even when I was just this kid and all, and as for Columbia, yeah, well, I guess I would study archaeology, anthropology or something like that, I mean given my background and all I think I might have an affinity for those subjects, although, you know, like don't ask, don't pin me down on this, and the guy, the first guy is just giving me this once, twice, this thrice over, and then it's like, "All right, Mister Sherman, you may leave," and I'm almost disappointed, more or less let's just say, because I was just getting started with my stories, you know, and I'd really like to find out a bit more about this Great Aunt Priscilla and some more about Columbia as well, but, "Sorry to have inconvenienced you, Mister Sherman," the guy says, and, "I guess you can't be too careful," I just tell him, I mean the guy's this real asshole and all but I guess he's got his job to do the same as everyone else.

And I'm not even going to go into how this is my first flight and all. I mean I haven't given the matter too much thought.

And, 'That's just like you, Bingo,' I tell myself when I'm already seated on the plane and all, I mean no going back, but make a decision, just any decision on the spur of the moment with little or no regard for consequences and it's like, 'This is your life, Bingo Sherman,' once again, I mean if I had a dollar, whatever, for every time I thought or said, 'This is your life, Bingo Sherman,' for all the different occasions on which I thought or said that, I'd be swimming in dough for sure. And the thing is I don't even know what I mean by that, 'This is your life, Bingo Sherman,' not really I guess.

And I've got this aisle seat. Which is both good and bad.

Good because I can move around I guess without having to disturb anyone else, and I'm thinking I'll be moving around a lot, I just feel it in my bones, and bad because I can't see out, not really, just glimpses here and there, but the thing about seeing, looking out is that it may not be such a hot idea, I mean until you start seeing the buildings, the roads, the cars, whatever grow smaller, you can sort of pretend you're not flying at all, just stuck in this moving cabin and all but not actually flying, up in the air, and the other thing is the flatness of the landscape below, and most of Florida is about as flat as you can get, but that flatness is truly depressing, I'm pretty sure it would be, but then, you know, wouldn't it be a hoot if we just flew over South Beach and all, and maybe even Frank's building, although it would take a lot of looking to pick out that, but, you know, let's just say that Frank and Linda would be up on top of the flat roof of the flat building in the flat city, and I'm just saying, but let's say they'd be standing there, looking up and waving, I mean what are the chances of that, but let's say they would be and I could see them and wave back, that'd be something I guess, and I don't even know what makes me think these crazy thoughts, these absolutely impossible thoughts, except that it's a lot better than thinking about crashing, which I guess I am, you know like exploding on impact with the earth below or this burial at sea or something, like I've always had this fear of a drowning death, you know, like don't ask but I always had, and then we're out over the ocean and all, and, 'Good luck, Bingo,' I'm thinking, and I'm probably as white as a sheet and sitting as stiff as a board or a corpse, you know, already like a corpse, and then this woman, real nice I guess, but this woman sitting next to me just leans over and asks, "Are you all right?" and, "What makes you think I'm not?" I just smile, and then it does get a bit better, not much I guess, but it does get a bit better after that.

But in general, you know, everything considered, the less said the better. Really.

And when we finally land, and I don't even care where any more, just so long as we do, but when we finally land I'm like ready to kiss the ground or something, I mean, 'Bingo Sherman land dweller,' I'm thinking, and the idea that this earth is just this planet zooming through space means nothing to me, I mean so long as it feels solid that's all I care about, and I doubt that anyone or anything will ever get me into the air again unless it's on some stupid roller coaster in some stupid amusement park, but, no, not even that, I'm pretty sure.

And on the ground, in the terminal I'm just touching, feeling my body all over to make sure I'm still in one piece and all, I mean it's like I've had my body scattered all over the East Coast or something, the ocean as well as the land and now it's time to make sure it's all back in one piece again.

And here's the thing.

The main thing, I guess. But here's the thing. I'm alive. You know.

Like, 'Bingo Sherman lives,' or something.

And that's a curious thing I guess, I mean the fact that one is alive and all, like so few people pause to consider, to realize, like, 'Holy shit, I'm alive!' you know, like everything, but just about everything in life tends to overwhelm I guess, you know, if it's not one thing it's another, but in that mess or whatever one almost always fails to take the very fact of life into account, I mean one is nearly always too busy just facing, confronting or even escaping these different things in life to pay attention to the very fact of life itself, and, 'This is a fine time to be thinking stuff like this,' I tell myself, as a joke or something, I mean here I am standing in the middle of nowhere, going nowhere and, for all I know, doing nothing, but absolutely nothing with my life, but in some ways it is I guess, I mean there's never a right or wrong time or place to start thinking about life as life, you know, to just let the thing sink in, whatever, and I guess I'm reminded of this guy, this 'Green Grocer' on TV and all, I think he's dead now but that's neither here nor there, but in addition to all the inane things Frank used to watch on TV, for a while he used to watch this 'Green Grocer' almost religiously, don't ask me why, I mean all it was is this three or four minute segment after the news of the day, whatever, but just this guy telling you about what was and wasn't a good buy as far as vegetables and fruits were concerned, I mean can you beat that, Frank who had never even scrambled an egg in his life, too busy· scrambling his brain I guess, but Frank just watching this show about veggies and fruits, but the few times I happened to catch it with him this guy, this 'Green Grocer' would always end his show by saying, "Remember, we're here for a good time, not a long time," and I don't even know if Frank knew what that meant, I mean you can take that just about any way you want, but I'm thinking of that now I guess, but in a kind of deeper sense than this 'Green Grocer' actually intended, I mean he was just this guy talking about fruits and vegetables and not any kind of a deep thinker, but, still, I'm thinking of it now like there's something, I don't know what, but something to what he said.

And.

"What about the Y," I ask the cabbie when I finally get into car, "what about the West Side Y?" like I'm thinking or hoping there is one, like that's the only destination I can come up with, and the cabbie is this swarthy turbaned type, from Pakistan or India I guess, and he's all serious like he's doing me this great big favor driving me because it's just interfering with his meditations or something, and like what are the chances of this guy, of this type of guy knowing anything about a West Side Y, I mean if it even exists, but then he just suddenly turns and smiles, I mean can you beat that, but he just turns and says, "You mean the one on Sixty-third and Central Park West?" and he's got this lovely British accent and all, I mean go figure, and I'm like, "Yeah, yeah, that's the one," even though I haven't the foggiest in the world, I mean this whole thing's just a shot in the dark, and like, "Sit back and enjoy, you're in good hands, my friend," he says, can you beat that, and I'm like, 'Welcome to New York, Bingo Sherman,' like I'm this world traveler or something, which is the last thing I ever wanted or even thought to be, but, 'Welcome to New York,' I'm thinking and just sit back and leave the driving to this Muslim or Hindu or whatever he is.

Like he knows what he's doing even if I don't.

And I guess I'll skip ahead.

I mean I don't want to linger on first impressions, driving across the Triborough Bridge and getting stuck in traffic on the East River Drive, I mean what's the point, but the thing is I'm depressed as hell by the sight of all these buildings, cars, roads, whatever, and I know it's supposed to be like some kind of revelation, you know, seeing New York for the first time and all, but all I am is depressed and getting more so with every passing minute, and the thing about me, I guess, but the thing about me is that I can get depressed or elated at the drop of a hat, and usually neither of them last very long, just temporary things I guess, so you can't go by me getting depressed and all, you just can't.

And it's not that I'm not amazed. I don't mean to suggest that. I'm both amazed and depressed I guess, although a bit more depressed than amazed I suppose. stupid roller coaster in some stupid amusement park, but, no, not even that, I'm pretty sure.

And on the ground, in the terminal I'm just touching, feeling my body all over to make sure I'm still in one piece and all, I mean it's like I've had my body scattered all over the East Coast or something, the ocean as well as the land and now it's time to make sure it's all back in one piece again.

And here's the thing.

The main thing, I guess. But here's the thing. I'm alive. You know.

Like, 'Bingo Sherman lives,' or something.

And that's a curious thing I guess, I mean the fact that one is alive and all, like so few people pause to consider, to realize, like, 'Holy shit, I'm alive!' you know, like everything, but just about everything in life tends to overwhelm I guess, you know, if it's not one thing it's another, but in that mess or whatever one almost always fails to take the very fact of life into account, I mean one is nearly always too busy just facing, confronting or even escaping these different things in life to pay attention to the very fact of life itself, and, 'This is a fine time to be thinking stuff like this,' I tell myself, as a joke or something, I mean here I am standing in the middle of nowhere, going nowhere and, for all I know, doing nothing, but absolutely nothing with my life, but in some ways it is I guess, I mean there's never a right or wrong time or place to start thinking about life as life, you know, to just let the thing sink in, whatever, and I guess I'm reminded of this guy, this 'Green Grocer' on TV and all, I think he's dead now but that's neither here nor there, but in addition to all the inane things Frank used to watch on TV, for a while he used to watch this 'Green Grocer' almost religiously, don't ask me why, I mean all it was is this three or four minute segment after the news of the day, whatever, but just this guy telling you about what was and wasn't a good buy as far as vegetables and fruits were concerned, I mean can you beat that, Frank who had never even scrambled an egg in his life, too busy· scrambling his brain I guess, but Frank just watching this show about veggies and fruits, but the few times I happened to catch it with him this guy, this 'Green Grocer' would always end his show by saying, "Remember, we're here for a good time, not a long time," and I don't even know if Frank knew what that meant, I mean you can take that just about any way you want, but I'm thinking of that now I guess, but in a kind of deeper sense than this 'Green Grocer' actually intended, I mean he was just this guy talking about fruits and vegetables and not any kind of a deep thinker, but, still, I'm thinking of it now like there's something, I don't know what, but something to what he said.

And.

"What about the Y," I ask the cabbie when I finally get into car, "what about the West Side Y?" like I'm thinking or hoping there is one, like that's the only destination I can come up with, and the cabbie is this swarthy turbaned type, from Pakistan or India I guess, and he's all serious like he's doing me this great big favor driving me because it's just interfering with his meditations or something, and like what are the chances of this guy, of this type of guy knowing anything about a West Side Y, I mean if it even exists, but then he just suddenly turns and smiles, I mean can you beat that, but he just turns and says, "You mean the one on Sixty-third and Central Park West?" and he's got this lovely British accent and all, I mean go figure, and I'm like, "Yeah, yeah, that's the one," even though I haven't the foggiest in the world, I mean this whole thing's just a shot in the dark, and like, "Sit back and enjoy, you're in good hands, my friend," he says, can you beat that, and I'm like, 'Welcome to New York, Bingo Sherman,' like I'm this world traveler or something, which is the last thing I ever wanted or even thought to be, but, 'Welcome to New York,' I'm thinking and just sit back and leave the driving to this Muslim or Hindu or whatever he is.

Like he knows what he's doing even if I don't.

And I guess I'll skip ahead.

I mean I don't want to linger on first impressions, driving across the Triborough Bridge and getting stuck in traffic on the East River Drive, I mean what's the point, but the thing is I'm depressed as hell by the sight of all these buildings, cars, roads, whatever, and I know it's supposed to be like some kind of revelation, you know, seeing New York for the first time and all, but all I am is depressed and getting more so with every passing minute, and the thing about me, I guess, but the thing about me is that I can get depressed or elated at the drop of a hat, and usually neither of them last very long, just temporary things I guess, so you can't go by me getting depressed and all, you just can't.

And it's not that I'm not amazed. I don't mean to suggest that. I'm both amazed and depressed I guess, although a bit more depressed than amazed I suppose. And then this Indian, Paki or whatever drops me on the corner of Sixty- third and Central Park West just where he said he would, and, "You just cross the street, sir, and it's right there," he just points, and I can't even see where he's pointing but I'm ready to get out just the same, I mean he could have dropped me off in Harlem and pointed and I would have gotten out just the same, and I give him this tremendous tip and all, why not, I mean I've got all this dough in my pocket although it's questionable how long it will or won't last, never mind, and, "Please, sir," he gives me this card, "just call this number whenever you're ready for your next ride," and I just put his card away like it's this thing of tremendous importance or something.

And, 'Here we go,' I tell myself. Like that.

But, 'Here we go, Bingo.' And let me tell you. This is some place.

I mean it's this Y and all and nothing like a hotel, but I feel like comfortable, really, from the moment I climb the stairs and step inside, and I doubt this would happen in some hotel, I mean the thing about hotels is that you always feel like this guest or something, and I can't even explain it, but this is like this great big mess of a place with all these different types just coming and going, and not pretentious, I guess that's what I mean, I mean men, women, kids, you name it, and some in groups I guess, these tourists from other countries out to see the world on the cheap, but then these old geezers as well, just coming for a swim or whatever, and the thing is no one really gives a shit, that's the thing, everyone just doing his or her own thing, and if there's one thing I like about a place, and I don't care what place, but if there's one thing I like it's no one giving a shit about what anyone else is up to, and there are even a couple of homeless types, just types I'm talking about, and I stand in the lobby or whatever for a spell just taking it all in, and if I wanted to I could probably just stand here for an hour or two without anyone bothering with me, and that's just the kind of place I like, it really is.

And then my room. You know.

It's just this hole in the wall up on the tenth floor, I mean it's nothing but this bed that feels like it rolls on wheels or something, and you can roll it wherever you like, toward or away from the window, whatever, and there's this tremendous view of the park with all the buildings surrounding it, and, 'Shit, holy shit,' I'm thinking, I mean this is really New York, and then I just sit on the edge of the bed and take it all in, and then I'm thinking,


'Christ, if only Frank were here to see this,' and I'm not even sure what he would make of this, Frank being Frank and all, but still I wish he were here so he could see what I'm seeing.

And then it just comes to me. Like that.

But I'll have to go out and find the nearest McDonald's, and I don't even know which way and all, no matter, and the thing is I could ask for directions at the desk but that's the last thing I want, I mean it's important that I search and find it on my own, don't ask, and it'll probably be somewhat different from the ones in Miami, I mean in some ways yes but in others no, and I'm not even hungry, I mean that's not why, but just to find it and go inside, and then like, 'You're hopeless, Bingo,' I tell myself, 'you really are,' I mean who comes to New York to look for a McDonald's, but the thing is I don't care, I just don't.

And it's like mild outside. Which is a good thing I guess.

I mean I haven't given my clothes too much thought, the appropriate clothes for New York, but it's pretty mild, and I don't know how long that'll last, this being New York, but I'm all right for the time being.

And I head west I guess. Away from the park. But here's the thing.

I go no farther than a block or two, you know, straight and then right on Columbus, whatever, but I'm already lost, just feeling lost I guess, and I don't mean physically, although that, too, I suppose, no, something else, I mean it's just all these people coming at you, at me from all these different directions, and everyone with the appearance of knowing where they're headed and what they're about, everyone but me I guess, and that's unsettling to say the least, and on top of that, you know, but on top of that this other feeling, I mean I've had it all my life, sometimes worse than others, but this yearning, whatever, and when it happens, like now, I don't even know what I'm yearning for, I mean that's the thing, I just don't, and that coupled with this feeling of being lost is enough to make me question not just why I'm in New York but why I'm anywhere at all, but I don't mean to make too much of this, I really don't, I'm just making a point I guess, simply observing.

And the thing about me, good or bad, I don't even know, but the thing about me is that I tend to observe myself as much as I observe everyone and everything around me, I mean it's like there's this one Bingo, whatever, just doing whatever he's doing and this other watching him do it, and I'm not saying always, nothing like that, but once in a while, like now I guess.

And it doesn't help. No. It really doesn't. So.

I just keep walking I guess. I mean what else? And then.

I do find this McDonald's after all, I actually do, and when I go inside what do I do but purchase this coupon for like fifty dollars, and that's quite a lot when you're talking McDonald's, and, "Fifty," this kid behind the counter says to me, "are you sure?" like I must be out of my mind or something, because I'm not even purchasing anything edible, just these five ten dollar coupons, but, "Yeah," I tell him, "that's it," and I just shove these coupons inside my pocket along with that cabbie's card, like some kind of insurance policy I suppose, although I don't want to go into this any more than that, I really don't.

So.

It's the middle of the night or something.

And I'm wide awake I guess, I mean I knew I wouldn't get too much sleep the first night, I just did, but I had no idea I'd be as wide awake as this, and out the window there are all these lights and all, I mean kind of in the distance and around the park, but, still, nothing but these lights and I'm like mesmerized or something, you know, what else, but, still, how long can that sort of thing last, and then I just shut my eyes, you know, like darkness is really what I'm after, but I can hear, you know, of course I can hear, and there are all these noises corning from out in the hall and even some of the rooms, and it's these kids I guess, these tourist groups from different parts of the world just returning from or maybe even leaving for the great big city outside, and I just bet this'll go on all night, I mean these kids have like energy to burn, arrived here with nothing but energy to conquer this great big city and all, and then what do I think of next, I mean what comes to mind but this stunning blonde I rode up in the elevator with a few hours ago, I mean just the two of us in this elevator and all, and she was from Denmark or Sweden or Holland or some place like that, and I'm just guessing but she must have been by the looks of her, you know, this kind of tall, dreamy blondes with nothing but this terrific smile in the way of communication, and what was I thinking then, in the elevator I mean, but what was I thinking but, 'Now here's the woman of my dreams,' like that, I mean it almost never fails, in the presence of a certain type of woman I skip

from A to Z in a flash, an instant I guess, and then it's like she's in the room with me, just standing there the way she stood in that elevator, I mean the room is still dark and all but she isn't, she's like lit from within, and then like, 'Watch it, watch yourself, Bingo,' I just tell myself, because there's nothing worse than some imaginary woman standing in your room in the middle of the night, I mean they can mess with your heart and flirt a lot more than any real one, I mean at least the real ones eventually turn out to be these ball busters but not the imaginary ones, they can drive you crazy for as long as your imagination's working and all which is like practically forever, and then, 'Maybe, maybe, Bingo, that's your destiny,' I tell myself, you know, to just fall in love with some imaginary woman and not a real one, at all, but like some ideal or idealized woman who'll like haunt you for the rest of your life, but then the thing is she's gone, her image I mean, and that's the thing with visions I guess, once you start analyzing them they just disappear, and that's okay I guess, I mean I've got enough to keep me awake without adding this young blond to the list.

And then, with my eyes still closed, I just start thinking of Frank and Linda, I mean the two of them together and with or without me in the picture, I mean I just don't know, and then I'm thinking how fucked up, I mean basically, but how fucked up all relationships are, I mean men, women, dogs, whatever, but there's this element to them that's just fucked up, and the best thing, you know, but the best thing is to just accept that from the start instead of thinking how marvelous, how great this relationship should or will be, I mean just to start with that, accept this fucked up part and then just take it from there, I mean you've got a lot less to lose and maybe more to gain with this approach, and pretty soon I'm like picturing myself back with the two, with the three of them, you know, with this great big cow of a dog, this Bingo and all, and I know that's hard to believe, I mean I hardly believe it myself but you never know what you'll feel or think from one moment to the next, you just don't.

And then I just turn on the TV and all.

And then it's like I'm back in Miami with Frank and Linda and watching some stupid show, you know, I mean I don't feel that different.

And then what comes on, I mean the first thing that comes on is this Nature channel, I mean go figure, and it's this special about this cave they've recently discovered in France and all1 this Chauvet Cave or something, and I'm thinking, 'Shit, holy shit, Frank would just eat this stuff up,' I mean whales or caves, what's the difference, but he could just watch this stuff from now until the moment he died, and there are these explorer and scholarly types going down into this cave and all, and one of them with this camera I guess and lights, but all of them with these soft lights on their helmets like miners, and the lights have to be soft I guess so as not to disturb these paintings on the walls, I mean like having been sealed off for like thirty thousand years or something they're probably like sensitive to light, whatever, and this is like the only group allowed into the cave to film and all, and this is when I imagine Frank and Linda and me exploring this cave and all, and no doubt I'd have to keep constantly reminding Frank not to touch, to disturb anything because this is like a sacred place or something, I mean it must have been once to the people who originally came in here to do whatever they did, worship, whatever, I mean no one really knows, but they didn't live here, I mean this guy with this beard and all, like the leader of the expedition or something has all these explanations as to why they couldn't have, I mean why these original people couldn't have lived here but just came to worship or something, and I'm thinking, 'Yeah, that makes sense,' I mean if you have to have some kind of religion, and I'm not even sure you do, but if you do it should just be this religion of life or something, I mean all the drawings on the wall are nothing but images of life itself, all these drawings of bison, horses, lions, whatever are nothing but images of life surrounding those people's lives, and they're really terrific, no question, just a few lines and they capture the spirit of all these animals, and there could have been little or no separation between the people drawing and then viewing and these images themselves, I mean you still get that feeling now, I mean after thousands and thousands of years you're still part of these images and they're part of you I guess, and then I just shut the sound off, because this guy with his whispered explanations is just getting on my nerves and all, I mean it's enough just to see these images and all, you need nothing more than that, and then it's Frank, Linda and me just staring at these images, and that's enough I guess, I mean what more do we need than that.

And then I just shut the set. I do.

And I don't know exactly what I'm feeling, something I guess but I don't know just what.

But then maybe, just maybe Frank, Linda and me are just this small tribe or clan or something, I mean without even knowing it, but we are, and what we have to do is to try to survive together, whatever, and that's something new for me, I mean all this time, practically all my life I thought of survival as this unique, this individual thing, you know, like, 'Bingo, if you don't look out for yourself, who will?' but maybe, just maybe that kind of survival is no survival at all, I'm just saying, and then I just get this flash, this image of Linda and all the way I often get these flashes, these images from practically out of nowhere, but Linda is standing naked and just staring at me, and this actually happened, I mean she was coming out of the shower and all with the bathroom door wide open and I just happened to be passing, and we both like just stood there and stared at one another, I mean nothing special, just staring at one another, and then what does she have but these tattoos on her inner thighs, and reading from left to right I guess, but on the left it said, 'If you lived here,' and on the right, 'you'd be home by now,' and that's pretty funny I guess, I mean it was then and even now, and the only reason I'm bringing this up now, I don't know, but because it fits somehow, you know, with everything else I've been thinking lately, and as I said I really don't know, but it just seems to fit.

And there's this kid at the information desk downstairs.

And perhaps he's mildly retarded or something, I mean I can't say for sure, but maybe he just has certain difficulties dealing with everything around him, and in that I guess he's no different from Frank or even me, you know, at times, but he's the sweetest kid imaginable, you know, just doing his job but always taking his time and always with the sweetest smile imaginable, and what he's doing in a place like this is really beyond me, but I make it a point to go up to him every chance I get, you know, on my way out or in, and I just ask him any question that comes to mind, it doesn't matter, like even the time of day or what time the cafeteria opens and closes, and then after he replies we just stare at one another, just stare and smile, and sometimes, yeah, sometimes for a pretty long time I guess, and it makes both of us feel pretty good I guess, I know it does me, and maybe that's the trouble with this city, you know, that no one, practically no one has the time to look at, let alone smile at you, in general, on the whole I guess, I mean everyone going about his or her business like it's the most important thing in the world, like there isn't any time to spare, and if like everyone's business is the most important thing in the world then, you know, like I'm not even sure what important means, like the other day I'm just headed into the park, like the park's become this refuge or something, but I'm just headed into the park and mulling things over, like, 'Of all the places in the city, Bingo, this is about the only one where I could see you work,' not making too much sense I guess, but I'm thinking of driving a carriage or running that merry-go-round or even just picking up the trash along these various walks and fields, but like no doubt these are union jobs and next to impossible to get, I told you I wasn't making too much sense, or someone, I don't know who, but maybe someone could hire me just to keep an eye on things in general, I mean you've got all these kids just playing and running around without anyone or not enough people to look out for them, I mean a city like this could certainly use some people to just look after things in general, no matter, but then what do I see and hear I guess but this really terrific looking woman in this amazing jogging outfit, it really was, and it must have been after her workout and all because she's heading out of the park with her dog on a leash I guess, and the dog's just this medium sized fluffy white one, and she, the dog I mean, just stopped to sniff this tree or patch of grass, whatever, and she, the woman I mean, just pulls on the leash and says, "Please, focus on the task at hand," I mean those were her exact, her very words, and I'm like, 'Can you believe it Bingo?' I mean saying this to this fluffy white dog, and that's exactly what I mean when I say that everyone's business is like the most important thing, I mean what else, and then what do I do but start thinking of Ronald McDonald and all, I mean he'd get a kick out of this woman for sure, I just bet, but on the whole a Ronald McDonald type wouldn't last in this city for long, or maybe he would but then pretty soon he'd turn into someone other than himself, you know, just saying, 'Please, focus on the task at hand,' to himself, and that's depressing, just that thought, it depressed the hell out of me at the time.

And I haven't had a decent shit in days.

And I don't mean to be crude or anything, but with me a shit is like a gauge as to how good or bad things are going, and I got that from my old man I guess, one of his more meaningful gifts to me, like "Shit well, be well," he used to say although with his drinking and all I doubt he himself ever had a decent shit in his life, no matter, but the thing is I lay a great store by a good shit and all, and, not to belabor the point or to go over the recent and uncomfortable past, but even when my mother was dying in the hospital I had this really amazing shit in that motel, like, 'Way to go, Bingo,' whatever, but not here, not for days now, and it's not that I haven't been eating because I have, but it's like this city constipates me or something, like the other day I almost walked into this fancy drugstore to purchase some enema just to flush things out of my system, and what did that remind me of but my mother who was like this great believer in enemas, you know, just flushing things out of her system once or twice a week, but that's neither here nor there I guess, but in the end I didn't bother going into that drugstore, like, 'Just let nature take her course, Bingo,' and the thing is even if I flushed it out this one time the shit would no doubt just start piling up again, I mean there are no quick fixes, easy solutions to certain things, there just aren't.

And another thing.

I've been having these bizarre dreams or visions, more visions than dreams I guess because I'm only half-asleep when they come, and they're all about Frank and Linda and me, I mean I wouldn't swear to it, they're just these visions and all but I'm pretty sure it's about the three of us, and the thing is at first it's just Linda and Frank I guess, I mean whatever's happening in these visions at first it's just Frank and Linda and I happen like somewhat later on the scene, but there are like all these cops, whatever surrounding them, and they're like in the middle of nowhere, but wherever they are the whole area has been sealed off or something, and it's like a kind of bust I guess, Frank for selling his stupid drugs and Linda for whatever, dancing naked in the street perhaps, I mean I'm just not sure, and at first I'm just watching from a distance, you know, and it's like I've never seen two souls more lost in my life, and I'm just watching, you know, and I don't know for how long but I'm just watching for a while, but then I guess I just step in, part this circle of cops and all and head for the middle where Frank and Linda are just standing or huddling together, and then I just embrace them or something, I mean I can't really tell, but just put my arms around them I guess, and then, 'A mistake,' I just yell out, 'there's been a terrible mistake!' and I'm addressing the cops I guess, all these cops surrounding us, and then I yell a bunch of other things besides but nothing as clear as that first, 'There's been a terrible mistake! and then the dream, the vision, whatever it is just ends there, I mean whether I wind up saving Frank and Linda and even myself is just left up in the air like that, but I just keep yelling and all and the dream, the vision just ends there. I mean, can you beat that? Or how's that for whatever's going on in my subconscious and all or somewhere in the back of my mind? I mean I guess my days, my weeks are numbered here. Whatever. But I guess they are.

I mean I don't even know what was going on in my mind and all when I came to New York, like starting a brand new life I guess, looking for a job, which is about the biggest laugh going, I mean what have I been doing since I got here except to make all these negative observations, comments to myself, I mean New York may be like the greatest city on earth, I just don't know, but filled with these endless possibilities, but if you don't belong here you just don't, and then what'll you do except make all these negative observations, comments to yourself, like it's only bound to get worse, not better, I'm pretty sure, but I'm just like waiting, you know, but just waiting for something to happen to let me put things into perspective once more and get the hell out of here, and then it happens, or they happen, two separate things or incidents, and then I'm like free or something, and I don't mean in general, you know, like totally, absolutely free which I guess I'll never be, but just free of this city and all, you know, 'Bingo Sherman of New York,' just free of all that nonsense.

But here we go, I guess, here we go.

The first event, incident, whatever is just seeing this car windshield washer on the corner of Fifth and Fifty-ninth, I mean this really ritzy corner of New York, but just this miserable windshield washer going from car to car with a rag in one hand and a spray can of some liquid in the other, and the thing, yeah, I guess the thing is he's like dancing as he goes, I mean he's got these really terrific moves and all, I mean he's dancing a hell of a lot more than he's actually cleaning windshields, and most people just wave him off or something, and when he does actually get to clean some windshields I wouldn't exactly call it cleaning, more like smudging than cleaning, and the people just handing him some change and all just to get him to stop, I mean he knows as much about cleaning windshields as some spider monkey in the Central Park Zoo, which is this really great place by the way, except for the animals being imprisoned and all, but the thing is he's dancing and all, the windshield washer I mean, I mean it's almost like his so-called windshield washing is just an excuse for his dancing and all, I mean what this guy really is just this terrific dancer and all but like most people only see him as this windshield washer, and a pretty bad, annoying one at that, but I just stand there, just leaning against this really stupid sculpture and watch him for a spell, and then what do I think of but Ronald McDonald, I mean this guy looks nothing like him and Ronald McDonald probably wouldn't be caught dead washing windshields, but, still, in a city like this you never know, Ronald McDonald might just have to wind up washing windshields and dancing and all.

And then I'm grateful, really grateful to this guy for reminding me of Ronald, for making him like come alive in this city.

And the second event or incident.

I'm on Times Square or somewhere, I mean I made myself this promise to visit Times Square once at least, big mistake of course, I mean it's like being in a whirlpool or something with the waters so churned up you can hardly see or think or breathe, but that's neither here nor there I guess, but I'm on Broadway somewhere and just looking, if that's the right word, but just hoping to come across something that isn't fake, artificial, but something that's at least half-way real, and then what do I come across but this singer and all leaning against a wall and accompanying herself on a guitar. And she's in this like ten gallon hat and bikini and all, but don't think of your beauty contestants, I mean that would be like the biggest mistake of your life, and while this woman is fairly thin and trim and all she's at least like fifty or sixty if she is a day, I mean she's like this living map of time or something, and I don't even know what she's singing, just some folk or pop tune from the past I guess, but that doesn't matter, and I'm not sure just what does, and she's got this sign, this homemade sign behind her that says, 'The Naked Cowgirl,' like that, and damn if she too doesn't remind me of Ronald McDonald, and the thing is I just stop and give her a few bills, I mean no one else seems to bother, to give a damn, and then we get into this conversation of sorts, you know how just one question and answer leads to the next and the next after that, but the thing is she's from Miami and all, I mean not originally, with a person like that you really can't tell where they're from originally and like you may not even feel like asking, but she spent all this time in Miami, and on South Beach of all places where she was doing pretty much what she's doing here and now, but this was like way before my time I guess, but she was like this 'Naked Cowgirl' even then, and now she's just traveling I guess, or, "Touring the country," as she puts it, and I'm just taken with her I guess, no particular reason, but just taken with her the way I always have been with Ronald McDonald, and we're just talking about all these places on the Beach and all, the ones that have changed but some that are still the same, and then she just looks at me and all, but just looks and asks, "Tell me, can you tell me what the fuck is going on?" and smiles, and that's this really great question as far as I'm concerned, I mean what else have I been asking myself especially since I arrived in New York but, 'Hey, Bingo, just what the fuck is going on?' and neither of us has an answer of course but like it's enough just to ask the question and all, and then we just bullshit some more about Miami and some other places as well I guess, and she's like thinking about this world tour or something, like, "If the Stones then why not me?" she smiles, and it's like this big joke or something, it really is, but it's the kind of joke I could hear Ronald McDonald making, I mean his entire life like this tremendous joke or something, and mine and the 'Naked Cowgirl's' as well I suppose, but like what else, I mean given all the alternatives what other way to go through life, and that about clinches it I guess, I mean talking to this 'Naked Cowgirl' on Times Square and all brings like this clarity to my thinking, and I don't want to make too much of this, I mean there was that windshield washer and perhaps a number of other things as well, but it's like I know what I've got to do, not really I guess, but at least I know I've got to get the hell out of New York and fly back to Miami.

I mean, what else? Really. What else? And.

I take this terrific dump on the plane, my best shit in weeks I guess, and if that's not a sign I don't know what is, you know, up above the clouds, whatever, and taking this tremendous shit, and it's like I'm already coming in for a landing, I mean I'm still thirty thousand feet above the earth, above Virginia or Washington, but it's like I'm already coming in for a landing.

And then it's like, 'Holy shit, look at all that flatness, that Miami flatness below,' but for some reason I don't mind, not at all.

And once I'm in the terminal and then in a cab, what do we pass, I mean what do I see but this brand new billboard, 'Thinking of a career change?

BUG BUSTERS! Now hiring,' and even though I've already gone that route before, mentally I guess, I mean, 'Bingo Sherman Pest Control,' still, I take it as a sign, I mean what else.

And I tell the cabbie, this Cuban exile, whatever, to take me up on Biscayne, I mean I'm not ready to go home just yet and anyway I've still got a lot of Frank's money so why not put it to some good use, and I tell him, "Keep the meter running," which he doesn't understand at first but then he does, but, "Keep it running," while I look for Grace and all, and I'm really not that optimistic, I mean not at all but why not give it a shot I figure, you know, it's like something I owe Grace or myself, either or both, but it's no go, you know, and then I just tell him to cross over and head back down on Collins, wherever, and, "Slow, slow down a bit," I tell him, and I'm just looking for this Fish Guy and all, I mean I'd just love to spot him there and stop and have a bit of a conversation no matter how one-sided, I really would, but instead of the Fish Guy all I see is this great big chicken, this Chicken Man I guess advertising this take-out place, but for some reason he doesn't appeal to me, I mean this Chicken Man really doesn't, so, "Okay," I tell the Cuban, "okay, drive on," but then we do pass this interesting hole-in-the-wall restaurant, I mean I've never seen it before, 'The Marmalade Lady,' and something about the name really appeals to me, it just does, and I'm thinking, 'Yeah, Bingo, yeah, maybe you'll take Frank and Linda to this restaurant tonight,' in the way of a celebration of my homecoming, whatever, but, 'Yeah, maybe you will,' and it's only then I tell the cabbie Frank's address and all, I mean it's like this great big secret I've been keeping from him, from myself all this time, and you can just see the relief on this Cuban's face, you really can that our journey, voyage, odyssey, whatever is finally over.

Just one more thing I guess.

As we turn the corner off Collins, what do I see but this handful of end- of-the-world demonstrators with signs that say, 'Repent! Repent!' and some others with quotes of certain passages from the Bible, I mean what else could they be, and like they're this really small group, the demonstrators I mean, and just quietly walking around in this circle and all, I mean they're really not bothering anybody, not me, certainly, although it's true I'm in this cab and all, but all they want is for people to repent, you know, meditate, withdraw into themselves before this certain end of the world, which is like right around the corner I guess, and like I have very little against that, you know, although not much for it either I guess, I mean the way I figure if you go through life thinking about repentance and all you'll hardly have any time for anything else, hardly any time to live is I guess what I mean, and if you're alive what else but live and all, I mean it stands to reason, and as for our approaching the end of the world, it's really not such a big deal, I mean the world ends millions of times every single minute of every single day, I mean for all these different people who just drop and all, and damn if I'm not thinking of the Green Grocer again, you know, "Here for a good time, not a long time," but the thing is in the end all these deaths, endings are private and all, I mean what else, and even if the world should suddenly end all at once what else would that be but these billions and billions of private deaths, I mean it's the single deaths that count as far as I can figure and not the fact that we would all die at once or something, I mean that would still be all these individual deaths, I don't see how they wouldn't.

But the thing of it is these demonstrators, whatever, don't make me feel bad or anything, just the opposite, I mean we know shit about life so why start worrying about death, and I don't mean never think about it, you know, because it's like all around you, but first start figuring out life, and then maybe, just maybe figuring out death will be like a cinch after that or it won't even matter.

I'm just saying.

But the thing is these demonstrators don't make me feel bad about death, all they're doing is making me feel pretty good about life.

I guess.

So.

I just walk into the apartment and all. What else? And the door is open.

It's nearly always open when Frank is home and he's like home practically all the time, and what are they doing, he and Linda I mean, the two of them together, but what are they doing but watching this stupid reality show or something, I mean it certainly looks and sounds like it or something equally ridiculous, I mean it's getting to be like everything on TV is this one big reality show, but fake of course, what else, and I'm thinking, 'Home, sweet home,' like that, but then they look up, Linda and Frank I mean, and it takes them a while I guess but then they do look up, and Linda's like, "Ah, the return of the Prodigal, I mean she can be pretty funny sometimes, come up with these cool allusions, and Frank's just staring and all, and at first I'm not even sure he can distinguish between one reality show and another, meaning me of course, but then he does get up and walk this really slow, this almost meditative walk towards me, and then we just stand there for a second or two, really, not much longer before we embrace and all, and like, "Shit, holy shit, Bingo boy," he's saying in the back of me, and I'm thinking, 'A good thing, yeah, it's a good thing I've come home.' And then Linda, you know, but Linda gets up as well, I mean what else is she going to do, and we make like this threesome in the middle of the room, and then for some reason all I can think of is the way she smells and all, and I even say, "What's that smell?" which doesn't come out exactly the way I intended, I mean the smell's not bad, it's all light and lemony and something I never smelled on her before, and she's just, "Oh, it's just this citrus antibacterial cream I'm using," which is like a joke or something, I mean it both is and isn't, at least the antibacterial part I guess, and then we just walk over to the kitchen table and all, we actually do, but the set is still on, like no one bothers to shut it, and it's 'Pregnant in High Heels,' or something, and it's all about these high society women or whatever who're going to have these babies but like once they're born they want to have very little to do with them, you know, delegate all the work to these nanny types, but that's really neither here nor there, because we're just sitting down at the kitchen table, I mean for once, the three of us together like that.

And then, like what? I don't know.

But we're just talking I guess. Just bullshitting a bit.

And later we're back in front of the TV and all, but this time like, "No more reality shows," I tell them, and, "Let's just see if there isn't something else on, like a good western or something," and damn if there isn't, it's something called 'Shootout at Medicine Bend,' and I just love how the titles, the names of some of these westerns leave practically nothing to the imagination, and it's about these three ex-soldiers cleaning up this corrupt town and all, standard stuff I guess, and even though it's not one of your greats of the thirties or forties, I mean it's still black-and-white but a lot more recent, it does have Randolph Scott in the starring role with a really young James Garner and Angie Dickinson supporting, and Randolph Scott is already this crusty old character, but he's still Randolph Scott, and I'm just looking and sighing like, "Randolph Scott," I guess, and I don't know how serious I am, a bit I guess, but I can see how neither Frank nor Linda think a tremendous lot of the flick and Linda's even like, "Bang, bang, bang," you know, but for my money it's a hell of a lot better than some reality show about desperate housewives or castaways or pregnant socialites, and anyway it's my first afternoon home, so what the hell I guess, I mean, really, what the hell.

And then just for fun or for no reason at all, but just for fun I guess, I try to picture Randolph Scott as Ronald McDonald or vice versa, I mean talk about your impossible combinations, but as a mental exercise it's pretty interesting and all, I mean Ronald McDonald just cleaning up this corrupt town and all or Randolph Scott entertaining all these screwed up kids just all over the world I guess.

And that's when it comes to me. I guess.

But why not the three of us, Frank, Linda and me, why not just buy this McDonald's franchise and all, I mean not here, there are plenty of them down here, but I'm thinking farther south, the Keys I guess, and I'm not even sure they haven't got all these McDonald's in the Keys, they probably have, but maybe not in some of the Keys, like Marathon or Key Largo I'm thinking, I mean we wouldn't have to go all the way down to Key West, just far enough south to get away from here, but I'm just like thinking you know, I mean it doesn't do any harm to have these different ideas.

And later. I guess.

But later off we go to this Marmalade Lady, I mean anything to get them out of the house, but I can like tell from the start the evening's going to be a bust, I mean the Marmalade Lady is no five star restaurant but still it's this pretty decent place and all, but Linda's this fussy eater, she just keeps sending back one dish after the next, and Frank's like, "You order, order me anything Bingo boy," which is nearly just as bad, but the thing is I've got my mind made up, and I don't mean just coming to the Marmalade Lady, but my mind made up about things in general, how we're going to turn our lives around.

I mean it's the determination that counts. Right? And sometimes you may have nothing, initially I mean, but nothing but this determination to go on, and maybe that's enough, you know, but like that's enough for starters I guess.

And Linda with this thing with her eyes.

I mean she's telling me how her vision's just blurry and all, not everyday but often, pretty often I guess, and I figure that's all we need, and she's deathly scared of doctors, ophthalmologists I guess, I mean she'd rather go blind than have herself examined, like, "They're my fucking eyes," she tells me, and no one's disputing that, and then she tells me this really stupid joke and all, I mean I've heard it before but it was about lawyers that time, and, "What do you call five hundred doctors on the bottom of the ocean?" she asks, and, "What?" I ask just to please her, and, "A start," she smiles, you know, a kind of average or worse than average joke, no matter, and then it's pretty clear we're not going to discuss her eyes any more, and I'm just picturing this blind exotic dancer, namely Linda, and that might be good for business but it sure as hell won't be for her, you know, just tapping her way to and from whatever girlie club she finds to work at, or using Bingo the cow as a seeing-eye dog or something.

And like that's all we need. You know.

Like we haven't got enough to worry about. And then here's something else.

Frank, you know, but Frank just starts talking to me about these E.L.E. and like, "What the hell are they?" I ask, and I shouldn't have, like the last thing you want to do with Frank is encourage him when he's got some kind of bizarre idea in his head, but, "Extinction Level Events," he explains, "like comets, earthquakes, tsunamis," and I don't even know where he got this idea from, I mean does it really matter, and it's not that I dismiss the possibility, not entirely I guess, but like why dwell on something no one will be able to do anything about, then as he goes on and on about this stuff I discover something else, and this really takes the cake, but it seems like he and Linda have discovered god or something, I mean you turn your back on some people, disappear for like a couple of weeks; and there's no telling what's going to happen, but they've become these regulars at this church of Saint Paul or San Pablo or something, and, "It's all built of coral," Frank explains as though that made any sort of difference, and I'm like, "You're shitting me, right?" but it's pretty obvious he's not, and it's not like this god thing's affecting the rest of their lives in any sort of obvious way, I mean Frank's still selling his stupid drugs and all and Linda, I guess I don't know, but Linda's doing whatever she's doing, but like what good is this god thing, whatever, if it doesn't affect your entire being, your entire life I guess, I mean for them, for Frank and Linda, god's just another reality show or something, I mean they can turn it on and off whenever the mood strikes, but Frank's like, "You just don't get it, do you, Bingo boy?" and it's like the first time I resent him calling me that, 'Bingo boy,' but, "No, I guess I don't," I just tell him, and like I'm really tempted to start this discussion about god as reality and god as image, and anyway I've been thinking a lot about this lately, no, not about god but just about things in general, how you have your images and your realities, whatever they may be, but how we always settle for images because the realities are so hard if not impossible to discover, but like good luck I guess, I mean I'd have an easier time with the Fish Man who's like no longer around, or even with my real or mythical Ronald McDonald, so I just let it go, I mean I'm not even sure what I'm trying to accomplish with someone like Frank and all.

And.

'Just get laid, Bingo,' I tell myself. Like that.

I mean it's high time I got laid, and I don't even care by whom or for how long, it doesn't matter, but once again I'm in this dry spell or something, I mean it's like either feast or famine with me and right now it's famine, and how can I expect to think clearly about anything at all if I don't get my rocks off, I mean jerking off has never been this really satisfying solution for me, it really hasn't, and I can't see someone like Ronald McDonald jerking off, the man yes but not the clown, but, anyway, 'Just get laid, Bingo,' I tell myself.

And leave it at that.

And.

I can't sleep. You know.

But it's like my first night back and, really, what did I expect, and even my nightmares, visions, whatever in New York were better than this, better than tossing and turning and just staring into the darkness, but I'm just wide awake, about as wide awake as when I first stepped off the plane, and, 'Face it, Bingo,' I tell myself, 'you're not going to sleep tonight and maybe never again in your life,' just kidding I guess but at the moment that's just how I feel, but it's like I just can't escape myself, I mean into sleep and all, I mean something in me just won't or can't let go, and I'm just thinking of now one thing, now another, and it's like it's not even me who's doing the thinking but just these thoughts that keep chasing each other around in my head, and then I'm just imagining this giant vacuum cleaner or something to suck up all the thoughts from my head and leave nothing but emptiness there, and like whoever said thinking's this terrific tool and all, I mean this great tool for solving any and all problems that come up, I mean if anything thinking just creates these problems that it's then incapable of solving, but that's like thinking as well, and I'm sick and tired of thinking, I really am.

So what do I do but just get up and go down to the pool and all, and I don't even know why unless it's to drown myself, but, no, I'm really not the type, I mean back home, back in the Panhandle there was this kid who hung himself, I mean I don't know how often he tried before he succeeded but then finally he did, but he was like disturbed from the get-go, you could tell, and even though I think myself this disturbed individual from time to time I'm really not the type to do away with myself, at least not so far, I mean that's pretty obvious, I mean things would have to be really out of whack, totally screwed up for me to even start considering it, like one of your impending E.L.E. events I guess, but, no, not even then, I mean if like you were born for no reason then why not just go the same way, you know, let life just take care of it all without you making the decision, but anyway down to the pool I go, and I've got this cigar I bought in New York in my pocket, like, 'Way to go, Bingo,' like I'm going to impersonate this tycoon or something by smoking this cheap cigar by this rinky-dink pool, or why not Arnold Schwarzenegger while I'm at it, you know, 'Conan the Barbarian' or 'Conan the Destroyer,' I mean these really awful, unwatchable movies, although don't say that to Frank, but the thing is Arnie really loves his cigars, not in these movies of course but off the set I'm sure, I mean even when he was governor and all what did he do but build this tent and all so he could smoke his cigars while running California, and while I'm no Schwarzenegger fan, you might have guessed, there is something almost admirable about the guy, you know, the way he doesn't give a shit about what anybody else thinks or says, but that's neither here nor there I guess, it really isn't.

So.

I'm just down by this pool and all and just puffing away, just circling this pool for a while and puffing away, and then down I flop into this lounge chair while still puffing away, and then, 'This is the life, Bingo, this is the life,' like that, but just kidding I guess, and then I'm just staring up at these stars and all, I mean what else am I going to do, but just staring up at these stars, and there are like billions and billions of them, I mean not that you can see them all, just a fraction of a fraction I guess, but they're there all right, and not just stars but like galaxies I guess, I mean billions of them, and then I start thinking of something I read in a magazine once, I forget which or when, doesn't matter, but in addition to all the stuff's that's visible there's all this other stuff that isn't, like dark matter or dark energy that even the scientists don't know shit about, I mean they're just guessing, but all this dark stuff that's like three quarters or even more of everything there is, and that's something I guess, like most of the stuff in the universe just made up of things you can't even see, and it makes you think I guess, it really does. 'Bingo Sherman, astrophysicist.' But just kidding I guess. And then I just doze off. Like that.

With the cigar still in my mouth. You know.

And then when I open my eyes, sooner or later I was bound to, but when I open my eyes who's standing there but Linda, I mean just standing there and staring at me, and the thing is she's stark naked, I mean I wouldn't make up something like that, I really wouldn't, but she's just stark naked and all and staring at me, and like, "Hello, Bingo, is everything under control?" and she's like whispering this, you know, the way people whisper a secret or something, and like, "What do you mean?" I ask, and it's like one thing to come down to this pool with a cigar in the middle of the night but quite another to come down stark naked and all but that's Linda I guess, I mean I'm not being judgmental or anything like that, and then what does she do but just spread her legs, I mean she's still standing and all but just spreads her legs, and it's like the second time I'm seeing her tattoos, and the first time really didn't count, I mean it was an accidental sighting, but you know, 'If you lived here,' on one thigh, and, 'you'd be home by now,' on the other, I mean she's as proud as shit of these tattoos, she really is, and like I just can't take my eyes off them, which is like understandable I guess, and, "It cost me fifty bucks," she says, "and that's a pretty good deal, don't you think?" and I'm like, "Yeah, you bet," and I'm just thinking what kind of place or joint would do this kind of job for only fifty bucks, but that doesn't matter I guess, and the next thing's like I'm sitting up and moving close for a better look, and the lettering's like all blue or aqua, I mean you can see it even though it's pretty dark, and then like I'm tracing all the letters with my finger you know, like from one side of her thigh to the other like I'm actually writing them, and she's like, "Don't forget the dash, the dash in the middle," and then she just moves closer or I do, and the thing is I don't know what I'm thinking or she, neither one of us, I guess we're just not thinking at all, and the thing is what have I been thinking or hoping for before I fell asleep with the cigar in my mouth I guess but to stop thinking and all, and now, like, here it is, and then I'm just exploring Linda down there I guess, and I'm like on this surveying job or something although with a number, any number of obvious differences, I don't have to tell you, and Linda's like my partner or something, like Bruce used to be I guess, I mean it takes two to survey, no question, and she's about as intrigued by the process as I am, I mean it's like Linda down there is this fascinating thing, object, whatever for us both, we just can't get enough of it is what, and we're like cooperating and all, I mean four hands and twenty fingers if you do the math and all, and it's like we're penetrating the secrets of the universe or something, and I'm exaggerating of course but not by much, only slightly, and it's like while she's spreading I'm digging or while I'm spreading she's digging, like we're taking turns I guess, and what do I do then, I mean really, but recall pictures of certain interstellar cloud formations or whatever that I must have seen I don't even know where, but it's like dark and pink and dark again, I'm only approximating, and it's like the deeper we go the more depth still remains, that's just the way it is, and she's like, "Yeah, Bingo, yeah," and I'm like, "Yeah, yeah," but without saying her name, I don't know why, and then I'm like, 'I bet I could climb in there, but just climb in there and disappear, in a manner of speaking I guess, but then what happens, what but that I lean too far forward or something and just fall out of this lounge chair or whatever it is, but no big deal, it's like we planned this all along, and then no sooner am I on the ground than I stretch out and Linda's right there on top of me, I mean we hardly skip a beat, and then we like ride the night or into or through the night, I mean she on top and I on the bottom but both of us riding I guess, and then like everything is light or dark or light and dark at once, and what else, really, what else remains to be said.

And the next morning, whenever, but it's close enough to morning because you can tell by the light the sun's about to rise, but the next morning Linda and I are just sitting at the kitchen table, I mean across from each other, and she's like, "The sun," and I just repeat it, like, "Yeah, the sun," I mean it's like that's all we can say and all, and the feeling's like if we started talking and all we would like never stop, and I guess maybe we would but that's the feeling I have, and Frank's not even up yet, I mean there are days, mornings I guess when Frank sleeps straight through till noon or even past, he's quite capable, but then he appears, makes an entrance I guess, and no one can make an entrance quite like Frank, I mean it's like he's both here and not here at the same time, I mean it's like he makes this entrance in your mind and all but not at all for real, and he's like, "Is that coffee I smell?" which of course he doesn't, you know, but that's just what he says, "Is that coffee I smell?" and after a while he's all smiles, and this is even before he sits down, but just all smiles like he's swallowed the ocean or something and it agreed with him, and then he sits down, you know, takes his time and all but does sit down, and then, "So, what have you kids been up to?" he asks, you know, still all smiles, and it's doubtful he knows what I think he knows but, still, this is Frank we're talking about and basically, in the end I mean it's impossible to tell what he does and doesn't know, and I can see that Linda with her blurry vision and all is thinking the same thing, but then like, "Linda's got this thing with her eyes," I just say, to change the subject and all which like never even came up in the first place, and, "What thing, what thing?" Frank asks and Linda's just shrugging her shoulders, and then I'm thinking, actually thinking that even going to a pharmacy might at least be something of a start, and then I just say, "What about the Saint Jesus pharmacy?" because I remember passing this place and all with this name that struck me at the time, and like if Linda and Frank found god then maybe she could be persuaded to go to this Saint Jesus pharmacy, but all she does is make this face and all, like Jesus or no Jesus she's not about to go into any pharmacy, and I doubt she would let even Jesus himself look at her eyes, I mean if he were around, but I seriously doubt she would.

And Frank's like, "Is the world coming to an end?" which is this thing with him, like he always wants to know if and when the world's coming to an end as though just knowing about it would make the slightest difference to him or to anyone else, and I just sit there looking at him, you know, like I'm trying to make up my mind about him, which I guess I never will, not in a million years, and then as he comes close I notice all these hairs, these really long hairs growing out of his nose and all, and, "Frank, why don't you just trim your nose hair?" I ask, but that's pretty much like asking Linda to have her eyes examined, and, "It's good for business," he just smiles, like he doesn't even know what he's talking about.

But then something else comes to me.

The way it always or usually or sometimes does.

And, "The fleet's in town," I tell them, which is something I read somewhere, that it's like fleet week or something, and even though none of us care that much about seeing a bunch of warships and all, I mean I'm pretty sure we don't, still, it's something for us to do, I mean the last thing I want is to just sit around the apartment and start mulling things over which I'm almost sure is bound to happen, so, " What do you say we just go down to the harbor and have a look?" and I can tell they don't know what to make of my suggestion, I mean they have no strong feelings about it one way or the other.

Still.

That doesn't matter.

I mean once in a while someone has to take charge and all. So.

What do I do but take them to McDonald's and all before we walk to the harbor, and Frank's like, "Shit, ah, shit," I mean his feelings about McDonald's are the exact opposite of mine and Linda's, but the thing is Frank can be persuaded to do pretty much anything at all except to stop selling his stupid drugs and all, and Linda's like, "The perfect morning after a perfect night," but I'm like, 'Nah, please, don't, like I'm not ready to start thinking about what happened between the two of us, let one start making references to it, I mean I still have no idea on Frank's possible take on the matter, so, "Let's just go," I tell them and, "What we need is a hearty breakfast," or something equally idiotic.

And then there or here we are I guess.

And it's strange, which is putting it mildly, but it's strange the three of us together at McDonald's, I mean I'm usually here by myself or that one time with Linda, but this is something entirely different, I mean how could it not be, and I'm thinking, 'This could be the start or the end of something, I really don't know which, and Linda and I have this Big Breakfast and all but all Frank wants are these home fries, these hash browns I guess, and he has four different orders, and I really don't care, I mean he's entitled, but who but Frank has nothing but hash browns for breakfast and all, I mean he's the only one I know.

So, that's it then.

Except that during the meal Linda gets up to get some powdered sugar for her griddle cakes, I mean she's got all the syrup in the world and then some, but, no, it's powdered sugar or nothing, and she even gives me this meaningful look like powdered sugar's supposed to have this hidden significance or something, which I don't get, I mean not at all, and McDonald's may be known for a lot of things but powdered sugar isn't one of them, but Linda's like dead set on it, like it's powdered sugar or nothing, and she's gone for a pretty long time I guess because at the counter no one really gets what she's after, I mean they do and they don't, but then what do you know, but the manager or someone does come up with this little plastic container of what looks like powdered sugar, I mean they must have had some of this stuff somewhere for like emergency purposes I guess, and Linda's like all smiles when she returns, I mean she couldn't be happier, and the two of us, Frank and me are just watching the way she sprinkles the stuff on her hot cakes, and then what happens but that with the very first bite she gets some of the stuff, the powdered sugar I mean, on her nose, and neither Frank nor I say anything because Linda looks really great with this touch of white on her nose.

And then it's like on, you know, on to see the fleet and all. And the color of the day is like gray and navy blue, I mean from the shore all you see are these warships, these destroyers I guess, and Linda's like, "Are they for real?" which is a pretty good question, because they really look like toys some giant might play with, or like if they're for real then we aren't or vice versa, and looking at them I get the same feeling I occasionally had in New York, like I'm on the verge of disappearing, and it's one thing to disappear because you choose to but quite another because you're dwarfed by these monstrous ships or buildings or whatever all around you.

And Frank's like, "Let's get the fuck out of here," which is pretty much the general consensus, and by then I don't even know what I expected or what I had in mind when I suggested we come down to view these ships and all, and like what was I thinking, I guess, but I often get these ideas that go nowhere in the end, they really don't.

I mean coming down to view these ships is a lot like my going to New York or my considering taking off for Kuwait, it just doesn't work, and I'll have to do a lot better than this I realize, I mean as far as coming up with ideas for both the short and the long runs, and it's like, 'Hey, Bingo, you do realize that after last night it's all on your shoulders,' and I don't even know why, but, 'It's all on your shoulders, Bingo boy,' I tell myself, like there's no escaping the fact.

And Frank's like walking and talking in his sleep.

And Linda doesn't think it's such a big deal, but with Linda it's hard to say what she does and doesn't consider a big deal, but Frank, who's otherwise this really deep sleeper and all, I mean you can hardly see him move or even breathe at times, but Frank just gets up in the middle of the night like he's searching for something, something he misplaced or never had in the first place, I just don't know, but he walks into Linda's room or mine and just stands there mumbling, talking to himself, but the thing is he's fast asleep, I mean Frank's neither smart nor good enough to fake something like that, and he's talking about god and drugs and Linda and me like in the same breath, I mean you really can't make out exactly what he's saying, just snatches here and there, but, "Frank, Frank," I tell him or Linda does, "Frank, come on, back to bed now," and we like put our arms around his shoulders, either Linda or me and guide him back to his bed, and the last thing we want is to wake him I guess, I mean he's in this one world and we're in another and the shock of pulling him from one into the other might be like too much for him, I don't know, but, "Frank, Frank, come on now," and the thing is he doesn't wake, he really doesn't, all he does is curl up on his bed in any old position and he's like dead to the world once more.

And it makes you think, I guess. It really does.

I mean this whole thing with Linda and me, the two of us being lovers, although I wouldn't exactly call us that, I'm not sure just what I'd call it, I mean like the last time we made love, and not the first time I'm talking about but the last after that, but the last time we fucked we did more laughing than fucking, that's a fact, I mean we fucked all right, I'm not saying, but there was a lot of laughing both before and after, like we bullshitted about Ronald McDonald among other things, did our own imitations I guess, and how can you take loving, fucking seriously with someone like Ronald McDonald on your mind, and the thing is Linda's not like the woman of my dreams, I mean how could she be, and I, you know, Bingo Sherman, how could I possibly be the man of hers, but I'm not complaining, don't get me wrong, I mean we have this terrific time and all, just laughing and fucking or fucking and laughing, either or, and Frank, you know, but Frank's like this unknown quantity, I mean neither Linda nor I know how he feels about what's going on, but that's something else altogether, I mean sooner or later we'll have to have this heart-to-heart or something, but for now, in the interim I don't even know what Linda and I are to each other, I mean I haven't got a clue.

You know.

Like I never thought fucking and laughing could be this natural fit or something, I mean in my mind I always connected fucking with this kind of desperation to find and then to hold on to something, I guess you know what I mean, I mean like you for me and I for you till death do us part or something, and maybe I'm like this last romantic son of a bitch, and wouldn't that be something, like, 'Bingo Sherman, this one woman man and all,' don't laugh, but if Linda's like the one woman for me, and I'm just saying, but if she is then I sure as hell don't know what's going on, I just don't.

And that's without even considering her tattoos. You know. 'If you lived here, you'd be home by now.' Like what are you supposed to think of something like that, and, again, I'm just thinking, wondering I guess, and then Frank, "Why don't the three of us get stoned?" which is like his way of suggesting a heart-to-heart or hearts-to-hearts for the three of us, like beating me to the punch I guess, and Linda's game of course but I'm like, "Gee, I'm not sure," because the last time I smoked pot all I did was get sick, started spinning around myself like I just jumped out of a plane without a parachute or something, like, 'Bingo Sherman pothead,' I was never very keen on the idea, but I guess it's just this one-time deal, and maybe I owe it to Frank and all, I mean if that's what it takes to get us all talking or whatever.

And Frank's got this really good stuff from Hawaii or someplace, I mean he won't even sell it, just keeping it for his personal use I guess, I mean the stuff he sells comes from South America via Panama or Mexico or wherever, I mean I don't even know, but certainly not from Hawaii, and the whole thing's like this religious ceremony or something, which is like the way it once was, not any more but once I guess, and it's just Linda, Frank and me, and not even Bingo, the dog I mean, I forgot to mention, but Bingo's taken off, headed for some imaginary hills while Linda was walking him one morning, and like good luck to him, I'm sure he'll make out in the short or perhaps the long run, I mean we never really bonded, his one true love, his sole focus of attention was Frank who like didn't even notice the dog wasn't around until Linda informed him of it, and like Frank's in charge of the whole evening now, and it's almost like a pleasure watching him roll these joints, you know, it's always a pleasure watching anyone do anything they care and know something about, and the TV's still on, I mean it nearly always is but no sound this time, CNN I guess because Frank just loves to watch these images, and then we just start in, you know, we might as well, and we're sitting on the floor, not the sofa, like we're camping out or something, and the first, the second and even the third hit does nothing at all, I mean I sort of knew they wouldn't, but Frank's like already with this big grin on his face and Linda with her eyes half shut, and all I'm doing or think I'm doing is trying to catch up and all, I mean just trying to get to this place where they've already arrived, you know, by the looks of it, and Frank's like, "Hey there, Bingo boy," all smiles, whatever, and Linda's like, "Hi there, stud muffin," and I'm just thinking, 'What are you doing with these losers, Bingo?' and it's not that I'm excluding myself, far from it, I mean if anyone's a born loser it's yours truly for sure, but there losers and losers I guess, I mean different types, different classes of losers, I mean you can't just say losers and lump everyone together like that, and basically I guess, I mean that's what I'm thinking, but basically there are happy and miserable losers, and Frank and Linda seem to be the happy and I the miserable sort, I mean it's okay with them to be these losers and all but not for me, I mean the last thing I ever wanted to be was this loser even though I sort of suspected I always was and would be, I mean the thing always was and will be somewhere in the back of my mind, it can't be helped, but I'm always trying not to be, just coming up with ideas, with ways of avoiding it, but then something happens, it does, and I don't know if it's the pot, this excellent weed from Hawaii or just that I'm sick and tired of analyzing every situation I find myself in, I mean how can you analyze anything at all, but I'm suddenly floating, and it's not just me, I mean personally, but like the whole world's floating and me along with it, I mean Frank, Linda, the apartment, just about everything I can see and touch and hear and smell and even imagine, I mean even those stupid images on stupid CNN, and it's like the whole world, the entire universe is floating, and, "Yeah, that makes sense," I say out loud, even though I don't even know what I'm saying, but I guess in some way I do, and, "You bet," Frank smiles, "you bet, Bingo boy," and it's not sense in any ordinary, in any intellectual way, which I guess it never is, but sense in some completely other, completely different way, I mean I don't even know what, and then we sort of move closer to each other, like this ever tightening circle or something, and nothing's left out, I mean that's the feeling I have, but nothing in the entire world is left out of this circle, and staring, you know, we're just like staring at each other, and Frank's no longer Frank and Linda no longer Linda, or maybe it's the other way around, that Frank's Frank and Linda's Linda for the very first time, and I don't know who I am or what they see me as being but maybe I'm truly Bingo Sherman for the very first time, and you know something like that won't last, I mean a part of you does but even that doesn't matter, and the thing is I no longer know what does and doesn't matter, which is like par for the course, but like even that doesn't matter, and Frank's saying, "Let's go look at the whales," which under ordinary circumstances would be this truly idiotic thing, I mean we're just huddled on the floor of this apartment and there's no way we're about to move, and the whales are thousands of miles away, in the Sea of Cortez or somewhere, but now, I mean right now it seems to make perfectly good sense, I mean hasn't Frank always wanted to go whale watching and all and so did I I guess, and Linda's like, "Whales, yeah, I wouldn't mind," and pretty soon we're out there watching these whales and all, and I don't even know where out there is, the only thing I do know is that's where we are, and then these giant creatures, whatever, swim really close so we can touch them and all, but, really, all we're doing is just touching each other, but it's really the whales, and Frank's like, "Yeah, yeah," and Linda and me are pretty much the same, I mean these whales are really something, and touching, stroking their skin and all is like touching, stroking silk or something, I mean they're not at all cold and slippery the way you might expect, although you might not, I really don't know, but like all we're doing is touching and stroking each other, which like goes without saying, I mean at one level, but then there's this other level I guess, where we're touching and stroking these whales and all, I mean it's like we're in this world that touches or even contains all these other worlds, like the difference among all these worlds is practically nonexistent, and beautiful, you know, and I realize how strange and even stupid this sounds, but I realize how beautiful everything is, I mean all these worlds just taken together, and Frank's like, "I love you, man," and, "I love you, Frank," and Linda's pretty much the same, and like I don't even know what happens after that, I mean everything or nothing, it really doesn't matter, and time, I guess, which is another thing, but time no longer has this hold on us, I mean we're either outside of time or become time itself, which amounts to pretty much the same thing, and then we like disappear or something, and I don't even know whether we're just out cold or simply disappear to reappear in some other world, I mean in all these other worlds, but we're like still hanging on to each other is the thing, I mean whatever happens to one of us happens to the other two as well, and we like disappear or reappear at the same time, we actually do.

So.

Then what do I do but run into this old guy, I mean I wouldn't exactly call him a friend and maybe not even an acquaintance, we just sort of stopped and talked on Collins several times before, I mean if the mood is right I'll just stop and talk to just about anybody I guess, and the thing about this guy is that from the very first he reminded me of this aged Randolph Scott or someone, just his appearance I'm talking about, but this aged Randolph Scott well after his career in the movies, I mean no longer a star or anything but in some ways still Randolph Scott and all, but the thing about this guy's that he's really something of a nut case, but, like, which of us isn't, I mean practically all the people I've ever met or even cared for have been these nut cases in one way or another, and he fancies himself this survivalist or something, I mean here, here we go again, and basically all he ever talks about are these canned foods, guns and ammo he's got stashed in his house or apartment, I mean his eyes just light up when he describes these different weapons he got through the mail or somewhere, and, "The Dutch," he tells me, "the Dutch have come up with this amazing pistol," and on and on he goes about how lightweight it is, some kind of titanium compound, and how the bullets can penetrate just about any known body armor, and I'm like, "Yeah, yeah," like I'm truly impressed or something, but then like, "And how long do you expect to hold out?" I just ask, you now, after this catastrophic event that leaves everyone else scrambling for food, water and other basic necessities, and he's like, "A month or two at the most," and like I don't get it, I really don't, I mean why not just die along with everyone else instead of trying to survive on your own for an extra month or two, "And what will you do while you're trying to survive and all?" I ask, and I can tell by the look on his face that no one, but no one has ever asked him that before, and he's like, "Watch old movies I guess," and that's pretty funny when you think of it, I mean I can just imagine Frank coming up with an answer like that, but that's where the resemblance ends because Frank's like anything but this survivalist, I mean you could call him just about anything at all but survivalist wouldn't be one of them, and, "What would be the point?" I ask, but by then it's becoming pretty obvious that I'm asking way too many questions for this survivalist's, this Randolph Scott's taste, so he just clams up, you know, just shrugs his shoulders and clams up, and it occurs to me then, you know, but it just occurs to me that his resemblance to Randolph Scott is like only skin deep, if that, I mean Randolph Scott may have been this loner and all but he was no survivalist, I mean basically he was out for everyone else and not so much himself, and from Randolph Scott what do I do but jump to Ronald McDonald, and this may not be any sort of natural progression but the thing is I just do, and once again I just can't picture Ronald McDonald as this survivalist, I mean he doesn't seem to care that much for himself, what he really cares about is just entertaining others I guess, and while I realize I'm thinking about only the image Randolph Scott and the image Ronald McDonald, that I don't know crap about the real Randolph Scott who like lived in this questionable relationship with Cary Grant one time, but like what does that matter, but I really don't know crap about either the real Randolph Scott or any and all of the real Ronald McDonalds, I mean for all I know they could have been survivalists to the core, you know, just look out for number one without any regard for anyone else, but for some reason no, I just don't think so, but the thing is that suddenly I've got like nothing to say to this guy, this survivalist I guess, nor he to me, and we like realize this pretty much at the same time, so he just nods I guess and I do the same, and, "You take care now," he says, and I, "Be seeing you," I guess, but like I'm really not looking forward to it, I'm just not.

And then I just keep on thinking some more. I guess.

And what I'm thinking is that the thing about life is that no one ever has or had it figured out, I mean it may look like you do or did, like if you're Donald Trump or Jesus Christ or someone, but, no, not even them, but like no one ever gets it right, you know, and I don't even know what that might mean, you know, to get life right and all, but that doesn't matter, the thing is no one ever does or did, and like we all wind up being these losers and all, Donald Trump and Jesus Christ included, like, 'Father, Father, why hast Thou forsaken me?' which is one of the few quotes I remember from the New Testament, but maybe even that doesn't matter, and perhaps, and I'm just saying, but perhaps the only thing that does matter are relationships, I mean when you look at life what are you really looking at, and, again, I'm just saying, but my guess is you're looking at nothing but relationships, and I don't care if they're all fucked up, I mean relationships of just these losers how could they not be, but, still, that's all we have, nothing but relationships.

And. Then.

I'm sort of glad Frank and Linda and I got high, this one time I guess which was enough as far as I'm concerned, but, still, I'm glad it happened, because what that did was to free you, me, I guess, from this constant need to figure things out, like there's really nothing to figure out, there are just all these relationships I guess, you know, and that's pretty much it.

And.

I'm feeling pretty good about things.

And I don't even know what those things are, but just feeling pretty good about things in general.

And then I can't wait to get home. You know. For no particular reason. But I just can't.

And Linda's this changed person or something.

And that may be just my perception, I mean I really can't tell, but Linda's this changed person and perhaps Frank as well.

And it could be that it's only me, you know, that I'm the only one who's this changed person, but I don't think so, I really don't.

I'll just skip ahead.

At this stage.

But I'll just skip ahead if that's all right with you. But Linda, let's just take Linda.

I mean Linda's no longer this exotic dancer, whatever, but, as strange or as unbelievable as this may sound, she's become this personal trainer or something, but I guess why not, I mean she's got the body, all the moves and even the personality I guess, and a couple of times a week she even leads this aerobic exercise group at the local gym, I mean this really upscale gym where at first they just took her on as a substitute but then like everyone just fell in love with her, in a manner of speaking, and now she's got this regular gig or something, and this is in no way to suggest that this sort of thing is my cup of tea, I mean sweating alone or in groups for your so-called body beautiful leaves me absolutely cold or lukewarm at best, but Linda's Linda, and who says she shouldn't pursue her calling wherever it takes her, but anyway she's become this local celebrity or something, the 'Neighbors' section of the paper ran this little article they called 'Fit for Life' where they had this pretty decent, not great but pretty decent photograph of her along with a number of quotes about all the things being fit meant to her, and even though afterwards she was like, "No, never, I never said that," the quotes were okay I guess if you like that sort of thing, but the best thing about it all is that in spite of her celebrity, whatever, we're still pretty much fucking, you know, just about every chance we get, and she's really into these different places for doing it, I don't mind, I mean we fuck in the gym after hours, in the backs of empty stores, and sometimes on the beach at night, I mean she's like this spontaneous spirit or whatever and I'm just doing my best to keep up with, and I'm not saying this is for keeps, for life or that she's like the love of my love, I mean as far as I know the love of my life may still be out there somewhere, you can never tell about these things, but this is the here and now and that's saying something or even quite a lot, but in general I stopped worrying about things of this sort, like where is the love of my life and all the rest of it, I mean worrying about it doesn't do any good, not one bit is my guess.

And then Frank.

Frank's like cut back on his selling activities, and I mean drastically, I mean if he hits the streets twice or even once a week I'm saying a lot, and I don't know if it's the organized competition and the lengths to which they're willing to go to corner the market, but Frank's like me in this, I guess, I mean he's really this miserable team player, if he can't do something on his own he'd rather not do it at all, but there may be a bit or even a lot more to it than this, you never know with Frank, but then what does he do, and, again, this may be a bit hard to credit, but what does he do but start working at this halfway house for runaways, and I know this sounds pretty incredible, I mean I for one can't even imagine it, but several times a week he takes this bus to the middle of nowhere to work with these troubled kids, and you've got to remember this is Frank we're talking about who most of the time can't even negotiate his way around the block without asking for directions, but he comes home with these stories about kids who're truly screwed up, I mean compared to them we're these stable, these model citizens, and, "Bingo," he'll say, "Bingo boy, you won't fucking believe this," and then on and on, and this is like a new Frank, you know, like some box of cereal that has 'New and Improved' stamped on it, and, again, I don't know how long this'll last, I mean everything's pretty much a phase with Frank, but, again, we're talking of the here and now, and the here and now is not that bad, pretty good in fact.

And.

As for me. As for me

I just walk into this McDonald's one afternoon, you know, the one where I'm this pretty much regular customer, but this time I walk in because of the sign in the window, 'Manager Wanted,' and even though I haven't given it much thought beforehand, none, really, I still just walk in and ask to see the manager who's still on the job until he finds the replacement, and he's this pretty cool guy, this weight lifter type with whom I've had several better than okay conversations, and, "I've come about the sign," I just tell him, and he says, "Come, come, let's sit down," and I can't tell how seriously he's going to take me, but at least he's ready to listen and talk, and wouldn't you know it, we sit down in the same booth where I usually sit as a customer, and that may or may not be some kind of sign, it really doesn't matter, but he's asking me all about my past experience, my relevant past experience, "What about life experience?" I ask, just kidding I guess, but then I tell him how I was this surveyor and all, and how surveyors have to have pretty sharp minds and eyes, and as far as I'm concerned that's relevant to any other job including managing a McDonald's, and I can tell he's interested at the very least he's asking all these questions about surveying which doesn't necessarily mean he's interested in me as a potential manager, but, still, we're having this great conversation, at one point he even points to my cap and says, "Chicago Bears, yeah, you betcha," like that, and, again, I really don't know what that means as far as my possible future as a McDonald's manager goes, but all the same it's nice, you know, really nice to hear, "Chicago Bears, yeah, you betcha." And then.

Out of nowhere I start telling him about some of my ideas for McDonald's, I mean this particular McDonald's, about how I'd like to make it different, a lot or just a bit, I don't even know, but just a bit from all the other McDonald's around, and I mean mostly the atmosphere I guess, I've got nothing against the food of course, but how I'd like to see these different flags just hanging from the ceiling, like you're in this sports stadium or something, I mean it's just an idea, and then, "Why all this canned music all the time?" I ask, "Why not some live entertainment once in a while?" and I'm thinking folk singers, whatever, even if it's 'The Naked Cowgirl' types, but I don't tell him that, no, we're just talking in general I guess, and once again, you know, I can see that he's interested, but like how that'll translate into my chances of becoming a manager I'm not at all sure.

And then.

Again, out of nowhere.

"And what gives with Ronald McDonald?" I ask him. And I tell him how surprised I am, disappointed I guess, although I don't say disappointed, just surprised, but how surprised I am that Ronald McDonald never visits this place, certainly not while I've been around, and he's like, "Yeah, I think you've got something there," and as manager, you know, I would see to it that he'd show up on a more or less regular basis, I tell him that, and, "Even if I have to dress up as Ronald McDonald myself," and he gets a kick out of that, I can tell, but, really, the truth is I wouldn't mind, in fact I'd sort of enjoy it, and I can see the guy appreciates this, or finds it amusing at the very least, "Because everyone loves Ronald McDonald," I add for good measure, and he's like, "Yeah, I think you're right," and then we're done with the interview, I mean not right away but pretty soon after that, and I don't even know what's going to happen, with the job I mean, but I'm glad of one thing at least, I'm glad I told him everyone loves Ronald McDonald, and he took it the right way, even though I'm not sure just what the right way is, but he took it the right way I think.